Leon and the Champion Chip

ALLEN KURZWEIL

Illustrations by BRET BERTHOLF

SCHOLASTIC INC.
New York Toronto London Auckland Sydney
Mexico City New Delhi Hong Kong Buenos Aires

This book is a work of fiction. References to real people, events, establishments, organizations, or locales are intended only to provide a sense of authenticity, and are used to advance the fictional narrative. All other characters, and all incidents and dialogue, are drawn from the author's imagination and are not to be construed as real.

The author would like to acknowledge the contributions of Donal O'Shea, Elizabeth T. Kennan Professor of Mathematics at Mount Holyoke College, and Suzy Williams of the Wheeler School Science Department.

ISBN-13: 978-0-439-92666-9
ISBN-10: 0-439-92666-1

Published by Scholastic Inc., 557 Broadway, New York, NY 10012, by arrangement with Greenwillow Books, an imprint of HarperCollins Publishers.

12 11 10 9 8 7 6 5 4 3 7 8 9 10 11/0

Printed in the U.S.A. 40

First Scholastic printing, November 2006

The text of this book is set in 12-point Goudy.
The display type is set in Garamouche.

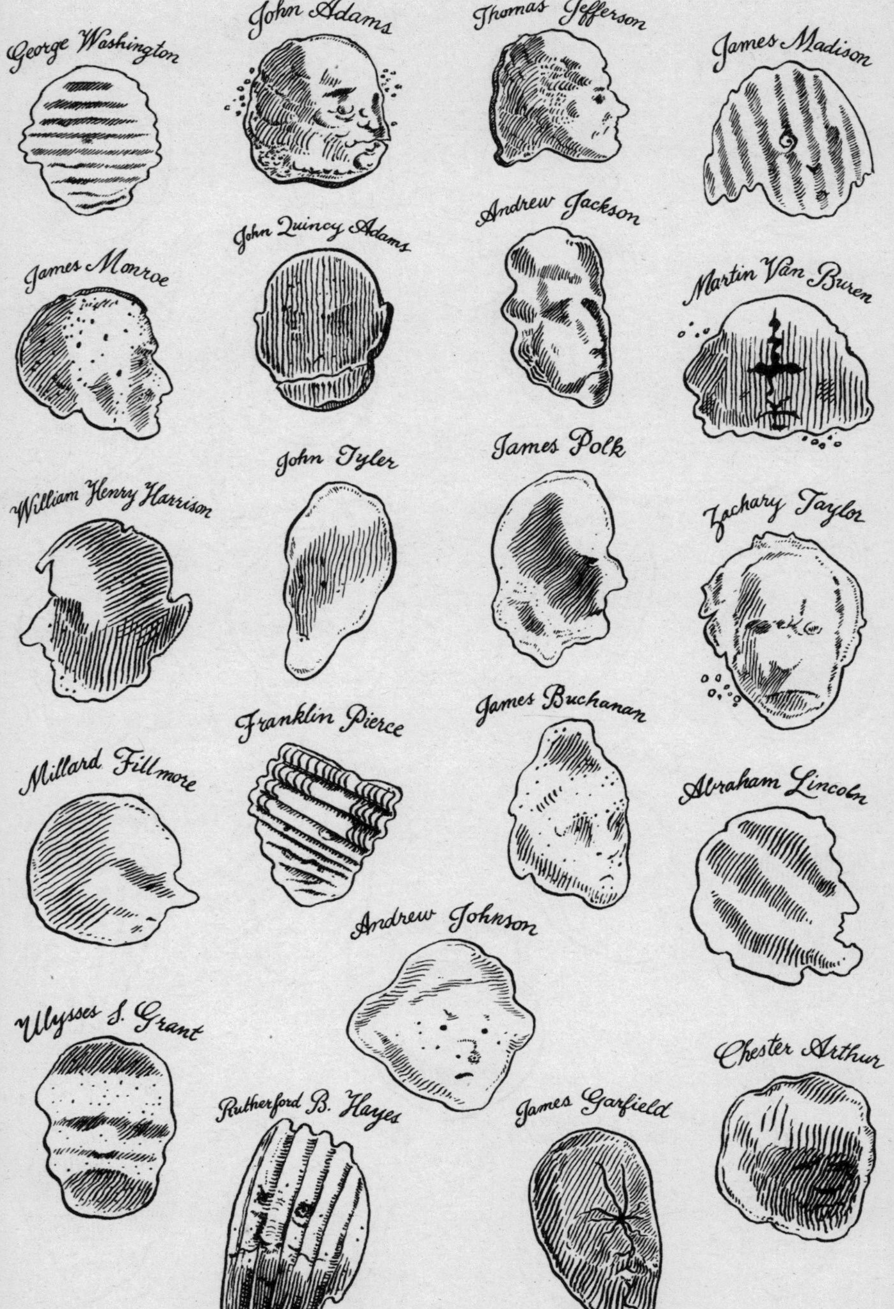
George Washington
John Adams
Thomas Jefferson
James Madison
James Monroe
John Quincy Adams
Andrew Jackson
Martin Van Buren
William Henry Harrison
John Tyler
James Polk
Zachary Taylor
Millard Fillmore
Franklin Pierce
James Buchanan
Abraham Lincoln
Andrew Johnson
Ulysses S. Grant
Rutherford B. Hayes
James Garfield
Chester Arthur

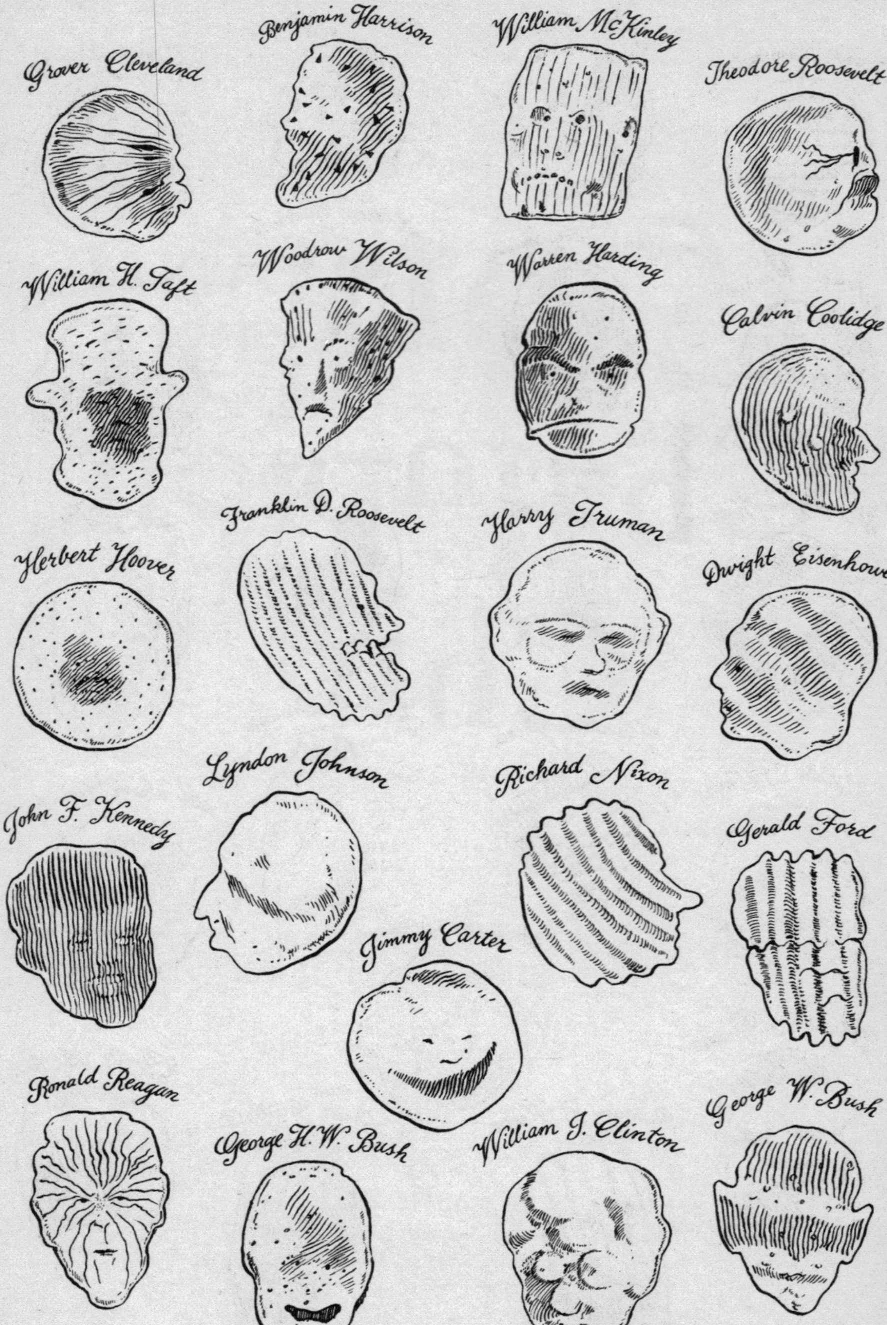
Grover Cleveland
Benjamin Harrison
William McKinley
Theodore Roosevelt
William H. Taft
Woodrow Wilson
Warren Harding
Calvin Coolidge
Herbert Hoover
Franklin D. Roosevelt
Harry Truman
Dwight Eisenhower
John F. Kennedy
Lyndon Johnson
Richard Nixon
Gerald Ford
Jimmy Carter
Ronald Reagan
George H. W. Bush
William J. Clinton
George W. Bush

Fox
Max

Table of Contents

spitting image ***noun*** [From Middle English. See ***spite.*** Date: circa 14th century] Perfect likeness of a person; exact image. Some experts think that "spit" is a corruption of "spirit." Others maintain that the phrase invokes magic—that armed with a sample of saliva ("spit") and a doll made to resemble a person ("image"), a sorcerer could cast all-powerful spells on the unsuspecting victim.

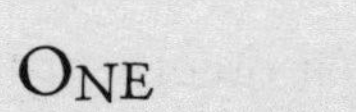

One

The Purple Pouch

The evening before the start of fifth grade, Leon Zeisel was feeling unusually chipper. He sat on his bed in Trimore Towers—the six-story, wedding cake-shaped one-star hotel he called home—and prepared for school.

Three-ring binder? . . . Check.

No. 2 pencils? . . . Check.

Pens? . . . Check.

Lab notebook? . . . Check.

After making sure all required materials were present and accounted for, Leon reached under his bed and pulled out a large purple pouch containing the *un*required item that was making him so chipper. Keen though he was to peek inside the pouch, Leon resisted temptation. He didn't want to jinx things.

He placed the school supplies—plus the pouch—into his backpack, hung the backpack on the doorknob, and pushed the extra item out of his mind.

For a while.

But in the middle of the night, Leon awoke with a start. A single word pulsed through his head.

The word beat quietly at first: POUCH! POUCH! POUCH!

But soon it got louder: POUCH! POUCH! POUCH!

Then louder still: POUCH! POUCH! POUCH!

Leon tried to ignore the chant. He couldn't. Eventually he hopped out of bed and padded over to the door, dragging his blanket behind him. He placed the blanket across the doorjamb, to keep light from seeping into the living room, then grabbed the backpack and switched on the lamp beside his bed.

As soon as his eyes adjusted, Leon unzipped the pack and removed the purple pouch. He took a breath. He squinched his eyes and clucked his tongue, a good-luck ritual performed to ward off worry. (And Leon Zeisel was feeling worried—*and* thrilled *and* antsy *and* eager.) He loosened the drawstrings of the pouch and extracted two objects: a small glass bottle filled with tarry brown liquid and a nine-inch-long, handmade rag doll. He set the bottle aside and directed his attention to the tiny doll—a boy dressed in an olive-drab army jacket. The boy had bright orange hair, a surly-looking mouth, and beady eyes that seemed to glower at Leon.

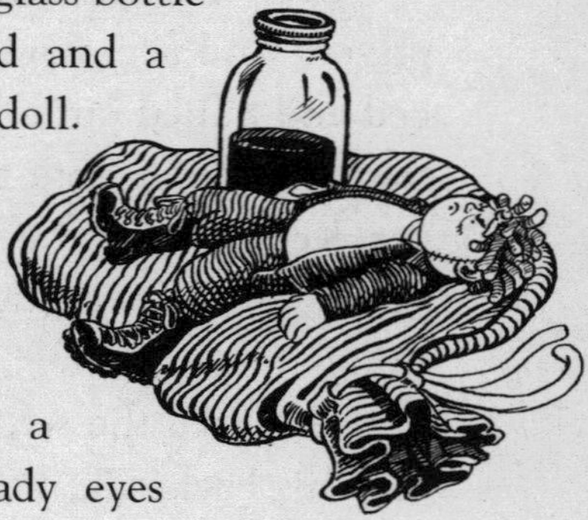

Leon glowered back. "You staring at me, Pumpkinhead?" he whispered sternly.

Pumpkinhead remained silent.

"Wipe that look off your face *now*, soldier!" Leon commanded in a low voice.

Pumpkinhead failed to obey the order.

"Okay, lamebrain, you asked for it." Leon dispensed a disciplinary noogie to show who was boss. Or rather, he made Pumpkinhead give *himself* a noogie by bunching up the tiny cloth fingers and grinding them into the figure's soft, stuffing-filled skull.

"And there's more where that came from," Leon promised.

Comforted by the one-way exchange, he began packing up. But as he reached for the bottle of brown liquid, he felt a slight tug on the leg of his pajamas. Suddenly his bed lamp came crashing down. A cord had wrapped around his shin.

Almost at once a voice called out from the living room. "Sweetie? You okay?"

"Fine," Leon managed as he groped about in the dark.

"What are you up to in there?"

Leon could hear the creaky springs of the pull-out couch, a sure sign his mother would soon burst in. "Just organizing stuff for school," he shot back, fumbling to re-pouch the bottle and rag doll.

The doorknob turned.

"What's blocking the door?" Emma Zeisel demanded.

Leon zipped up his backpack seconds before his mother pushed the blanket aside. She entered the bedroom and flipped on the wall switch.

Sniffing the air, she said, "I smell something fishy. You've been going through that collection of yours, haven't you?"

"No, Mom. It's just back-to-school jitters," Leon improvised.

"Well, jitters or no jitters, this is no time for mischief—not the night before the start of fifth grade. Get it?"

"Got it."

"Good," said Emma Zeisel firmly as she picked up the blanket. "Now get your behind back in bed."

As soon as Leon was under the sheets, his mother gave the blanket a single expert flick. It landed over her son with pinpoint accuracy. Quickly and effortlessly, she tucked in the corners. "There we go," she said, fluffing up the pillow. She gave her son a kiss and returned the bed lamp to the nightstand. "I'd tell you 'Lights out,' but you seem to have taken care of that all by yourself."

"I was just—"

"Hush now, and get some shut-eye," she scolded gently. "You have to be up by six-thirty to walk Trudy Lite."

"Six-*thirty*?" Leon whined.

"At the latest, sweetie. You're the one who told Napoleon you wanted to get to school before the first bell. Remember, he's picking you up at a quarter to eight on the dot."

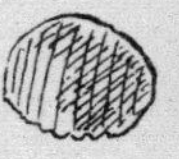

Two

The Moodometer

At 7:45 sharp the following morning, Leon pushed through the hotel's revolving door (twice) and hopped into an ancient yellow cab idling by the curb. He greeted the driver, a finely dressed Haitian man with a glistening smile made all the more sparkly by a shiny silver tooth.

"Bonjour, Napoleon!"

"Bonjour, Monsieur Leon! It has been too long, *mon ami*. How have we been?"

"Awesome," said Leon.

"Awesome?" Napoleon repeated disapprovingly. "Can you not be more exact?"

Leon knew what Napoleon wanted to hear. The cabby liked answers with numbers. A great day was an eight. A okay day was a four. A lousy day was a two.

Leon had come prepared. "If you really want me to be exact," he said, "we'd better use this." He handed Napoleon a small cardboard measuring device.

"For me?" Napoleon asked as he admired the handmade dial.

"Yup," said Leon. "I call it a 'moodometer.' It's like

an odometer, except that it indicates mood instead of miles."

Napoleon immediately propped the device on his dashboard. "Monsieur Leon, I am . . ." He finished his thought by nudging the needle to nine: PUMPED!

"And to answer your question," said Leon, "I'd give my summer an eight. It'd be higher, except for flute lessons, plus Mom keeps sticking me with more and more chores."

"Chores are good," said Napoleon.

"Not when it means picking up poodle poop at six-thirty in the morning!"

"That is true," Napoleon conceded. "Is that all you must do?"

"Are you kidding?" said Leon. He launched into an account of his expanded responsibilities. "I don't mind handling the VIP board. That's actually kind of fun. But now I have to do that *plus* walk Trudy Lite, *plus* clean cages, *plus* once I had to change a chimp's diapers." Leon winced at the memory. "I should've been paid double for *that* chore."

Napoleon chuckled. "Sometimes, Monsieur Leon, I wonder whether you live in a hotel or in a zoo."

"Mom says the same thing. She thinks we should sell tickets and peanuts to the folks who sit in the lobby. But that's the great thing about our all-pets-welcome policy. We get the best guests in town—except for that super-annoying Trudy Lite."

"I am sure you can control her," Napoleon said confidently. "You have a way with the beasts."

"You think so?" said Leon.

"I do," said Napoleon.

"Hope you're right," said Leon, giving the pouch in his backpack a squeeze.

THREE

A Spitting Image

Leon climbed the limestone steps of the Classical School and planted himself under the entrance flag ten minutes before the morning bell. He looked around nervously for his two best friends: Lily-Matisse, the strong-willed (and strong-armed) daughter of the school's art teacher, and P.W., a smart-alecky kid from Thailand whose full name—Phya Winit Dhabanandana—was too long for attendance forms.

Leon hadn't seen his buddies all summer. P.W. had spent the time with relatives in Bangkok. Lily-Matisse had gone off to gymnastics camp. The two, rounding the corner soon after Napoleon honked good-bye, made a beeline toward Leon.

"*So?*" said P.W. "Did you finish?"

"Yup," said Leon.

"When?" Lily-Matisse demanded.

"Two days ago."

"You brought him with you, right?" P.W. pressed.

Leon gave his backpack a tender pat. "He's right in here."

"Excellent," said P.W. "This is going to be so unbelievably sweet."

"If it works," Lily-Matisse cautioned.

"Have you guys seen you-know-who?" asked Leon.

P.W. lifted his wrist to his mouth and made a staticky sound. "That's a negative."

Lily-Matisse rolled her eyes.

"Okay," said Leon. "Where should we set up?"

"Over behind the trash can," P.W. suggested. "It's protected and in range. Plus it'll give us a clear shot of the entrance."

"Sounds good," said Leon.

Crouched behind the trash can, Leon unzipped his backpack and removed the large purple pouch. He turned to Lily-Matisse. "Care to do the honors?"

"Definitely!" she said.

"Hold it," said P.W. "Aren't we forgetting something?"

"What?" Leon asked.

"The pledge," said P.W.

Lily-Matisse made another face. "We already pledged last year."

"Maybe," said P.W. "But it's like a magazine subscription. You gotta renew."

Lily-Matisse and P.W. both looked at Leon. He could tell P.W. was a bit jealous that Lily-Matisse got

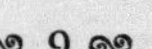

to hold the bag. "P.W. does have a point," he said diplomatically.

"Whatever," said Lily-Matisse. "Crossmyheart-hopetodiestickaneedleinmyeye. There. Satisfied?"

"No," said P.W. "You forgot the most important part."

"He's right," said Leon.

Lily-Matisse grudgingly sealed the oath by spitting, or at least pretending to spit. "Okay, your turn."

After the boys repeated the pledge (and spat copiously), Lily-Matisse slipped her hands inside the pouch and began extracting Pumpkinhead.

"Yow!" P.W. cried as soon as he saw the face.

Lily-Matisse was equally impressed. "He's perfect, Leon! How did you make him so, I don't know . . ."

"Gruesome?" P.W. proposed.

"Actually," said Lily-Matisse, "I was going to say real looking."

"It wasn't that hard," Leon said humbly. "I had that class picture Mr. Groot took at the medieval carnival."

"That is one nasty scowl!" said P.W.

"How'd you get his eyes to look so beady?" asked Lily-Matisse.

"Beads," said Leon.

"C'mon, let's see the rest of him!" urged P.W.

Gingerly Lily-Matisse continued the extraction, pausing again when Pumpkinhead was halfway free.

"The army jacket is incredible!" she cooed. "The buttonholes are amazing!"

"Oh, for crying out loud," P.W. exclaimed. "Will you hurry up!"

"Cool your jets," Lily-Matisse snapped. "It's not like pulling a rabbit out of a hat."

"No," said P.W. "This magic is way cooler."

"We'll see," said Lily-Matisse.

"Yes, we will, Miss Skeptical," said P.W. "Just because—"

"Guys," Leon interjected. "Let's pick up the pace."

"But I might damage something," said Lily-Matisse.

"No, you won't," Leon reassured her. "I double-stitched every seam. After all, Pumpkinhead has to be *extremely* flexible."

Lily-Matisse giggled. "What are you planning?"

"Guess," said Leon.

"A backflip?"

Leon smiled and shook his head. "Nah."

"Yeah, that's not nearly harsh enough," said P.W. "You're going to make him do a striptease in the lunchroom, aren't you?"

"Not exactly," said Leon, "but you're getting warmer."

"So it's clothing related?" Lily-Matisse conjectured.

"Yup," said Leon, his smile widening.

"Don't tell me he's going to moon Principal Birdwhistle!" said Lily-Matisse.

"Nope," said Leon. "But you guys are so hot you're burning up!"

There was a brief silence before P.W. came up with the answer. "Got it!" he exclaimed. "A wedgie!"

"Bingo!" Leon said. "Only not your ordinary standard-issue wedgie. I'll be taking things turbo."

"A *turbo*wedgie?" Lily-Matisse said dubiously.

"Right," said Leon. "Instead of just yanking on the underwear, I'm going to add a spinning motion, like this." He jerked his hand upward and twirled it overhead, as if handling a lasso. "I got the idea watching an old western on TV."

"Well, yee-ha!" P.W. whooped. "Ride 'em, cowboy!"

Lily-Matisse sighed. "Couldn't you have Pumpkinhead make him do something acrobatic, like a handstand on the salad bar?"

"Trust me," said Leon, "a turbowedgie *is* acrobatic."

Lily-Matisse gave a shrug and freed Pumpkinhead from the purple pouch. "Here," she said coolly, handing the figure to Leon.

"Thanks," he said, miffed by her lukewarm response. "And can you give me the bottle, too?"

Lily-Matisse grimaced. Without a word, P.W. took over, grabbing the pouch and removing the bottle of brown liquid.

"That stuff is *so* gross," Lily-Matisse said from a safe distance.

"Just think of it as starter fluid," said P.W.

"It's *not* starter fluid," she said. "It's teacher's spit and chewing tobacco and I'm not going anywhere near it."

"In that case," said P.W., "make yourself useful and recon the perimeter."

"Huh?"

"He means, be lookout," Leon explained.

"Oh," said Lily-Matisse. "What's the sign if I see him coming?"

"Just whistle," said P.W., before turning his attention to Leon. "Ready?"

Leon took a deep breath and nodded.

P.W. gave the spit bottle a vigorous shake. "Commence spit application in three, two, one . . ." He unscrewed the lid.

Leon did a quick squinch-and-cluck before accepting the bottle. Slowly and steadily he tilted it, watching as the spit traveled down the side of the glass like cold molasses. After a glob of the liquid landed on the midsection of the figure, he righted the bottle. "Done," he announced solemnly.

"You sure?" said P.W.

"Positive."

P.W. reclaimed the bottle. Just as he finished screwing the lid back on, Lily-Matisse, posted at the top of the school steps, began whistling like a songbird.

"Oh, yeah!" cried P.W. with unsuppressed joy. "Mission control, we have established visual contact. Target in sight. Repeat. Target in sight!"

FOUR

The Target

The target had many nicknames. Lumpkin the Pumpkin. The Lethal Launcher. Hank the Tank. All the aliases hinted at what was obvious to anyone who met him. Henry Lumpkin, Jr. (that was his full name, though woe to any classmate who called him "Henry" or "Junior" to his face), was big—*very* big! And he was mean—*very* mean!

He was a class bully in a class all his own. He picked on girls and he picked on boys. He picked on kids who were older, on kids who were younger, and on kids exactly his age. Although he wasn't particularly smart, Lumpkin did display an unnatural aptitude for whomping and whipping, punching, pushing and poking, smashing and mashing, teasing and taunting. He took an active interest in all matters military, and displayed that interest whenever, and on whomever, possible.

Yet while Lumpkin was an equal-opportunity bully, he had always paid particular attention to Leon.

During preschool, the attacks were pretty crude—playground kicks, lunch-line pokes, and the occasional snatched nap blanket. But as Lumpkin got bigger (and bigger and bigger), he refined his methods. By second grade he had perfected tripping. Third grade saw the introduction of the Howlitzer (alias the Ow!itzer or, when the victim was a girl, the How-It-Hurts-Her), a move that sent its victim flying into the closest available wall. For each of these innovations, Leon had been an unwilling test subject.

All that seemed about to change.

Lily-Matisse rejoined the boys behind the trash can.

"Payback time!" P.W. declared. "Think about it. No more rope burns."

"*If* it works," said Lily-Matisse.

"Oh, it'll work," P.W. said. "Won't it, Leon?"

Leon remained silent. He was too busy preparing Pumpkinhead.

"And when it does work," P.W. continued, "there'll be no more purple nurples or noogies or dead arms or dead legs or 'kick me' signs or wet willies or—"

Lily-Matisse cut him off. "What's a wet willie again?"

"Amateurs," P.W. sniffed. "Remember the time Lumpkin licked his finger, stuck it into Antoinette's ear, and swirled it all around?"

Lily-Matisse groaned. "*That's* a wet willie?"

"Last time I checked," said P.W.

"Keep it down," said Leon. "He'll be in range soon."

They watched and waited.

"Sheesh!" Lily-Matisse exclaimed. "He's even huger than last year!"

"His army jacket barely fits him!" P.W. marveled.

"That's not the piece of clothing he has to worry about," said Leon, pinching the rubber band holding up Pumpkinhead's tiny underpants.

Three sets of eyes (four, if one included the glass beads stitched into the doll's head) focused on the carrot-topped bully lumbering toward the limestone steps.

"Range?" Leon inquired.

"About forty feet," said P.W.

Leon lined up the shot like a big-game hunter, hunching slightly forward and planting his feet.

"Thirty-five feet," said P.W., his voice beginning to tremble.

Leon pointed the bead eyes of the doll at the beady eyes of his human likeness.

"Steady," P.W. warned. "Just a few more feet."

Suddenly Leon felt his hand yanked by Lily-Matisse.

"What the heck are you doing!" sputtered P.W.

"Teachers!" she exclaimed.

Leon froze. He had no choice but to suspend the

attack until Coach Kasperitis and Miss Hagmeyer, the dreaded fourth-grade teacher, disappeared through the entrance of the school.

"Okay," said P.W. "The coast is clear."

"Hey, Lumpkin's moving away!" said Lily-Matisse.

Leon frantically worked Pumpkinhead's limbs, but with no effect on Lumpkin.

"Darn!" said P.W. "He must be just out of range."

The three watched the bully trip an unsuspecting third grader. Not content to leave the kid sprawled on the pavement, he then *accidentally* kicked his victim's backpack into the gutter. By the time the ambush was over, a steady stream of first graders, holding their parents' hands, began climbing the school steps.

Leon craned his neck. "I can't see him!"

"Hold on," said P.W. "He'll resurface."

"No," said Leon. "I'm going in."

"Ten-four," said P.W., "but you'll need cover." He gave Lily-Matisse a knowing look, which she acknowledged with a nod. The two closed ranks to create a human shield.

"Perfect," said Leon, scooting up behind.

The surveillance resumed.

"Thirty-five feet," P.W. whispered. "Thirty feet—wait. He may be going after another kid . . . no, false alarm. Here he comes. Steady . . . *steady* . . . hold on just a little more . . . twenty-five feet. Target in range. *Repeat!* Target in range!"

Leon aimed, jerked, and twirled, swinging Pumpkinhead around once, twice, three times over his head, with the doll's underpants acting as the sling.

An agonizing few seconds elapsed before P.W. announced the sad news. "Failure to launch," he said with a sigh. "Repeat. Failure to launch."

Leon lowered his arms.

"What happened?" Lily-Matisse asked as gently as possible.

"You mean what *didn't* happen," Leon snapped. "Maybe someone didn't shake up the spit enough."

"Hey, hold on," P.W. said. "I shook the bottle plenty. Maybe *someone* didn't apply enough spit."

"I used the right amount," Leon grumbled.

"Look, guys," said Lily-Matisse, "it's no one's fault. Re-shake the bottle, add some more spit, and try again. Lumpkin is still in range."

They headed back to the staging area behind the trash can. After the necessary prep work, Leon gave Pumpkinhead another overhead turbowedgie.

"Nada," said P.W. "Miss Skeptical was right. The action figure is a bust."

Before Leon could respond, Lily-Matisse cut him off. "Lumpkin's spotted us! He's heading over!"

"Quick!" P.W. cried. "Hide the evidence!"

Frazzled by the launch failure, Leon was slow to react.

"*Hurry!*" cried Lily-Matisse.

P.W. grabbed Pumpkinhead, shoved him inside the

pouch, and deftly lobbed the incriminating package into the nearby trash can.

"Well, well," said Lumpkin. "If it isn't my good buddy Leon *Zit*-sel, plus his two dorky friends, P.U. and Silly-Matisse." He eyed the trash can. "Whatcha doin'?"

"Practicing free throws," said P.W.

"Just tossing away his lunch," Leon improvised a little more plausibly. "His mom keeps giving him squid sandwiches."

Lumpkin held out his hand. "Give me five!"

Leon hesitantly slapped his archenemy's upturned palm—or tried to. Within seconds he felt beefy fingers squeezing his wrist like a shop clamp.

"Stop it!" said Lily-Matisse.

"What's the matter?" Lumpkin sneered. "Don't you want Leon to be the first to experience my brand-new patented blood bracelet?"

Leon kept stone silent as his hand began to throb.

"Cut it out," said P.W. "How'll you explain the grip marks when Leon goes to Principal Birdwhistle?"

Lumpkin paused to consider the logic. "Maybe you're right," he said, releasing his hold. "We wouldn't want *Zit*-sel here to tattle on the very first day of school."

The next thing Leon knew, he was in a headlock. "The true beauty of the noogie," Lumpkin said, "is that it never leaves a mark."

Five long seconds elapsed before Leon felt a knuckle bone bear down on his scalp. If the blood bracelet felt like a shop clamp, the noogie was a drill.

"*Ow!*" Leon hollered.

"How original," Lumpkin crowed.

Only after Leon began whimpering did Lumpkin release him.

Leon staggered away, his head (and wrist) throbbing.

Once he was sure Lumpkin had moved on, Leon returned to the trash can to retrieve Pumpkinhead. He reached in and groped about.

"I can't feel it," he told his friends. "Must be all the way at the bottom." He hiked himself onto the rim of the container. Cautiously he extended an arm into the can and moved it around in small, investigative circles.

"No good," he said. "I'll have to go deeper."

He counted to three, took a breath, and stuck his head into the canister, stretching his hands blindly until the fingertips of his left hand brushed against something promising. He stretched a little more and . . .

"Gotcha!" he said, grabbing hold of the pouch.

Still balancing on the rim, doing his best not to breathe, Leon began to back himself out of the trash can.

All of sudden he felt something take hold of his

ankles. The next thing he knew, he was slipping.

"Easy does it," an all-too-familiar voice purred. "We wouldn't want Zit-sel to hurt himself."

Within seconds Leon found himself scrunched upside down in the trash. "Hey, let me out of here!" he howled, his legs flailing.

Voices came from all sides. "Pull him out!" "Touch him and you're dead!" "He'll suffocate!" "Tough, he deserved that dunkin'." "The bell's about to ring!"

The last prediction proved correct. The school bell did ring, after which Lumpkin's voice and the voices of Leon's friends died away, leaving him alone in dark, smelly silence.

FIVE

A Practice Flush

On his own and powerless, trapped inside a stinky, sticky trash can, Leon struggled to get free. He couldn't. His arms were pinned beneath him.

"Hey, you in there," someone chirped.

"I'm stuck!" Leon moaned.

"No kidding. Hold on—or rather, don't hold on. Just relax."

Relax? Leon said to himself. In a trash can?

"Okay," said the voice. "Here goes. Three, two, one . . ."

Leon felt a tug. Suddenly his whole body started to uncrumple. It was as if someone had hit the Rewind button on the previous few minutes of his life. The next thing he knew, he was squinting into the sun. He shielded his eyes and found himself looking at a thin, bald man with a very bushy beard.

"You okay?" the man asked pleasantly.

"Kind of," said Leon.

"What's in the pouch?"

Leon had forgotten all about the pouch clutched in his hand. "Um, lunch."

"Pretty fancy lunch sack you got there," said the man. "You sure you're okay? You look like, well, garbage."

Leon managed a smile.

"How'd you end up in there?"

"Slipped," said Leon.

"Slipped? Into a trash can?"

Leon nodded. He wasn't about to rat.

The man scratched his beard. "What's your name?"

"Leon Zeisel."

"Well, if you slipped *into* a trash can headfirst, Leon Zeisel, you defied the laws of gravity."

Leon shrugged.

"We'd better get inside," the man said, turning for the entrance of the school. "Second bell's already rung, and it's never wise to be tardy on the first day of class."

Leon tensed. It took him a moment to figure out why. Then he knew. "Tardy," he realized, was a word only teachers used.

For the rest of the day, Leon tried to keep a low profile. He hoped no one would talk about his trash can dunking.

Yeah, right, he told himself. Fat chance!

At assembly, walking past a row of sixth graders, he heard someone joke, "Hey, isn't that the kid who got *canned?*" And at gym, when Coach Kasperitis warned the class against trash-talking, Lumpkin yelled out, "If we can't *trash*-talk, then we can't talk about Zit-sel."

Leon fumed. When the recess bell rang, he took refuge in the boys' room. He checked the stalls and was relieved to find them empty. He entered the one farthest from the door and sat down. He removed Pumpkinhead from the pouch and stared at the figure's grim features.

What's the deal? he asked himself. Why don't you work like the last spitting image?

Leon brooded for a while about the success of his previous handiwork—the figure of his fourth-grade teacher, Miss Hagmeyer. With a careful application of teacher's spit, that earlier doll had worked like a charm (perhaps because it *was* a charm).

Pumpkinhead was a different story, and one that now seemed doomed to end badly.

Leon stood up and turned to face the toilet. He gave the miniature likeness of his archenemy a long, hard squeeze before beginning a countdown.

Five . . . four . . . three . . .

He hesitated. Headfirst or feet first? he wondered. Headfirst, *definitely*!

He dangled Pumpkinhead by the ankles over the bowl and started over.

Five . . . four . . . three . . . two . . .

He was stopped by another concern.

Release Pumpkinhead and *then* flush? Or flush *first* and then release? Or (a third option) drop and flush *at exactly the same time*?

Figuring a practice flush try might help him decide, Leon yanked on the tank handle. There was a weak *whoosh*, followed by a feeble gurgle, after which the water in the bowl slowly whirled away.

The Classical School was an ancient building, and its plumbing was just as old. Leon guesstimated it was fifty-fifty Pumpkinhead might not clear the drain. He imagined the miniature Lumpkin bobbing, like a dead halibut, on the surface of the water. The thought pleased him—until he realized the larger-than-life Lumpkin would probably find out. Plus there was a chance Principal Birdwhistle might learn about the floater. That wouldn't be pretty either.

In the end Leon nixed the dunking idea.

Ten minutes of recess remained. Not knowing where else to go, he dragged himself onto the playground.

P.W. and Lily-Matisse tried waving him over to the basketball court (where Lily-Matisse was winning a game of one-on-one). But Leon chose to sit on his own, under the giant maple shading the middle of the yard.

He glanced about. Reminders of his vanished power were everywhere. The jungle gym? That was where he had first revealed his supernatural abilities to P.W. and Lily-Matisse by forcing Miss Hagmeyer to perform one-handed pull-ups. The spot where Lumpkin was now teasing Antoinette Brede? That was where, again thanks to the earlier spitting image, Miss Hagmeyer had executed a stunning series of double-Dutch moves that culminated in a septuple twist—a 2520!—between a pair of spinning jump ropes.

But that was fourth grade, Leon said to himself, and this is fifth.

School began at 8:05 and ended promptly at three. Those six hours and fifty-five minutes were the longest six hours and fifty-five minutes Leon had ever endured—ever. Which might explain why, when the final bell *finally* sounded, he bolted like a racehorse.

He took the school steps two at a time, turning his head away as he passed the trash can that had caused him so much grief. In that split second, he caught sight of an ominous green-orange blur that prompted him to pick up the pace.

Halfway down the street, he glanced back, hoping he had imagined the ominous green-orange blur.

He hadn't. In fact, the ominous green-orange blur was gaining. And the closer it got, the less blurry (and the more ominous) it became.

Leon broke into an all-out gallop. He was in the homestretch, twenty feet from Napoleon's taxi, when he felt the first *thwack*!

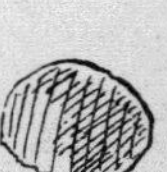

He stumbled, but didn't fall.

Then came the second *thwack*!—the one that dislodged his backpack and caused him to tumble.

"Wipeout!" Lumpkin cried out triumphantly as he dashed away.

Leon dusted himself off, thankful that his backpack had pillowed the fall.

Six

The Twofer

Napoleon turned and flashed a silver-toothed smile at his favorite passenger. "So, Monsieur Leon, how was the very first day of school? Still an eight?"

"No!" replied Leon as he got into the cab.

"Your mood, it went down?"

"Yes!"

"How far did it descend? To a seven?"

"Worse."

"A six?"

"More like *negative* six, okay?" Leon said angrily as he fumbled with the seat belt.

Napoleon looked through the rearview mirror. "A nasty teacher?"

"No."

"A nasty student?"

"Yeah," Leon acknowledged bitterly. "Now can we get going?"

Napoleon knew better than to press. For the next

few minutes, he drove without saying a word.

"I bet you," he said at last, "I can raise your mood to a five by the time we reach the hotel."

"No possible way," said Leon. He heard the click of the glove compartment, followed by a crinkling. "Is that what I think it is?" he asked.

"Perhaps," Napoleon responded coyly.

The crinkling grew louder.

"Plain?" said Leon.

"Non."

Leon leaned forward, his chest straining against the seat belt. "Sour cream and chives?"

"Hmm, *non*."

Leon sensed some hesitation and adjusted his next guess accordingly. "Sour cream and *onion*?"

"Non."

"Chives and cheddar cheese?"

"Non."

"Got it!" said Leon. "Mesquite barbeque. You know that's one of my favorite flavors."

"Sorry," said Napoleon. "Try again."

"Peppercorn?"

"Non."

"Edvard's Munch Madness—'the chip that'll make you scream!' "

"Guess again."

Leon pulled out all the stops. "Lickety Chips? Ho-Hums? Goody Two-Chews? Fandangos?"

"Non, non, non . . . non!" The cab filled with laughter.

Leon persisted: "Willy Winkle Krinkle Kuts?"

"Non."

"Cousin Ray's Low-Fat Kosher Dill Pickle Delights?"

"Non."

"Furtles Double Crunchers?"

"Non."

"Okay, already. I give up!"

Napoleon ended the guessing game by tossing the source of the crinkling into the backseat.

"Wow!" Leon exclaimed as soon as he saw the label. "Pinocchio Sour Cream and Clam Artificially Flavored Ripple Potato Chips! Where'd you get these?"

"A passenger," said Napoleon. "I've been saving them for a special moment."

"I have sixteen or seventeen sour creams," said Leon, "but this is my first *clam.*" He turned the package over to see where it was made. "Dynamite! They're from Maine!"

"Is that good, Monsieur Leon?"

"Better than good," said Leon. "I don't have a single bag from Maine." He inspected the package closely. "Listen to this poem. 'Nobody tires of Pinocchio fryers. / If folks say they do? / Well, we say they're liars!' "

"We should find out if that is so," Napoleon proposed.

"You read my mind," said Leon as he gently pulled apart the bag's heat-sealed seam, careful to minimize damage.

The taxi quickly filled with the distinctive odor of clam.

Leon reached forward with the open bag. "Care to do the honors?"

"*Mon dieu*," Napoleon exclaimed, waving a hand in front of his nose before rolling down the window.

"I'll take that as a no," said Leon, helping himself to a clam chip.

Within seconds he was rolling down *his* window. "Yuck!" he cried, spitting out the chip. "They taste even worse than they smell—not that I'm complaining. My first clam *and* my first Maine all in a single bag? That's one fine twofer!"

"Does that mean I win the challenge, Monsieur Leon?"

"I guess so."

As Napoleon adjusted the needle on the moodometer to five, Leon realized that potato chips had almost made him forget the botched turbowedgie, the trash can, the teasing, the taunts, and the tripping. Potato chips had almost made him forget Lumpkin. Almost.

But not quite.

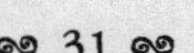

Seven

The Collection

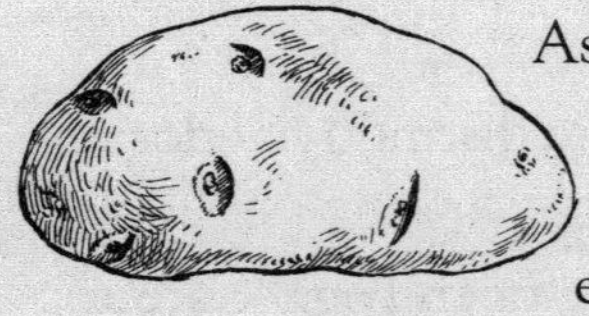

As soon as the taxi dropped him off, Leon spun through the revolving door (twice) and headed for the elevator.

He didn't make it.

Maria, the Trimore Towers housekeeper, blocked his path. "Not so fast, Leonito. Where you running?"

"Upstairs," said Leon. "I just got a twofer."

"Sorry, that twofer, she must wait. Your mother wants to see you."

"All right," Leon sighed before he made his way to the reception desk.

"Hey there, sweetie," said Emma Zeisel. "How was school?"

"Fine," Leon answered, figuring the less said, the better. "Look what Napoleon gave me." He showed off the twofer.

"*Clam* chips?" said Emma Zeisel dubiously.

"Yup—plus they're from Maine."

"Does that mean you've polished off New England?"

"Almost," said Leon. "I'm still missing Rhode Island. Can I go upstairs?"

"As soon as you update the VIP board. The

Barnstable Beekeepers will be swarming the place any minute."

"Can you handle it, Mom? *Please?*"

"Tell you what," said Emma Zeisel. "I'll do the board if you shell out one of those clam chips."

"I'm not sure that's a good idea," said Leon.

"Shell out a clam or no deal."

Leon presented the open bag to his mom. She reached in and took a chip. The gagging started almost at once and was followed by a quick dash to the tiny office behind the reception desk. When Emma Zeisel reemerged, she was looking a little green.

"I tried to warn you," said Leon.

Leon's mother managed a nod and waved her son away.

He took the elevator to the fifth floor. After a brief pit stop at the hallway garbage chute to dump the clam chips from the bag of Pinocchios, he let himself into the tiny two-room suite he shared with his mom. Once inside he went straight for the old metal footlocker stowed under his bed. He popped open the lid and removed an empty plastic sleeve. He slotted the chip bag into the transparent protector and placed it on the carpet. Then he took out the rest of his collection and spread it all around him.

Not bad, he said to himself. Not bad at all.

Empty potato chip bags—dozens and dozens of them—formed a crazy quilt of bright, bold colors, with not a double or damaged bag in the whole extraordinary bunch.

Leon had always loved potato chips. Always. He had been gobbling up chips for as long as he could remember. His collection, however, had a briefer history.

It all started in the middle of fourth grade. For Leon's tenth birthday, Maria had surprised him with a subscription to the Worldwide Chip of the Month Club. Membership entitled Leon to a monthly sampler of six different kinds of potato chips. After eating the chips, Leon decided to save the bags and mark the name of each sample on a little checklist included with the first shipment.

For a while the monthly packages kept Leon happy. But at a certain point, he discovered that the club failed to include samples of smaller, hard-to-find brands. That's when he decided to take matters into his own hands. He used his salary—with Emma Zeisel's authorization, the hotel bookkeeper cut him an allowance check in the amount of ten dollars every two weeks—to buy brands of chips the club had overlooked.

Did Leon stop there? No, he did not. Soon he began recruiting friends and family to help boost his holdings. Maria kept a lookout for stray chip bags left behind in the hotel rooms she cleaned, and Napoleon agreed to do the same when tidying up his taxi. Was that where Leon stopped? Again, no.

He added still more samples by writing directly to potato chip makers all over the country. It was amazing how many companies sent free samples when informed that their donations would be added to the permanent holdings of the Leon Zeisel Potato Chip Collection.

Surely Leon *must* have ended his pursuits there? Once more, the answer is no.

As the collection grew, so did Leon's ambitions. He started making special trips to the public library, where he compiled a master list of national and international potato chip makers. Furthermore, whenever foreign visitors stayed at the hotel, Leon would match their hometowns—helpfully listed in the Trimore Towers guest register—to the master chip list. If the visitors came from someplace near a potato chip factory that hadn't provided a sample, Leon would approach the guest and explain the situation. Since many visitors took pride in their local brand of chip, they often agreed to mail Leon a sample of the bag in question. Did it matter that some of the chips arrived crushed to the size of breakfast flakes? Not to Leon. He tasted the crumbs and preserved the bag like a first-edition comic book.

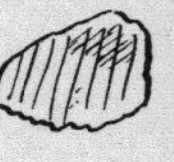

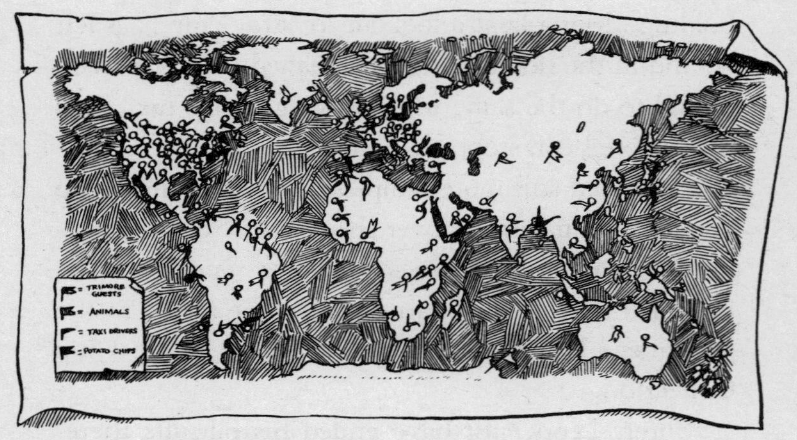

Besides collecting bags and keeping a checklist, Leon also maintained a geographical record of his potato chip holdings by noting the origin of every bag on a map of the world that hung above his bed. Each and every specimen that earned a place in the footlocker also received a flag marker on the map.

Leon kept a box of flag pins in his desk. The flag pins came in four colors (green, red, blue, and yellow). The variety proved useful, since Leon collected tons of stuff besides chips.

Blue flags marked the nationalities of the human visitors who checked into Trimore Towers.

Red flags recorded the birthplace of the animal guests. (For example, at the end of fourth grade when a group of emperor penguins booked a suite, Leon got to poke a red flag in Antarctica.)

Green flags were reserved for taxi drivers. Every

time Leon took a cab, he would ask the driver where he or she was from. He'd then flag that country on his map. (The taxi driver collection, it should be noted, dried up once Napoleon took Leon under his wing.)

And the yellow pins? The yellow pins, logically enough, were reserved for potato chips. Which explains why Leon fished one of those from his flag box and plunged it into Maine.

With the new conquest declared, Leon sat back and surveyed his holdings. Twenty-two states. Eight brands from Pennsylvania alone. *All* of New England (except for Rhode Island). Eleven countries in South America. Nine more from Asia, including a bag of squid-flavored chips sent by a Japanese VIP whose feisty Akita puppy Leon had happily walked three times a day during the entire month of July.

The ding-dong of an old-fashioned door chime interrupted his territorial inspection.

"Who is it?" Leon called out.

"Room service, Herr Zeisel," came the reply.

"Coming!" Leon jumped off his bed and cleared a path through his collection. He undid the chain on the front door and allowed a plump, pink-cheeked woman to enter the front room of the suite.

"Hey, Frau H!"

"Hey yourself, you little stinker, you," said Frau Haffenreffer, setting down a heavy tray on the table next to the pull-out couch.

"Whatcha got?"

"Dinner from my coffee shop."

"Mom pretty busy?"

"*Ja.* A new group is just now checking in."

"Must be the beekeepers," Leon speculated.

"*Ja.* Your mother told me the whole place is buzzing!"

Leon rolled his eyes. "I'm sure she did."

Emma Zeisel loved jokes and puns almost as much as Leon loved potato chips. The lamer the better. Guests who attended the auto show *drove* her crazy. The rabbit breeder convention kept things *hopping*. The West Coast Mime Company left her *speechless*. Leon was sure his mom had demanded he *shell* out a clam chip just to make a joke.

"So, anyway," said Frau Haffenreffer, "here is your dinner. You're the only one I give my personal room service."

"Thanks," said Leon, eyeing the dinner tray. "Let's see what we've got." He lifted the first of three dome-shaped food warmers. "Hmm," he said noncommittally. He removed the second dome, poked at the food underneath, and licked his fingertip. That prompted another "hmm."

"So?" Frau Haffenreffer asked nervously.

Leon refused to comment until he had lifted the third and final dome. Once he had, he let out a sigh.

"It's not okay?" said Frau Haffenreffer. "Tell me!"

"No," Leon replied. "It is *not* okay, Frau H. It's . . . *perfect*."

He waved his hand over the three-course meal. "PB&J (extra J). A bag of Billy Bob Barbeque Potato Chips. And, to finish things off, a platter of Haffenreffer dough balls. Now *that's* what I call dinner!"

"You little stinker, you!" Frau Haffenreffer said, pinching Leon's cheek. "You just make sure you eat everything up. And don't forget to leave the tray in the hall for Maria."

Frau Haffenreffer bustled toward the door. "Ach, and something else. Your mother—she wanted me to tell you she has some doggone good news for you."

"Let me guess," said Leon. "The toy poodle in three-oh-nine checked out."

Frau Haffenreffer gave him a startled look. "How did you know that?" she said.

"Because," said Leon, "Mom can't resist doggone jokes."

After polishing off his three-course dinner, Leon worked on the collection. Comforted by the soothing crinkle of foil, he felt his mood climb into the low sevens by the time he prepared for bed. But that was

before he noticed a mysterious black splotch on the bottom of his backpack. He undid the zipper and stuck his hand inside.

He felt something wet and slimy.

A queasy feeling came over him as he dumped the contents of his pack. Brown gunk covered everything—his three-ring binder, his No. 2 pencils, the purple pouch.

Leon was forced to replay the humiliating attack that had ended the school day. He *thought* he'd been lucky when the backpack pillowed his fall. Now he knew better. The spit bottle inside the pouch had smashed on impact. He hadn't gotten hurt, but Pumpkinhead was another matter.

In a rage, Leon grabbed the dripping pouch by the drawstring, dropped it into one of the metal domes resting on the dinner tray, and used the dome to carry the mess to the bathroom.

"*Sayonara*, Pumpkinhead!" he said bitterly as he tipped the dome. The pouch landed in the toilet with a *plouf*!

He banged on the toilet handle and waited for the damaged doll to disappear. Seconds later he let out a curse. The Trimore Towers toilets proved every bit as feeble as the toilets at school.

Leon retrieved the other two metal domes and used them to extract the pouch from the bowl. He dropped the pouch onto a dinner plate, which he took to the garbage chute. He pulled on the heavy handle and tilted the plate. The pouch plopped into the bin.

All that remained was to release the door handle and send the pouch on its final voyage—first in a free fall to a basement Dumpster, then to the hotel trash compactor, and from there to a garbage truck that would haul it to a landfill beyond the city limits.

Leon decided to take one last look before letting go. He loosened the drawstrings of the pouch and shook out the contents into the open bin.

The sight was horrible—a disgusting stew of saliva, broken glass, and cloth. Shards from the shattered bottle had sliced through Pumpkinhead's arms, legs, and face. Panty hose stuffing oozed out of the wounded figure's substantial rump and tiny head.

"Time for a Lumpkin Dunkin'—Zeisel style!" Leon announced bitterly. And with that, he slammed the chute door shut.

EIGHT

Sparks

Even though he no longer had to deal with Pumpkinhead and could sleep later than usual, thanks to Trudy Lite's departure, Leon was feeling miffed when Napoleon picked him up the next morning.

"A three," he said when pressed for a reading. "Three and a half, tops."

"I am sorry to hear that, Monsieur Leon. I wish I could adjust your mood like so." Napoleon reached over and fiddled with the needle on the moodometer so that it pointed to GREAT!

"Yeah, well, you can't," Leon said glumly.

His mood stayed in the low threes for most of the morning, then dropped to the mid-twos after Lumpkin tripped him, accidentally on purpose, during a third-period fire drill.

He measured a tiny improvement at lunchtime after discovering that Frau Haffenreffer had packed a bag of Krispee Krunchy Salt 'n' Vinegar Potato Chips in his lunch sack. (It was a brand he needed for his collection.) But then Lumpkin snatched the bag away. Within seconds he had devoured the chips and destroyed the package, which sent Leon's mood needle to the danger zone of CRUMMY.

During recess Leon swished two shots from the free throw line in a fierce game of H-O-R-S-E. That raised his mood to four. Yet comfort again proved fleeting.

"Lumpkin wants the ball," Lumpkin announced before Leon could secure the win.

"But Lily-Matisse is at H-O-R-S," said Leon, "and she's about to get an E."

"Tough!" Lumpkin barked. "Give me the ball now, or I'll knock the stuffing out of you."

Leon was tempted to satisfy the request by launching the basketball at Lumpkin's head. He resisted the impulse, knowing it would trigger a swift and brutal counterattack.

"Take it," he said, releasing the ball.

His mood dropped below two, and there it stayed until last period.

The school day ended with science, a subject taught in a big old basement laboratory next to Mr. Groot's woodshop. Leon had never set foot inside the lab. It was off-limits until fifth grade. As soon as he entered, he understood why.

The lab was filled with lots of serious-looking equipment. There were Bunsen burners, safety goggles, and racks of test tubes and beakers. Three glass tanks—containing tropical fish, a turtle, and a pair of lazy geckos—took up one wall of the lab. A giant

plastic python stretched across a locked cabinet filled with chemicals.

Leon joined his two friends near a lab sink.

"You're off the hook," said P.W. "Looks like Hank the Tank is going after the new kid."

"Who is she?" asked Leon.

"Florence Parmigiano," said Lily-Matisse. "Mom told me I have to be nice to her."

"From the looks of things," said Leon, "she should have told Lumpkin."

"Yeah," P.W. agreed. "Lumpkin's going to eat her up alive."

Before Lumpkin could make a quick meal out of Florence Parmigiano, a brilliant flash lit up the lab.

"Welcome, fellow researchers!" a voice chirped from the back of the room as a dazzling pinwheel, the size of a Frisbee, began spinning and shedding sparks near the blackboard. Even before Leon turned, he knew that the voice belonged to the bald bearded man who had rescued him from the trash.

"That's the science teacher," Lily-Matisse whispered. "He's new. Mom told me he's a little weird. And given how loosey-goosey she is, that means he must *really* be out there."

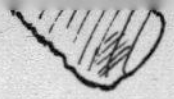

"No kidding," said P.W. "What clued her in? The bright green high-top sneakers? The wild-man beard? Or was it the ponytail running down his back?"

"Knock it off," Leon said protectively. "Cut the guy some slack."

The science teacher made his way to the front of the room, and as he passed Leon he whispered, "Ah, the boy who defies gravity." With the pinwheel still spinning, the teacher grabbed a stick of chalk off the ledge of the blackboard. He drew a pair of jagged lightning bolts and, between them, wrote the word "park" so that the blackboard looked like this:

He put down the chalk and wiggled the fingers of one hand, which appeared to make the pinwheel stop. "My name is Franklin Sparks," he informed the class. "Everyone grab a seat."

"Don't we have *assigned* seating?" asked Antoinette Brede expectantly.

"Not exactly," said Mr. Sparks. "My seating rule is

simple. You can't sit next to the same person twice in a row. And before anyone asks me why, I'll tell you. Great science tends to emerge from unexpected combinations." As the students swapped looks of amazement, Mr. Sparks pulled a clipboard from a beat-up leather satchel. "I'll have to take attendance," he said, "at least till I learn who you are. Sound off when you hear your name." He glanced at the clipboard. "Zeisel, Leon?"

"Here!" Antoinette Brede called out.

"Here!" cried Leon a split second later.

Mr. Sparks turned to Antoinette Brede. "You don't look like a Leon." Antoinette turned red. Leon was also a little embarrassed, though pleased. His surname usually meant the end of the line, the back of the bus, the last to be called.

"Scientifically speaking," said Mr. Sparks, once attendance had been taken, "a spark is a glittering spit of energy that travels between two conductors. Well, I'm going to be one of those two conductors. All of you will be the other!" He wiggled his fingers at the pinwheel, hocus-pocus style, and once more, as if by supernatural force, sparks began to fly.

"You see that?" P.W. whispered to Leon. "He's got a remote in his pocket."

Leon didn't respond. He couldn't. He was entranced. The little sparks Mr. Sparks had set off triggered much bigger sparks in his head. He found himself thinking about his dad, who had worked as a pyrotechnician—the fancy word for fireworks designer—until an accident had taken his life. Leon remembered very little about his dad, but what he did remember usually involved big, bright, colorful bursts of light.

"Um, Mr. Sparks?" It was Antoinette.

"Please don't interrupt."

"But, Mr. Sparks. Your sleeve!"

A spark from the pinwheel had landed on his shirt cuff.

"Oh," he said. "Nothing to worry about. A science teacher always takes precautions when it comes to matters of safety." He dashed over to the sink and turned on the tap. "Problem solved," he said as a wisp of smoke rose toward the ceiling.

Lumpkin couldn't control himself. "Hey, Mr. Sparks," he shouted, rocking back and forth on his stool. "*Students* aren't allowed to be clumsy. Don't you know our school saying? It's 'Nimble fingers make for nimble minds!' "

"And don't *you* know that nimble fifth graders avoid annoying their science teachers?" Mr. Sparks shot back.

A chorus of oohs filled the room. Lumpkin abruptly stopped rocking. Leon, P.W., and Lily-Matisse exchanged approving looks.

Mr. Sparks squeezed the water from his sleeve and

said, "All kidding aside, I am indeed familiar with the motto of the school. It is one I endorse wholeheartedly. After all, the type of hands-on science we will be performing requires nimble fingers."

For the next few minutes, Mr. Sparks discussed lab reports and field trips and the science fair held at the end of the year. But just as he started to sound like a normal science teacher, talking about normal science teacher things, he again did something *ab*normal.

He unbuttoned his shirt.

"I know, I know," said Mr. Sparks. "Teachers should never undress in class. But this wet sleeve is a nuisance." He stripped down to a T-shirt that showed a picture of a white-haired old man sticking out his tongue. The T-shirt said:

"ANYONE WHO HAS NEVER MADE A MISTAKE HAS NEVER TRIED ANYTHING NEW."
—ALBERT EINSTEIN

Mr. Sparks tapped the face of the scientist. "Einstein got that right," he told the giggling class. "Science *demands* mistakes. And accidents. And failure. They're the building blocks of grand discovery."

The pinwheel in Leon's brain started to spin again. Mistakes? he said to himself. I know all about mistakes. And accidents. And failures. Pumpkinhead is proof of that. More sparks flew. If Einstein's right, maybe the launch failure was a *good* thing. Words spun about in his head. *Mistakes . . . gravity . . . spit of energy . . . grand discovery.*

All of a sudden, the words came together, and when they did, Leon's mood needle began to rise. *Four . . . five . . . six . . .*

NINE

The First R

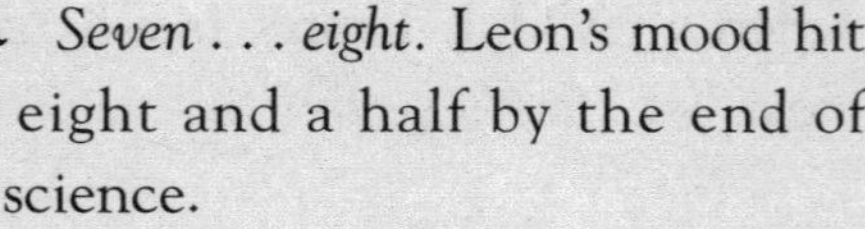

Seven . . . eight. Leon's mood hit eight and a half by the end of science.

"I've made a decision," he informed Lily-Matisse and P.W. as soon as they'd left the lab.

"About?" said P.W.

"About Pumpkinhead."

"Which one?" Lily-Matisse asked. "The human or the doll?"

"It's an *action figure*, not a doll," P.W. grumbled.

"Whatever," Lily-Matisse snapped.

"Guys," Leon interjected. "Focus. I'm talking about *both* Pumpkinheads."

"That's a relief," said P.W. "I got worried that you might've bailed on the whole project."

"I almost did," Leon admitted.

"So what's changed your mind?" Lily-Matisse asked.

Leon stuck out his tongue.

"Einstein?" said P.W.

"Yup—and Sparks. I figure if accidents, mistakes,

and failures lead to discovery, we're pretty much set."

P.W. grinned. "So what's the plan?"

"Not here," said Leon. "Let's go over the details at my place—if that's okay with you guys."

He didn't have to ask twice. Both Lily-Matisse and P.W. loved Leon's hotel and its menagerie of guests.

"Better get my mom to call your parents," said Lily-Matisse. Once permissions were secured, the three fifth graders dashed down the school steps and piled into the yellow cab parked at the end of the block. It pleased Napoleon to see Leon with his two best friends. He tried to ask his usual question, but Leon cut him off.

"Eight-point-five and rising!"

Leon refused to discuss specifics in the taxi. Lily-Matisse and P.W. both knew why. Napoleon might overhear, and that would violate the crossmy-hearthopetodiestickaneedleinmyeye spit pledge the three had sworn soon after Leon discovered his special powers. The conversation in the cab focused on science, and on the bald, bearded, ponytailed, green-sneakered teacher who taught it.

Leon said, "Mr. Sparks may be out there, and he may be a little bit clumsy, but I think he rocks."

"Me, too," said Lily-Matisse.

"No argument from me," said P.W. "And man oh man, was it sweet watching him shut Lumpkin down with that crack about nimble students!"

"Not as sweet as it will be when *we* shut Lumpkin down," Leon said with renewed confidence.

A few minutes later, Napoleon pulled up to the hotel and released his passengers. Before the cab drove off, Leon asked if P.W. and Lily-Matisse could be picked up around five.

"Bien sûr," Napoleon confirmed with a silver-toothed smile.

"That means 'sure thing,'" Leon explained.

The three thanked the driver and pushed through the revolving door (twice).

"Holy moly," P.W. exclaimed as soon as he'd set foot inside the lobby. The air was filled with dense smoke and an odd, steady buzzing.

"What's going on?" asked Lily-Matisse, waving a hand in front of her eyes.

"No idea," Leon replied. He led his friends to the reception desk, where Emma Zeisel was looking unusually flustered.

"Mom?" said Leon.

"It's those bumbling beekeepers," she complained. "One of them dropped a hive in the coffee shop."

Lily-Matisse and P.W cracked up. Leon rolled his eyes.

"What's with the smoke, Ms. Z?" P.W. asked.

Emma Zeisel pointed to a man wearing a bright white jumpsuit and a wire mesh helmet. "You see the

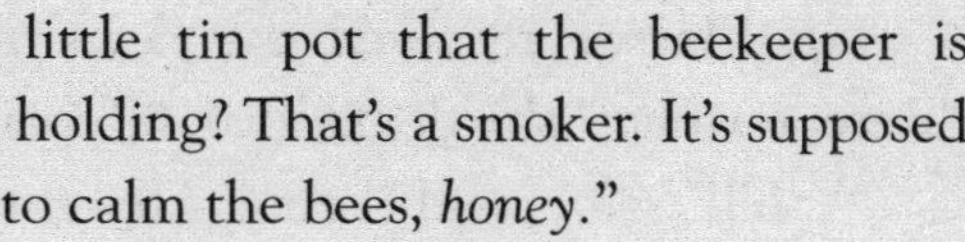

little tin pot that the beekeeper is holding? That's a smoker. It's supposed to calm the bees, *honey*."

"Anyone get stung, Mom?"

"Not yet, thank heavens. But just to be safe, you three should make a bee-line to the elevator."

"What about the VIP signboard?" Leon asked.

Emma Zeisel checked a list behind the reception desk. "You can change the board later," she said. "The International Ferret Festival won't be arriving until tomorrow afternoon."

Leon, Lily-Matisse, and P.W. did what they were told and headed for the elevator. "Okay, 'fess up," P.W. said as soon as they were safely inside. "How are we shutting Lumpkin down?"

"Have you guys ever heard of the three R's?" Leon asked as he jabbed a button marked B.

"Duh!" said Lily-Matisse. "Reading, writing and 'rithmetic."

"Not *those* three R's," Leon teased.

"Okay, I'll bite," said P.W. "Which ones are *you* talking about?"

"Glad you asked," said Leon as the elevator doors opened. "I'm talking about rescue, repair, and reanimation."

"I like what I'm hearing," said P.W.

Lily-Matisse received the news more tentatively. "Rescue what?" she demanded. "Repair what?"

"You'll see," said Leon. He guided his friends through the basement, to a door marked HOUSEKEEPING. "We've got to pick up some stuff before we hit the garbage room."

"And we're going to the garbage room *why*?" Lily-Matisse asked nervously.

"To perform the first R," said Leon.

"What exactly are we supposed to be rescuing?" said Lily-Matisse.

"Pumpkinhead."

"What's Pumpkinhead doing in the garbage room?" she asked.

"I tossed him."

"Why?"

"Lily-Matisse!" P.W. cut in sharply. "Stop giving Leon the third degree."

"It's okay," said Leon. "I do have to explain the situation. Remember how Lumpkin attacked me after school yesterday? Well, when I fell I landed on the spit bottle. It got smashed. Everything got all goopy and torn up. I was so bummed, I tossed the mess away."

"Everything?" said Lily-Matisse. "Even the pouch?"

"Even the pouch," Leon confessed.

"But I made you that pouch for your tenth birthday," Lily-Matisse said sullenly.

"I know," said Leon. "And I feel bad about that.

But we'll get it back. I promise." Leon opened the door to Housekeeping. "Okay, let's see." He looked around the cluttered room. "We'll need a broomstick, a pair of rubber gloves, and a plastic bag."

The first two items were easy enough to locate, but the bags proved tougher to find.

"Hold on," said Leon. He walked over to a trash can, tugged off the black plastic can liner, and reached inside for a fresh bag.

"How'd you know there'd be a spare?" asked P.W.

"Old housekeeping trick," said Leon. "Maria always stashes extras inside the cans."

"Is that everything?" P.W. asked impatiently.

"Don't rush me," said Leon. "We'll also need Maria's sewing basket."

"Better write her a note," Lily-Matisse advised.

"Good idea," said Leon. "What should I say we're using the stuff for?"

"How about telling her it's for a science project?" P.W. suggested.

"Perfect," said Leon. "And, actually, that *is* what we're doing."

He scribbled a note:

"You're not returning the science project," Lily-Matisse quibbled. "You're returning the stuff. The note's confusing."

"Hey, can we keep things moving here?" said P.W. "The note's fine."

"Just one more thing, and we'll be all set," said Leon. He scrounged up a big jug from a closet of cleaning products. "When you live in a hotel with an all-pets-welcome policy, this stuff is a must!"

Lily-Matisse looked at the label and grimaced. " 'Poop-B-Gone'?"

"Maria calls it her 'miracle potion,' " Leon said as he led his friends down a narrow corridor.

The garbage room was dark and hot. A network of water pipes crisscrossed the ceiling. Wire fencing cut the space in half, and it was the caged-off half that contained a dozen or so wheeled Dumpsters and a singularly nasty-looking machine that had a thick metal pole rising up from the middle.

"What *is* that?" P.W. asked.

"The trash masher," said Leon.

"Oh, great," Lily-Matisse said miserably. "I bet my pouch has been crushed like a pancake."

"Not a chance," Leon reassured her. "The trash masher is directly below the reception desk and makes such a huge racket that we only smoosh things on Sunday nights, when no one's in the lobby."

P.W. yanked down on a heavy padlock that secured

the cage. "Hey, Leon, did you bring the key for this thing?"

"It's locked?"

"Affirmative," said P.W.

"Darn. I'll have to find Maria. Be right back."

"Hold on," said Lily-Matisse. Quick as a whip, she bent her knees, sprang into the air, and grabbed hold of an overhead water pipe. "Watch and learn," she said, dangling off the ground.

She swung her legs up and around the pipe and slithered through the narrow gap at the top of the cage.

"*Nice* move," said Leon as she dropped down on the far side.

Lily-Matisse blushed. "Gymnastics camp," she said.

Leon shoved the rubber gloves and the broomstick through the fencing. "You'll probably want these," he said. "Could be nasty in there."

"Which Dumpster is the stuff in?" Lily-Matisse asked.

"No idea," said Leon.

"Super," said Lily-Matisse as she snapped on the gloves. "I'm going to have to eenie-meenie-minie my way through garbage."

"No, you won't," said P.W. "If Leon dumped Pumpkinhead last night, it makes sense to check the Dumpster underneath the garbage chute first."

"He's right," said Leon.

Lily-Matisse peered into the bin positioned underneath the mouth of the chute. "Empty," she announced.

"Check the one next to it," P.W. called out.

Lily-Matisse followed his advice. "Nope," she said. "Just recycled stuff. Newspapers and cardboard." She moved on.

"Yuck!" she cried. "What a stink!"

"Our guests tend to have a lot of accidents," Leon told her.

"It's not a poopy smell," she observed. "It's more fishy."

"Really?" Leon said excitedly. "I tossed some clam-flavored potato chips a few hours before I got rid of Pumpkinhead and the pouch."

Lily-Matisse probed the Dumpster with the broomstick. "I see it!" she called out. A carefully aimed poke harpooned the soiled pouch. Pumpkinhead, however, proved elusive. "I can't find him," she said.

"Then what are you waiting for?" P.W. shouted. "Dive in!"

"Are you nuts?" cried Lily-Matisse.

"He's right," said Leon. "It's the only way."

Reluctantly Lily-Matisse took a running jump and vaulted into the Dumpster. When she resurfaced, she was clutching Pumpkinhead in her rubber-gloved hand.

"Way to go!" Leon yelled.

"Not bad," P.W. allowed.

Lily-Matisse hopped out of the Dumpster and returned with the rescued items. She peeled off the gloves and pushed them through the fencing, then passed back the broomstick and the pouch. But once again Pumpkinhead caused headaches.

"He won't fit through," said Lily-Matisse. "The holes are too small."

"We can see that," said P.W.

"Toss him over the top," Leon suggested.

After a couple of tries, Pumpkinhead cleared the fencing and landed on the cement floor with a *plop*!

"He looks like a dead jellyfish," said P.W.

Leon placed Pumpkinhead and the pouch inside the plastic bag snatched from Housekeeping.

"Is that it?" said Lily-Matisse. "Can I come back over?"

"That's a roger," said P.W.

Lily-Matisse jumped up, grabbed hold of the water pipe, and shinnied back to freedom. As soon as she dropped down, she let Leon and P.W. have it. "I got slime all over my brand-new sneakers!"

"Stop your bellyaching," said P.W. "Look on the positive side. We've just completed the first of the three R's."

"And don't worry about your sneakers," Leon quickly added. "We'll clean them up upstairs."

Ten

The Second R

The first R—rescue—went off without a hitch. The second R—repair—would be trickier. Up in the bathroom of his apartment, Leon put on a pair of rubber gloves and extracted the two soiled objects recovered from the trash.

"The pouch is okay, just stained," he declared.

"And Pumpkinhead?" P.W. asked anxiously.

The silence that followed made it clear the action figure hadn't been so lucky. The free fall down the garbage chute had added more damage to an already battered body.

"Take the slivers out first," Lily-Matisse advised. "They can be super-dangerous."

"I'm on it," said Leon. He found a pair of tweezers in the bathroom cabinet and used them to pick out the bits of broken bottle.

"What's next, doc?" asked P.W.

"Despitification," said Leon.

"Count me out!" Lily-Matisse said adamantly.

"What a surprise," said P.W.

"Hey, leave her alone," said Leon. "She just dove into a Dumpster."

"Fair enough," P.W. acknowledged. "Sorry."

"Apology accepted," said Lily-Matisse.

Leon turned to P.W. "You despitify the pouch, I'll work on the doll."

"What about my sneakers?" Lily-Matisse pressed.

"We'll get to them, I swear," said Leon. "Can one of you grab the Poop-B-Gone?"

Lily-Matisse backed off as soon as she heard the name.

"I'll get it," said P.W. He picked up the jug. "Hey, listen to this." He began to read the label out loud:

"Take the POOP-B-GONE Challenge!
We're sure this potion is entirely able
To clean the things on this label
And if it doesn't, in the time
It takes to read the following rhyme,
Poop-B-Gone will GUARANTEE
To reimburse the purchase fee!*"

He took a deep breath and continued:

"Crud, mud, raspberry juice,
Ground-in dirt—tough or loose.
Spills on twills, grease on sweats,

Nasty fluids expelled by pets.
Grass, grout, Limburger cheese,
Guano, glue marks, Darjeeling teas.
Lipstick, pen marks, makeup, mold,
Coffee stains (new and old)."

He took another deep breath:

"Light caulk, white chalk, silver tarnish,
Asphalt, crayon, yellowed varnish.
Scuff marks, mucus, bacon fat,
Scotch tape, whisky, things that *splat!*"

And another breath:

"Fruit punch, cola, lager beers,
Decals, wet paint, pesky smears.
Chocolate sprinkles, powdered sugar,
Old folks' pee and baby booger.
Red wine, pickle brine, French champagne,
Candle wax on carpet stain.
Muck, mulch, horse manure,
Gunk belonging in the sewer."

And another:

"Grease, tallow, oil, blubber,
Skid marks caused by bike wheel rubber.

Pasta sauce, steamer trunk labels,
Ghastly rings on antique tables.
Rust, must, all known inks,
Stubborn clogs in backed-up sinks.
Grit, grime, bathtub scum,
Residue of bubblegum.
So rest assured, the list is long,
Of mess addressed by POOP-B-GONE!

*Operating time: one minute or less.
(Please wear gloves when handling mess.)"

"It doesn't mention spit," Lily-Matisse noted.

"Sure it does," said P.W., still catching his breath. "'Nasty fluids expelled by pets' . . . that means spit."

"Maybe it does, maybe it doesn't," said Lily-Matisse. "Pet spit and teacher spit aren't the same."

"Yes, they are," said P.W. "Spit is spit. There's no chemical difference, right, Leon?"

"I have no idea. But the sooner you guys stop arguing, the sooner we'll find out."

Leon grabbed the jug and poured a goodly amount of Poop-B-Gone on the pouch and Pumpkinhead. He allowed the potion to fizz for a few seconds before attacking the drenched areas with a washcloth. Less than a minute later, the stains had disappeared.

"Maria was right," said P.W. "That stuff is magic."

Lily-Matisse looked at Pumpkinhead and said,

"Let's just hope that magic doesn't counteract the magic in the doll."

"Action figure!" P.W. exclaimed.

"Guys," said Leon as he grabbed a hair dryer mounted to the wall. "Less fighting, more helping, okay? P.W., you blow-dry Pumpkinhead. Lily-Matisse, you clear off the table near the couch."

By the time Pumpkinhead was dry, Lily-Matisse had finished in the living room. "The operating room is ready, doctor," she announced.

"Wow," said Leon, surveying the sewing instruments neatly arranged on a hotel towel. "Nice job."

"Thanks."

"You even threaded the needles," Leon noted gratefully.

"I figured it'd speed things up," said Lily-Matisse.

"Not bad," P.W. admitted. "There's only one problem." He disappeared into Leon's bedroom.

"What are you looking for?" Leon called after him.

"You'll see," P.W. shouted back.

While waiting, Leon surveyed the operating table. "One long knitting needle. Four threaded sewing needles. One pincushion with pins. Three spools of thread. That's pretty much all I need, except for a pair of scissors."

Lily-Matisse rifled through the sewing basket and found the missing instrument. Just then P.W. reappeared.

"My bed lamp?" said Leon.

"Yup," said P.W. He plugged the lamp into an outlet and aimed it at the surface of the table. "This should help," he said, flicking on the switch.

"You're right," said Leon.

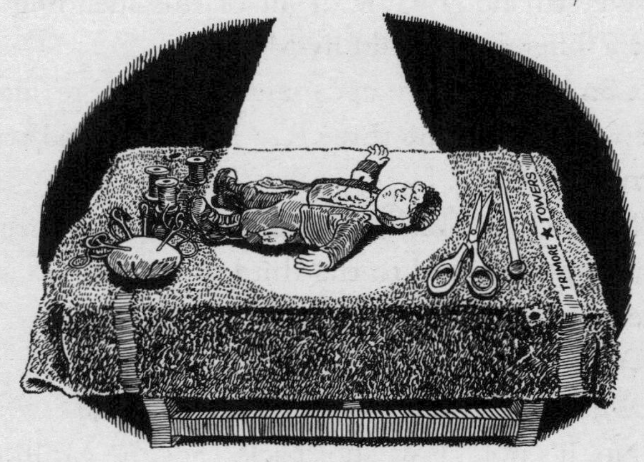

For the next twenty minutes, Leon sewed in silence, displaying the agility of a master tailor. It seemed hard to believe that a kid who'd had trouble tying his laces at the start of fourth grade now wielded needle and thread with a surgeon's precision.

He started at the feet and slowly moved his way up the body. His method was the same at each trouble spot. First he would reinsert the panty hose stuffing that had popped out. Then he would pin the rip, stitch it, and tie off the thread. Some of the smaller cuts required nothing more than a simple, straightforward running stitch. But a number of larger holes demanded complex double- and triple-stitch repairs.

"What's the prognosis, doc?" P.W. asked as Leon was suturing the last of the trouble spots, a gash just below Lumpkin's hairline.

"Pretty good."

"We still don't know if all of this mending will make a difference," said Lily-Matisse.

"Can you lighten up?" said P.W. "We're almost done with two of the three R's. That's not bad for an afternoon's work."

"Maybe," said Lily-Matisse. "But rescue and repair are a snap compared to the third R. There's no guarantee we'll be able to reanimate the doll."

P.W. snapped. "Stop calling it a doll!"

"Well, that's what it is," said Lily-Matisse.

"No, it's not," P.W. shot back. "For the gazillionth time, my sister plays with *dolls*. What Leon is repairing is an *action figure*."

"So far it hasn't been all that active," said Lily-Matisse. "*In*action figure is more like it."

Leon looked up from his repair. "Guys! Cool it. Just come up with a name you can both live with, okay?"

Lily-Matisse frowned at P.W. "What do *you* want to call it?"

"Well," said P.W., "since Leon called the first spitting image of Lumpkin 'Pumpkinhead,' let's call this new and improved version 'Pumpkinhead two-point-oh.'"

"Works for me," said Leon.

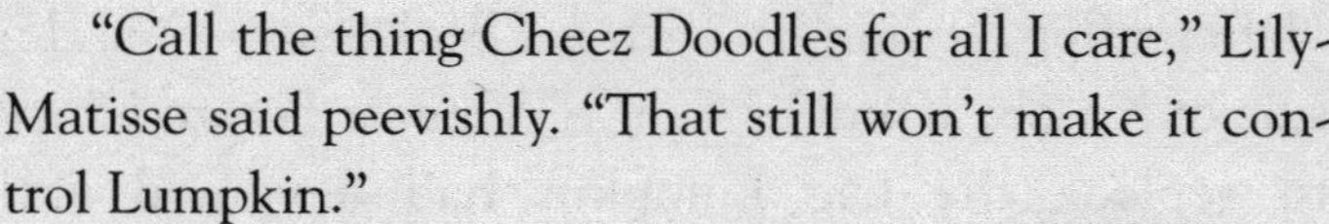

"Call the thing Cheez Doodles for all I care," Lily-Matisse said peevishly. "That still won't make it control Lumpkin."

Leon sat up and dropped his sewing needle on the towel. "All done," he announced.

"Not entirely," said Lily-Matisse. "Aren't you forgetting something?" She tapped her sneakers.

"I don't remember 'Dumpster dirt' listed on the Poop-B-Gone label," said P.W.

"I did promise her," said Leon.

By the time Pumpkinhead 2.0 was ready for action (and Lily-Matisse's sneakers had been cleaned), the air in the lobby had cleared and the beekeeper with the smoker had left.

"Where's the bee guy?" Leon asked his mom.

"I told him to buzz off," said Emma Zeisel. "The smoke was bothering the VIPs. Speaking of which, here's the list for tomorrow. We've got some last-minute additions that'll make Maria very happy."

After Leon said good-bye to Lily-Matisse and P.W., he updated the VIP board, then headed over to the coffee shop, where Frau

Haffenreffer set him up with a PB&J (extra J) and a side of Krispee Krunchy Salt 'n' Vinegar Potato Chips to replace the bag Lumpkin had devoured and destroyed. After dinner, Leon worked on his collection until he went to bed. He fell asleep thinking about all the things he could do to Lumpkin if and when Pumpkinhead 2.0 started working.

That's one huge if and when, Leon told himself, moments before nodding off.

ELEVEN

Thin-Sliced Deep-Fried Tubers

"So why isn't the magic working?" said Lily-Matisse.

"How am I supposed to know?" said Leon.

"It's got to be the spit," said P.W.

"Possibly," said Leon, clearly unconvinced.

The three were sitting in the science lab, waiting for the start of class. Tests on Pumpkinhead 2.0, like his predecessor, had ended in disappointment, despite repeated trials during recess, lunch, and gym.

"You know what I think the problem is?" said Leon. "I think—"

"Can it," said Lily-Matisse. "Here comes Sparks."

The science teacher strode into class, bright green high-tops slapping against the laboratory linoleum. He planted himself on a stool at the front of the room and, without fireworks or flaming sleeves, posed a two-part question.

"What is science?" he asked. "And where do we find it?"

Antoinette Brede raised her hand. "In textbooks?"

Mr. Sparks made a face. "No, no, *nooo,*" he replied emphatically. "That's the *last* place one finds science. Before we do anything else, I want all of you to take down the following formula." He faced the blackboard and wrote:

Textbooks = the ENEMY of Science!

He turned back to the class and said, "You have a far better chance of finding science in that fish tank over there, on the bottom of my Converse All-Stars, or in the things you do after school."

Mr. Sparks abruptly grabbed the inflated plastic python off the chemical cabinet and playfully bonked Antoinette Brede's desk. "Forget about textbooks and name a passion."

"Horseback riding," Antoinette Brede said at once.

"Perfect," said Mr. Sparks. "If you really want to understand horseback riding, Antoinette, you have to know about breeds and bloodlines. In other words, you should study the science of genetics."

Mr. Sparks spun around with the python. *Bonk!* He clunked P.W.'s desk. "Okay, kiddo, out with it—name a passion."

"Legos!" P.W. exclaimed.

"Do you have the medieval castle set?" asked Mr. Sparks.

"How'd you know?"

"Educated guess. Would it surprise you to learn that we could spend an entire week on the science of the Lego drawbridge? Force, gravity, counterweight, leverage, pulleys, gears."

"Awesome," said P.W. "Let's do it!"

A number of students moaned.

"Sorry, P.W.," Mr. Sparks said. "Not everyone seems to share your passion for interlocking building bricks." *Bonk!* The python landed on the desk of the new girl. "Name a passion, Florence."

"Actually, Mr. Sparks, everybody calls me Flossy."

"Okay, Flossy, what do you love doing when you aren't stuck in school?"

"I like to watch wrestling," she replied hesitantly.

"No kidding?" said Mr. Sparks. "Me, too. Who's your favorite wrestler?"

"Sergeant Slaughter, definitely."

"What do you think is his best move?"

"The atomic noogie or the cobra clutch," said Flossy Parmigiano. "Probably the clutch."

"Well," said Mr. Sparks, "if you want truly to appreciate the beauty of the atomic noogie or the cobra clutch (or the frankensteiner, the elbow smash, the scorpion deathlock, or the hip-hop drop), you've got to know about fulcrums and levers, and about controlling the center of gravity. When Sergeant Slaughter performs that thing with his forearm—" Mr. Sparks interrupted himself. "What's the name of that move?"

"The flying burrito?"

"That's the one. When Sergeant Slaughter does a flying burrito, he's also giving his audience a lesson in basic mechanics."

The fifth graders listened in stunned silence as Mr. Sparks pinned scientific principles to each of their after-school interests. He bonked Lily-Matisse's desk. "What rocks your boat?"

"Gymnastics."

"What's *your* toughest move?"

"Hmm." Lily-Matisse gave the question careful consideration. "Probably a no-handed aerial cartwheel," she eventually said.

"What exactly *is* a no-handed aerial cartwheel?" asked Mr. Sparks.

Without missing a beat, Lily-Matisse stood up, took two steps, and hurtled herself forward, arms over head, and without touching her hands to the ground, kicked her legs (first the back one, then the front) over her body and twisted around, nailing a perfect landing that she rounded off with a short, precise upturn of the head.

"Wow!" exclaimed Mr. Sparks over the cheers of the class. "That's the whole package. Torque, trajectory, momentum, inertia, gravity. We could spend a month, maybe more, studying the physics of the no-handed aerial cartwheel!"

"No way!" P.W. shouted. "Legos!"

"Gymnastics!" Lily-Matisse shot back.

"Horseback riding!" Antoinette advocated.

"Wrestling!" proposed Flossy Parmigiano.

"Okay, guys, settle down," said Mr. Sparks.

Bonk! The python head came down on the desk of the next unsuspecting student.

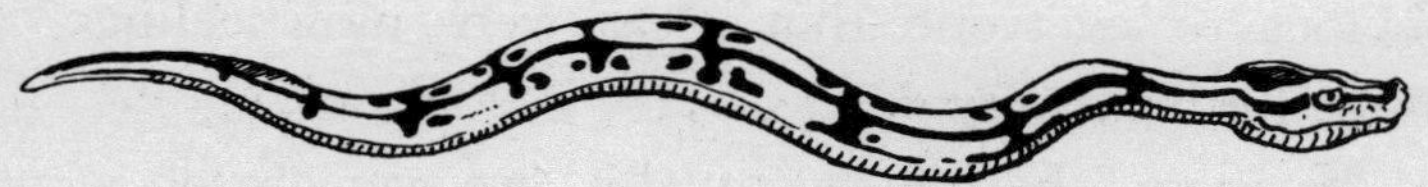

"Your turn, kiddo. What are you crazy about?"

Leon had had plenty of time to think about the question, and he was ready with an answer he felt sure would stump Mr. Sparks.

"Potato chips," he said.

For a moment no one in the class said a word. Then, all at once, the lab was rocked by explosions of laughter and applause even louder than the one triggered by the no-handed aerial cartwheel.

P.W. started a chant: "Chips! Chips! Chips! Chips!" His classmates soon joined in.

Mr. Sparks allowed the cheer to run its course. When the room quieted down, he said, "Observational analysis suggests widespread support for thin-sliced, deep-fried tubers. Is that a valid hypothesis?"

"YES!" the whole class shouted.

"So no one is *anti*-potato chip?"

"NO!"

Flossy Parmigiano raised her hand. "Mr. Sparks? I love chips and all, but I'm not allowed to eat them at home."

"Well, we're not at home, are we, Flossy?"

"We sure aren't," Flossy Parmigiano said appreciatively.

For a long moment, Mr. Sparks stood silent, rocking back and forth on the heels of his high-tops. It was obvious to everyone that ideas were pinwheeling inside his head.

"Suppose," he said eventually, "we were to do a unit on potato chips?"

"A whole unit?" Thomas Warchowski blurted out excitedly. "No way!"

"Perhaps you're right," said Mr. Sparks. "The idea *is* outrageous. It is absurd to think we could study potato chips for four weeks. Forget I even brought it up."

Moans of discontent spread through the lab.

"Thanks a bunch, Warchowski," Lumpkin snarled menacingly.

"There's no need for disappointment," said Mr. Sparks. "Perhaps I failed to make myself clear. I only meant that the subject is much too complex. Potato chips deserve—no, I take that back, they *demand*—an entire year of study."

Once more the class started laughing.

"I am quite serious," said Mr. Sparks. "How would all of you feel if we spent the next nine months investigating the science of potato chips?"

"Potato chips and nothing but potato chips?" said P.W.

"That's the idea," said Mr. Sparks.

"Count me in!" said Leon.

"Me, too," said Thomas Warchowski.

"Me, three," said Lily-Matisse.

Very quickly everyone in the class had expressed support for the potato chip proposal.

"Fine," said Mr. Sparks. "It's settled. I want all of you to raise your right hands and repeat after me."

"What about lefties?" said Leon.

"Lefties still raise their right hands," Mr. Sparks clarified. "Everyone ready to pledge allegiance to the bag?"

Eighteen right hands went up, palm out.

"Now repeat after me," said Mr. Sparks. "I agree . . ."

"I agree . . ."

"To study chips . . ."

"To study chips . . ."

"The whole universe of chips . . ."

"The whole universe of chips . . ."

"And nothing but chips . . ."

"And nothing but chips . . ."

"For the next nine months."

"For the next nine months."

"Okay, then," said Mr. Sparks. "The potato chip pact has been sealed with the pledge. Your first homework assignment is to bring in a favorite bag of research material."

And so began the Year of the Chip.

TWELVE

The First Assignment

"Well," said Mr. Sparks at the start of the next lab. "What are you waiting for? Come up front and hand in your homework."

A mountain of potato chip bags quickly formed on the top of his lab bench. Leon eyed the pile like a miner hunting for gold but quickly concluded there was nothing worth prospecting.

Mr. Sparks picked through the mound. "I see we've got some of the usual suspects. Oh, but here's one I haven't seen before." He tapped a bag. "Who brought these Wall Street Blue Chips?"

"I did," said Antoinette Brede. "They're terribly gourmet and the only ones Nanny allows in the house."

"And these salt-free low-fat kale chips?" asked Mr. Sparks.

"Those are mine," Flossy Parmigiano acknowledged unhappily. "They're superhigh in calcium and they taste like burnt cardboard. My dad doesn't allow me to eat normal chips."

"Hmm, low-fat?" said Mr. Sparks. "They may not taste that good, Flossy, but they'll come in handy in a future experiment." He continued to excavate. "Now here's an interesting-looking bag. Garden of Eatin' Chips. Who brought these?"

Leon raised his hand.

"Where'd you get them?" Mr. Sparks asked.

"My friend Maria gave me a membership to the Worldwide Chip of the Month Club. This bag was part of my August shipment. They're pretty tasty. Kind of a cross between a Wisdom and a Fandango."

"In case you haven't noticed, Leon is crazy about chips," said Lily-Matisse.

"So I gather," said Mr. Sparks. "Well, it's always helpful to have an expert on hand." He dug deeper into the pile. "Whoa! Who brought these?"

"Guilty," P.W. said with a smirk. "My aunt sends them to us from Thailand."

"Is that all one word?" Mr. Sparks asked, tapping the label.

"Yup. It's the old-fashioned Thai word for Bangkok," P.W. explained. "The *Guinness* says it's the longest word in the world," he added proudly.

"How do you pronounce it?" asked Flossy Parmigiano.

"Just the way it's spelled," P.W. said with a straight face.

Everyone laughed. P.W. grabbed the bag, took a deep breath, and read the name in its entirety:

"Krungthepmahanakornamornratanakosinmahintarayutthayamahadilokphopnopparatrajathaniburiromudomrajaniwesmahasatharnamornphimarnavatarnsathitsakkattiyavisanukamprasit."

"Most impressive," said Mr. Sparks.

"We usually just call 'em Bangkok chips," P.W. said. "Basil and pork is my favorite flavor, but my mom goes for these green tea ones."

"Hey, is this language class or science?" Lumpkin complained.

"Perhaps you have a point, Henry," said Mr. Sparks. "We should get started on today's assignment."

The lesson began as soon as everyone was seated.

"Does anyone know how many different species of living things there are in the world?" Mr. Sparks asked.

Hands shot up.

"Thomas?"

"A million?" Thomas Warchowski ventured.

"Multiply that number by a hundred, and you'd be about right."

"A hundred million?"

"Give or take," said Mr. Sparks. "Now, as you might imagine, it's easy enough to distinguish, say, a panther from a python, or a mushroom from a muskrat. But some differences are harder to detect. For instance, take birds. How do you tell a yellow-bellied flycatcher from a yellow-bellied sapsucker? The biologist's answer is: You learn how to classify and how to create a key. That is today's assignment."

"I bet the yellow we'll be studying isn't bird bellies," P.W. speculated.

"How right you are," said Mr. Sparks, beckoning the class to join him around his desk. "Time to brainstorm properties of potato chips," he said as he lined up eight bags from his stockpile. "Can anyone come up with a yes or no question that will distinguish some of these chips from others?"

"How about, 'Is the chip flavored?'" suggested Lily-Matisse.

"Excellent," said Mr. Sparks. He wrote down FLAVORED and NOT FLAVORED. "Anyone else have a mutually exclusive property that will help us classify our thin-sliced deep-fried tubers?"

"How about shape?" said Thomas Warchowski.

"Turn that into a yes or no question," said Mr. Sparks.

"'Is the chip crinkle cut?'"

"Perfect," said Mr. Sparks. He wrote down CRINKLE CUT and NOT CRINKLE CUT.

The question-and-answer session continued until he had a long list of properties that helped differentiate each brand of chip from the others.

"Right," said Mr. Sparks. "Now let's see how we can use this information. Suppose I say to you, Thomas, I have a non-crinkle cut, flavored, non-low-fat potato chip. Can you tell me which of these eight it might be?"

Thomas looked at the pile and said, "Nope."

"You can't?" said Mr. Sparks disappointedly.

"Well, I know which one it is. I just can't *say* it," Thomas explained. "It's P.W.'s chip—the one with the superlong name."

"Fair enough," said Mr. Sparks. "But you see my point? By coming up with yes/no questions that isolate differences, we can create a key that enables us to classify potato chips."

"Cool," said Thomas. "Does that mean I get to eat all the chips in the bag?"

"Afraid not," said Mr. Sparks. "We'll be using these samples in next week's experiment."

"That stinks!" Lumpkin grumbled.

"I feel your pain," said Mr. Sparks. "But you can take comfort in knowing that the ability to classify—to draw distinctions—is crucial to the scientist's understanding of the natural world. Without that ability, we couldn't tell a potato chip from a lump of coal."

Or a lump of coal from a Lumpkin, Leon said to himself. Mr. Sparks's lesson got him thinking. If classification could aid the scientist in understanding the *natural* world, maybe it could help with the *super*natural, too.

THIRTEEN

One, Two, Three . . . Spit!

Leon, as it turned out, wasn't the only one who drew insight from the first potato chip assignment. Lily-Matisse and P.W. also connected the science class to Pumpkinhead 2.0. So much so that the three had a powwow about the lesson at lunch the following day.

"I think we've got to work up a classification of the spitting images to figure out why one worked and one didn't," said P.W.

Lily-Matisse paused between bites of an open-faced grilled-cheese sandwich. "The difference is pretty obvious," she said. "One worked, the other doesn't."

"Still P.W. has a point," said Leon. "If we can isolate the key differences in construction, we might be able to figure out why Pumpkinhead isn't functioning."

"I guess," said Lily-Matisse, not all that convinced.

"Okay, then," said P.W. "Here's what we know. Point one. Last year Leon made a mini-Hag that looked *exactly* like Miss Hagmeyer. Point two, Lumpkin got hold of that spitting image and stained it with teacher's spit. Immediately after that—this is

point three—Leon here discovered that moving the spitting image of the Hag moved the Hag herself."

"Right," said Lily-Matisse. "Remember when—"

"Hey, don't interrupt," said P.W.

Lily-Matisse ignored him. "Remember, Leon, when you used the Hag doll to make the real Hag do pull-ups on the jungle gym?"

"That *was* pretty sweet," said Leon. "But personally, I liked the food fight better. How often do you see teachers throwing cottage cheese at each other?"

"Give me a break!" said P.W. "How can you compare pull-ups and projectile lunch food to Leon's supremo move?"

"Which was what, in *your* humble opinion?" said Lily-Matisse.

"The septuple twist," said P.W. "Man oh man. Seeing the Hag complete a 2520 while jumping rope! Now *that* was something!"

They all laughed.

"Too bad we don't have that power right now," said Lily-Matisse. She glanced over at Lumpkin, who was planted in front of a steam table, ladling mounds of ground beef onto a grinder roll.

"If we had Pumpkinhead two-point-oh working right now," said Leon, "that beef wouldn't be going on a roll."

"Well, he's not working," said Lily-Matisse.

"Which is why we should get back to the scientific analysis," said P.W. "Now where was I?"

"Point four," Leon prompted.

"Thank you, point four. You spent the summer working on a spitting image of Lumpkin, which—"

Leon finished the sentence. "Which hasn't done diddly."

P.W. nodded. "Now let's run through differences and similarities between the real Lumpkin and his spitting image."

"We should work our way from the top down, starting with the hair," Lily-Matisse suggested.

Leon retrieved the pouch from his backpack and, after checking that the coast was clear, pushed up on the bottom to expose the head of the inactive action figure.

"Tell me his hair color doesn't match," said Leon.

P.W. and Lily-Matisse glanced back and forth between the spitting image and the bully.

"It's perfect," Lily-Matisse acknowledged.

"I agree," said P.W. "So it's not the hair that's causing the interference. What about the jacket? Are you sure you got the right specs?"

Lily-Matisse looked puzzled. "Specs? Lumpkin doesn't wear spectacles."

"*Specifications*," P.W. clarified.

"I got the right specs," said Leon. "Check for

yourselves." He removed Pumpkinhead 2.0 from the pouch. Again Lily-Matisse and P.W. ping-ponged their glances between the supersized bully and his pint-sized clone.

Once more they were in total agreement—the two jackets, except for the obvious difference in size, were identical.

"Okay, so the jacket passes," said P.W. "What about the pants and the boots?"

"The pants seem fine to me," said Lily-Matisse, "but it's impossible to compare boots from over here."

"I'm on it," said P.W. He walked over to where Lumpkin had seated himself and dropped a spoon on the floor. While picking it up, he sneaked a peek at the bully's army-issue footgear.

Back at the table, P.W. shook his head in disbelief. "You're incredible, Leon. Even the laces match—eight perfect crisscrosses!"

"I told you," said Leon. "I customized everything."

"So it's definitely not the clothing that's causing problems," said Lily-Matisse. "How about the insides? Maybe the stuffing isn't absorbing the spit the same way."

"It can't be that," said Leon. "I used the Hag's old panty hose for both spitting images."

"So that leaves only one variable," said P.W. He started making moist smacking sounds with his lips.

"Spit?" said Leon.

"Roger that," said P.W.

Lily-Matisse winced.

"No way," said Leon. "I applied teacher's spit from the exact same source—Coach Kasperitis."

"Hey! Wait a minute!" said P.W. "That's it."

"What's it?" said Leon.

"Think!" said P.W. "If you need teacher's spit to activate the spitting image of a teacher, then it only makes sense that to control a kid you would need . . ."

"Kid spit!" said Leon.

"Exactimundo," said P.W. "Using the coach's spit on Pumpkinhead two-point-oh is like using triple A batteries in a Game Boy. It'll never work."

"I'm afraid to ask," said Lily-Matisse. "What's next?"

"Isn't it obvious?" said P.W. He drained his milk, disappeared under the table, and resurfaced moments later, holding a milk carton that was no longer empty. "Someone grab a straw."

"Gag me," said Lily-Matisse.

Leon fetched a straw and returned to the table. "Here you go," he told P.W. "I'll let you do the honors."

P.W. suctioned up some spit, which he dabbed on the stomach of Pumpkinhead 2.0. He then tapped the straw on each shoulder of the spitting image and said, "I dub thee Pumpkinhead two-point-one."

Moments later the three fifth graders (and the

recharged, renamed doll) regrouped behind a tray station, where they observed the ugly spectacle of a lunching Lumpkin.

"Look at the way he's inhaling that sloppy joe," said Lily-Matisse.

"Yeah, it's disgusting," P.W. marveled. "Though not as disgusting as when Leon is finished with him."

"Am I in range?" Leon asked.

"Absolutely," said P.W. "You're in spitting distance of the target."

"Ha-ha," said Lily-Matisse.

"Okay, now," said Leon as he prepared to take aim.

"One sloppy Lumpkin coming up!" P.W. wisecracked.

"Shush!" Leon ordered. He leveled Pumpkinhead 2.1 at the unsuspecting target and began to move the figure's tiny arms so that Lumpkin would stick his ground beef sandwich into his own right ear.

The sandwich suddenly disappeared. Sadly for Leon, it did so into Lumpkin's mouth.

"Well, we know *my* spit doesn't work," said P.W. "You're up next, Leon."

Back at their table, Leon ducked down and harvested some saliva. After a quick reapplication and renaming ceremony ("I dub thee Pumpkinhead two-point-two," P.W. intoned), it was back to the tray station for another round of tests.

Again nothing happened.

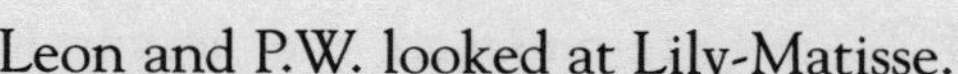

Leon and P.W. looked at Lily-Matisse.

"No way," she said before they even asked. "I'll barf."

"But your spit *has* to work, Lily-Matisse," P.W. said.

"Why does my spit *have* to work?"

"Think about it," said P.W. "The Hag is a woman, the coach is a man. They're opposites. We used man spit on a woman figure. It makes sense that a boy figure needs *girl* spit."

"C'mon, Lily-Matisse," urged Leon.

"Hock a loogie for the team," P.W. cajoled.

Lily-Matisse tried to resist, but her friends' begging soon overwhelmed her. "Enough already. I'll do it, but not in public."

"Fair enough," said Leon.

Lily-Matisse went to the girls' room and returned a minute later looking a little green. "Take it," she said, holding out a small paper cup.

P.W. looked inside. "Is that all you could come up with?"

"Hey, I'm not a seasoned professional like some folks I know."

Leon glanced into the cup. "Don't worry, Lily-Matisse. There's plenty."

Lunch was winding down, so they had to act fast. Leon poured some girl spit onto the already damp belly of Pumpkinhead 2.2. While they waited for the liquid to absorb, P.W. re-re-re-renamed the action figure Pumpkinhead 2.3.

It took some doing, but Leon managed to find a spot close to where Lumpkin was bussing his tray. He raised Pumpkinhead 2.3 and fired off a shot.

"You see that!" P.W. cried out.

"See what?" said Lily-Matisse.

"Lumpkin twitched."

"I didn't see any twitching," said Lily-Matisse.

"Leon?" said P.W.

Leon moved the arms of Pumpkinhead 2.3 up and down to verify P.W.'s wishful analysis. "False alarm," he said at last. "The jerking was Lumpkin all on his own."

FOURTEEN

The Great Potato Chip Flameout

The failures of Pumpkinhead (versions 1 through 2.3) weighed heavily on Leon as he entered the science lab. It was all fine and dandy to undertake rescue and repair, but unless he could master the third R—reanimation—the whole salvage operation would provide no payoff whatsoever, and Lumpkin would keep behaving like Lumpkin.

"Okay," Mr. Sparks chirped. "So we've learned about the importance of classification, right?"

"Right!" the class shouted.

"And we've analyzed all the qualities a potato chip can possess, right?"

"Right!"

"Wrong!" Mr. Sparks shot back. "There are tons we haven't considered."

"Like what?" said Thomas Warchowski.

"Well, have we asked ourselves whether any or all potato chips can *burn*?"

"Du-uh," said Lumpkin. "*Of course* potato chips burn. Everything burns."

" 'Du-uh' and 'of course' are terms scientists tend to shy away from," said Mr. Sparks.

"I think Henry's wrong," said Antoinette Brede. "If chips could catch on fire, grown-ups wouldn't let us near them."

"Some parents don't," said Flossy Parmigiano.

"Sorry to break it to you, girls," said Thomas Warchowski, "but Henry's right. Chips *do* burn. I mean, think about it. Potato chips are food, right? And all food is energy, right? And all energy burns, right? Therefore . . . potato chips burn."

"Except potato chips *aren't* food," said Flossy Parmigiano. "At least not according to my dad."

"Flossy and Antoinette are right," said P.W. "Who ever heard of a potato chip catching fire?" He grabbed a bag and looked it over. "I don't see anything on the label that says, 'Warning: Keep away from flames.' "

"Seems to me class opinion is pretty divided," said Mr. Sparks. He walked over to the blackboard and wrote:

Hypothesis #1: Potato chips are flammable.
Hypothesis #2: Potato chips are NOT flammable.

"Whenever a scientist is faced with two contradictory hypotheses, it is often best to confront the problem experimentally." Mr. Sparks reached under his bench and pulled out a pair of safety glasses. "Well, what are you pyromaniacs waiting for? Grab eye protection, tie your hair back if it's long like mine, and gather around!"

Once the whole class was properly goggled, Mr. Sparks placed a sturdy ring stand on his bench top and fitted the stand with an alligator clip. "Hmm, let's see. Perhaps we should start things off with one of these green tea chips from Bangkok— you'll forgive me, P.W., if I don't say the full name."

"No problem," said P.W.

Mr. Sparks plucked a green tea chip from the bag and gingerly clamped it between the jaws of the clip. He then pulled out a box of safety matches and, without fanfare, struck a match. Everyone watched as he placed the match underneath the chip. It lit up like a candle.

"Boo-yah!" Lumpkin yowled, gyrating his rump like a running back showboating after scoring a touchdown.

"I welcome enthusiasm," said Mr. Sparks. "But before you get too excited, Henry, perhaps we should see if other chips generate the same illuminating reaction. After all, proving a hypothesis requires repeatable results."

Mr. Sparks removed one of Flossy's salt-free, low-fat kale chips from its recycled paper bag and clipped it in place. He struck another match and directed the flame under the kale chip. It smoldered and blackened but refused to catch.

"Hey, wait a minute!" said Lumpkin. "That chip must be defective."

"Let's try another from the same bag," Mr. Sparks said calmly. He repeated the procedure. Again the kale chip refused to ignite.

"Maybe the *first* chip was defective," said Lily-Matisse.

Mr. Sparks removed another green tea chip, clamped it in place, and struck a match. Once more the chip caught on fire, producing a steady, yellow flame that burned for nearly a minute.

"So what can we conclude?" Mr. Sparks asked the class.

"That not all chips are created equal?" Leon suggested.

"Correct," said Mr. Sparks.

"But what's making my chip fireproof?" asked Flossy Parmigiano.

"Ah," said Mr. Sparks. "If I answered that question, you wouldn't have a chance to set all these chips on fire. Now break into groups and test the flammability of the chips we classified last week. See if you can isolate the variable that explains why some chips burn like bandits and others only smolder."

Mr. Sparks outlined the procedure. "Take a chip from each bag. Burn it—or try to—and write down your observations. The height and color of the flame. The brightness. The duration. You can measure the burn time using that big old wall clock above the door."

"No, we can't," said Thomas Warchowski. "That clock's busted."

"In that case, share your watches," said Mr. Sparks. "The point is, analyze both the data you gather today and the data collected last class.

"And one last thing. Keep good records. Lab notebooks often hide secrets that only reveal themselves later!"

Within minutes the groups were announcing their results.

"Orange chips burn better than yellow chips!" said Flossy Parmigiano.

"Sour creams burn better than plains," said Antoinette Brede.

"Crinkle cuts light up more than non-crinkle cuts," said Lily-Matisse.

"Anyone want a barbequed barbeque chip?" Thomas Warchowski called out.

Thirty minutes and a box of safety matches later, the groups all came to the same conclusion: Kale chips were the only ones that were flameproof.

"So, let's address Flossy's question one more time," said Mr. Sparks, holding up a kale chip. "Why is this chip different from all other chips?"

"How are we supposed to figure that out?" Lumpkin grumbled.

"By thinking scientifically," said Mr. Sparks. "By analyzing the collected data."

Thomas Warchowski ventured a guess. "Is it because they're salt-free?"

"You tell me," said Mr. Sparks. "Justify your reasoning."

"Well, I checked my notes from last week—only one chip is salt-free."

"That's not true," said Leon. He knew the ingredients of all the chips by heart. "You must be reading the chart wrong." He ran over and grabbed the Wall Street Blue Chips. "See, Antoinette's chips are salt-free, too, and they burn like paper."

"Let me see," said Thomas Warchowski. He read the label. "You're right," he said glumly. "No salt."

"Don't be too hard on yourself, Thomas," said Mr. Sparks. "I keep telling you guys, mistakes are often the scientist's greatest ally. Take space travel. Every time NASA sends up a rocket and something goes wrong, they convene an FRB—that stands for Failure Review Board. Many of the greatest developments in the history of modern aeronautics have emerged from FRB meetings focused on errors. Check through your notebooks and see if you can find the key variable affecting flammability."

For a few minutes, the only sound in the lab was the rustle of turning pages.

"I've got it!" yelled Flossy Parmigiano. "I know why my chips don't burn. It's because they're low-fat!"

"Justify the hypothesis," Mr. Sparks said formally.

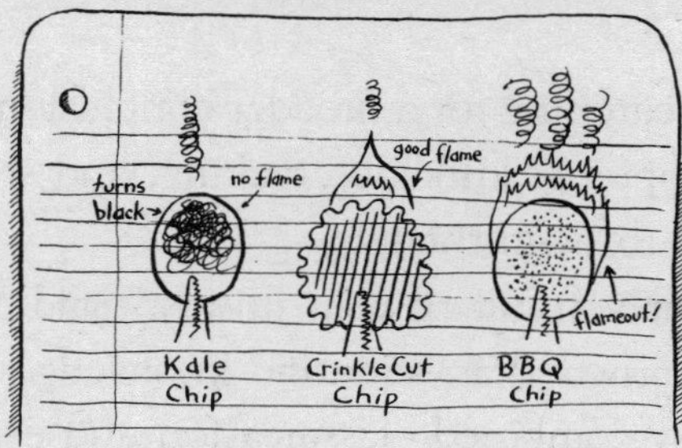

"Well, I double-checked my notebook *and* all the bags. Kale chips are the only ones that are low-fat."

"Hey, that makes sense," said P.W. "In fourth grade we learned about tallow candles—and tallow's a kind of fat."

"Well done," said Mr. Sparks. "You have very ably found the key variable that explains why low-fat chips are flameproof. Fat is indeed an *excellent* source of energy."

Leon leaned over and whispered to Lily-Matisse, "Maybe that explains Lumpkin's bully power."

"The flame," Mr. Sparks continued, "indicates that fuel is present. That's what generates an *exothermic* reaction, which is a jazzy way of saying that heat has been freed."

The bell rang.

"And *that's* the school's way of saying it's time for *us* to be freed!" P.W. wisecracked.

"Not so fast," said Mr. Sparks. "Let's wrap things up. What have we learned?"

"That Flossy's chips burn as bad as they taste?" said Thomas Warchowski.

"I suppose that's true," Mr. Sparks acknowledged.

"But I'm searching for a broader conclusion."

Foot tapping, knuckle cracking, and stool swiveling spread through the lab.

"I'll put you out of your misery," said Mr. Sparks. "We've learned that scientific knowledge is cumulative. Flossy combined classification and experimentation to solve the stubborn mystery of the flameproof chip. By doing so, she showed us that breakthroughs often piggyback on past discovery. Now scram!"

As the fifth graders were filing out of the lab, Mr. Sparks stopped them in their tracks. "Hold on!" he said. "I almost forgot. A good scientist always puts things away."

The news prompted widespread groans until Mr. Sparks reached into a bag of chips and said, "Anyone want to help me get rid of this extra research material?"

There was a stampede back to the teacher's bench. The fifth graders devoured the chips that hadn't been set on fire. One student, however, chose not to assist with cleanup, despite a deep-felt love for deep-fried tubers. Leon resisted the feeding frenzy because he was too busy chewing over Mr. Sparks's comments about experimentation, about reviewing failure, and about the methods best suited to unlocking a stubborn mystery.

FIFTEEN

Fathead

Leon convened a Failure Review Board of his own as soon as lab let out. "We've got to go over all the problems with the final R one more time," he told his two best friends.

"Agreed," said P.W. "If it's good enough for NASA, it's good enough for me."

"I don't know," said Lily-Matisse. "I'm kind of tired of all this."

"But we need you," said Leon. "I mean, you keep the best notes of anyone in the whole class."

The compliment did the trick. "Oh, okay," said Lily-Matisse. "But I'm not handling any spit, and that's final."

"Fine," said Leon. "Besides, I don't think spit's the problem. Something else is causing the malfunction."

"You know what we need," said P.W. "We need the *original* spitting image of the Hag. If we had that, we could compare it scientifically with Pumpkinhead two-point-three."

"You're kidding, right?" said Leon. "How are we

supposed to get the Hag to give back her doll?"

"Sweet-talk her, Leon," said Lily-Matisse. "After all, you're the very best sweet talker in the class."

"But—"

"But nothing," said P.W. "Without the original, we'll never produce a Pumpkinhead that works."

Despite grave reservations, Leon returned to his fourth-grade classroom. As soon as he peered inside, his palms turned clammy. Nothing had changed. The room still had the sinister sewing posters, the padlocked supply cabinet, the yarn-and-spool chart logging student productivity.

Leon spotted Miss Hagmeyer at the far end of the room. She had her back to him. Dressed all in black from head to toe, she cut a grim figure.

Before entering, Leon clucked and blinked for good luck.

"Mr. Zeisel?" a voice called out. "*Still* have that nasty clucking habit, do you?"

Leon stood flabbergasted at the entrance until Miss Hagmeyer reminded him of her unusual powers by lifting the fringe of her unnaturally black hair just enough to expose a large and gnarled ear. "My hearing never fails me."

Leon took a deep breath, entered the room, and approached his former teacher. "Good afternoon, Miss Hagmeyer. How *are* you today?"

"Suspicious—that's how I am, Mr. Zeisel." She brandished a dagger-sized sewing needle. "What brings you back to my little lair—and on a Friday afternoon, no less?"

Leon kept to his script. "I was hoping to borrow that sewing assignment I made for you at the end of last year."

"You mean the Hag doll? Yes, I know that's what you and your partners in crime called it. Why, Mr. Zeisel, should I lend her to you?"

"I need the doll for a project, Miss Hagmeyer. I don't know if you remember, but I told you at the end of last year that I wanted to make another animile."

"That does ring a bell," Miss Hagmeyer admitted. "And I am pleasantly surprised you remember the word 'animile.'"

"I wish I remembered more," said Leon. "I've hit a snag and was hoping to study the old doll to see what I'm doing wrong."

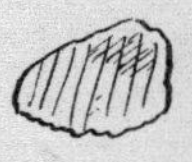

Miss Hagmeyer inspected her former student closely. "This new animile, are you making it for a worthy cause?"

What cause could be worthier than taming Henry Lumpkin? "A *very* worthy cause," Leon answered.

Miss Hagmeyer let her former student stew for a long minute before she said, "Come with me."

Leon followed Miss Hagmeyer to the supply cabinet at the back of the room and watched her fish a key from the pocket of her black cape. She undid the padlock and hooked it onto the cabinet latch.

"A place for everything and everything in its place," Miss Hagmeyer intoned as she flung open the doors to reveal a treasure house of sewing supplies. Below an array of scissors and racks of thread, the cabinet gave way to dozens of drawers, most of which contained (according to their meticulous cursive labels) the body parts of various creatures. There were noses and ears, flippers and fins, snouts, trunks, tails, and a particularly rich assortment of eyeballs.

Only one compartment remained unlabeled, and it was into that one Miss Hagmeyer reached.

"I keep *your* handiwork in my stuffing drawer, Mr. Zeisel. Why, you may ask?"

Leon remained silent.

"I shall tell you," said Miss Hagmeyer as she plunged her hands deep into a mass of shredded panty hose. "Stuffing is a perfect pillow." She pulled out the spitting image Leon had made at the end of the previous year.

"Here you are, Mr. Zeisel. But understand this. I want her back in my hands before class begins on Monday. And she had better be neat and tidy, safe and sound."

"But—"

"No ifs, ands, or buts, Mr. Zeisel. You either accept my conditions or return my animile at once."

* * *

Lily-Matisse and P.W. were waiting in the street.

"Mission accomplished?" P.W. asked.

"Yup," said Leon. "But the Hag expects the doll back first thing Monday morning."

"So?" said P.W.

"So," said Leon, "there's a big poultry convention booked into the hotel. I won't have time to do much this weekend."

"I'm busy, too," said Lily-Matisse. "Gym meet upstate."

"Don't sweat it," said P.W. "I'll work up an analysis on my own."

"You sure?" said Leon.

"Positive," said P.W.

With some reluctance, Leon handed P.W. the Hag doll and Pumpkinhead 2.3. "Be super-careful," he said. "And don't forget, get here early on Monday."

Leon was antsy on Friday, nervous on Saturday, and a wreck by Sunday night. He called P.W. to make sure the doll was safe.

"Relax," said P.W. "Go tend to your chickens. Everything's A-OK at my end. The comparative analysis is coming along great."

"You're *sure?*"

"Chill, Leon. I didn't light the Hag doll on fire, and I didn't stick firecrackers under Pumpkinhead's army jacket. You'll have

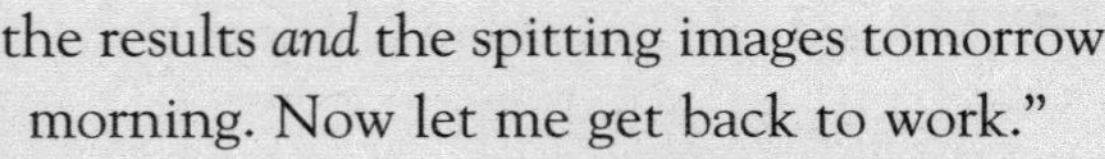

the results *and* the spitting images tomorrow morning. Now let me get back to work."

Leon hung up the phone and tried to distract himself by working on his chip collection. He went to bed early that night but found it impossible to sleep. (The clucking in the hallway didn't help matters.) Well past midnight, he took the elevator to the lobby and asked his mom if he could bunk down in the back office.

"Sure thing, sweetie," said Emma Zeisel. And as she often did, she whipped together a makeshift bed out of two beat-up leather armchairs and some hotel linen. Bundled up near his mom, Leon managed to nod off, but his slumber was brief and troubled. A long, drawn-out nightmare put the Hag doll in jeopardy, sending her first down the hotel's garbage chute and then into the hands of Henry Lumpkin, who squeezed her until all her seams burst, releasing a cloud of panty hose.

Leon awoke in a cold sweat. He felt his whole body shaking. And it wasn't just his body that shook. The walls shook, too. And the chairs. And even the keys in the little cubbyholes behind the reception desk.

Leon let out a yelp, which brought his mother running.

"It's only the trash masher, sweetie," she said, brushing the hair off her son's moist brow. "Creates quite a racket, doesn't it?"

"Yeah," Leon said groggily, relieved to learn the source of the rumbling.

The next day P.W., Leon, and Lily-Matisse all arrived early at school and immediately got down to business behind the playground maple.

"Did you uncover something?" Leon asked.

"That's a roger."

"You're kidding, right?" said Lily-Matisse.

"No, Miss Minus Sign, I'm *not* kidding." P.W. removed a large roll of paper from his pack and unfurled it. The paper was covered with charts and numbers, as well as front and side views of the Hag doll and Pumpkinhead 2.3.

Lily-Matisse's eyes widened. "What *is* all that?"

"The results of my failure review," said P.W. "I spent the weekend comparing weights, heights, leg lengths, arm lengths, waist size, and head diameter."

"And you took all those measurements why?" Lily-Matisse asked skeptically.

"To check for biometric inconsistencies," P.W. said.

"And did you find any?" Leon asked.

P.W. nodded. "One. But it's a biggie. I'm pretty sure Pumpkinhead two-point-three has a serious problem with his head."

"So does Lumpkin," said Leon.

"No, I mean the size of Pumpkinhead two-point-three's head is totally out of whack," P.W. clarified. "Even taking into account the Hag's gigantic ears, you've made the new noggin way too small."

"It *has* to be small," Lily-Matisse said. "After all, Lumpkin is a pea brain."

"Maybe," said P.W. "But his actual skull size is pretty close to normal."

"So what are you saying?" Leon asked.

"Simple," said P.W. "You're going to have to give Pumpkinhead two-point-three more wadding upstairs." He tapped his forehead.

"How much more wadding?"

P.W. pointed to a chart marked CRANIAL DIMENSIONS. "According to my calculations, you'll need to enlarge the head by two inches around the ears."

"But I don't have enough panty hose to do that," Leon said.

"Then you'll just have to get more," said P.W. "Check my measurements. The numbers don't lie."

Lily-Matisse studied the figures. "P.W.'s right," she said, none too pleased to confirm the accuracy of his analysis. "You've got no choice, Leon.

You have to blow up Lumpkin's head."

"Well, I guess when you put it *that* way . . ."

Leon made it back to his old fourth-grade classroom just as the first bell rang.

"Did you find the loan useful, Mr. Zeisel?"

"I did, Miss Hagmeyer, thanks so much. I figured out the problem."

"And what was it, Mr. Zeisel?"

"I ran out of panty hose," said Leon.

He waited for Miss Hagmeyer to take the bait. "Is that a plea, Mr. Zeisel?"

"Yup," said Leon.

Miss Hagmeyer ran her bony fingers over her spitting image while she considered the request. Leon knew she was inspecting the doll for the tiniest rip or blemish. Finding none, her manner softened. "Go help yourself," she said. "The cabinet is unlocked."

That very same afternoon, Leon fetched the sewing basket from Housekeeping and carried it up to his tiny suite. He chained the door and unrolled P.W.'s blueprints on the living-room floor, weighing down the corners with four plastic shampoo bottles that said, "Try the Trimore! Where we try more every day!"

He studied the charts and took various supplemental measurements of Pumpkinhead 2.3 to confirm the Small Head Hypothesis.

This won't be easy, he said to himself.

He wasn't sure where to cut open the skull. In the end he chose a seam that ran along the scalp line. The first few snips were tricky, but after that things fell into place. He removed the thread and implanted some additional stuffing behind the eyes and ears. After he stitched the seam shut, he took a new measurement and matched the results to the numbers on P.W.'s chart.

At first he thought he had made a horrible mistake, but further consideration revealed the problem. He had used Maria's centimeter tape, whereas P.W. had done his calculations with a ruler marked in inches. Remeasurement confirmed that his repair was right on the money.

The operation didn't stop there. It couldn't. Although the outside dimensions of the head were now perfect, the panty hose implants had disfigured the face. That meant more poking and probing to realign the nose, ears, and eyes. By the time the job was done, it was nearly midnight.

"You don't look so hot," Lily-Matisse told Leon when she saw him at recess the next day.

"Who cares how *he* looks?" said P.W. "It's Pumpkinhead that matters."

Leon showed off the results of the surgery. "This is as good as I can do," he said.

"It's terrific, Leon," Lily-Matisse gushed.

"Man oh man, is it sweet," P.W. cooed. He whipped

out a pencil and tapped it on the figure's shoulders. "I hereby do dub thee Pumpkinhead version three-point-oh. Go in peace."

"Can we stop with the *version* stuff? Two-point-three. Three-point-oh. It's confusing."

"Well, what do *you* want to call him?" P.W. demanded.

"I was thinking of 'Fathead,'" said Lily-Matisse.

"I can live with Fathead," said Leon. "How about you, P.W.?"

"I guess—so long as we take him out for a test spin right here, right now."

"You read my mind," said Leon.

Lily-Matisse reluctantly supplied some spit, which P.W., less reluctantly, worked into Fathead's stomach.

"You may fire at will," P.W. announced once he was done.

It was easy enough to locate Lumpkin. He was causing trouble on the jungle gym.

"Okay," said Leon. "Here goes." He began flexing Fathead's beefy arms.

Lily-Matisse and P.W. watched the target closely.

"Did he just twitch?" asked Lily-Matisse.

"*Yeeesss!*" P.W. shouted. "That definitely was a twitch."

"Sorry to break it to you guys," said Leon, "but that was just Lumpkin being Lumpkin."

"Are you sure?" said P.W.

"Positive," said Leon. "Fathead isn't doing anything. I'd feel it if he were."

"Try a few more moves," said P.W.

"All right, but I'm telling you, I'm not feeling it." Leon continued to work the limbs like joysticks. After five minutes P.W. was forced to admit that the Small Head Hypothesis, and the surgery it prompted, had failed to fix the faults that had hobbled all previous Pumpkinheads.

"We have to face facts," said Lily-Matisse soberly. "Fathead lacks energy."

"He's not the only one," Leon said, glumly repouching his powerless puppet.

"I'll tell you one thing that *doesn't* lack energy," said P.W. indignantly. He pointed at the top of the monkey bars.

"Lumpkin is king of the jungle gym!" the bully was shouting as he pounded his chest Tarzan style. "Lumpkin is king of the jungle!"

Sixteen

The Potato Clock

Mr. Sparks glanced toward the broken wall clock at the start of the next lab.

"Potato chip *time*!" he declared.

The emphasis on the word "time," plus the glance, caught Leon's attention. He could smell lame jokes a mile off. "This has something to do with that clock, doesn't it, Mr. Sparks?"

"It does indeed, Leon. We can't have a science lab without proper timekeepers." Mr. Sparks turned to the blackboard. "Here's what we'll do to remedy the problem." He wrote:

- One Potato
- One empty potato chip can
- Two copper pennies
- Two galvanized nails
- One battery-operated digital clock (batteries not included)
- Three alligator-clip wires

Antoinette Brede's hand shot up faster than a bottle rocket. "Aren't you forgetting something, Mr. Sparks?"

"What would that be, Antoinette?"

"The batteries, of course. How can we run a battery-operated clock without batteries?"

"Do you remember what I said about using 'of course'?" said Mr. Sparks.

"That it's not scientific?" said Antoinette.

"Correct," said Mr. Sparks. "I did not forget about the batteries. In fact, I listed them first."

All eyes turned to the blackboard. "Potatoes?" everyone shouted.

"Potatoes," Mr. Sparks confirmed before passing out a handout:

How to Make a Potato Clock

1. Cut two one-inch rings off a potato chip can.
2. Cut a potato in half.
3. Sit potato halves on the two rings.
4. Jab a penny halfway into each potato half.
5. Jab a galvanized nail into each potato half, making sure to pick a spot far away from the penny.
6. Clamp one end of the *first* alligator-clip wire to the penny and the other end to one of the battery terminals on the digital clock.

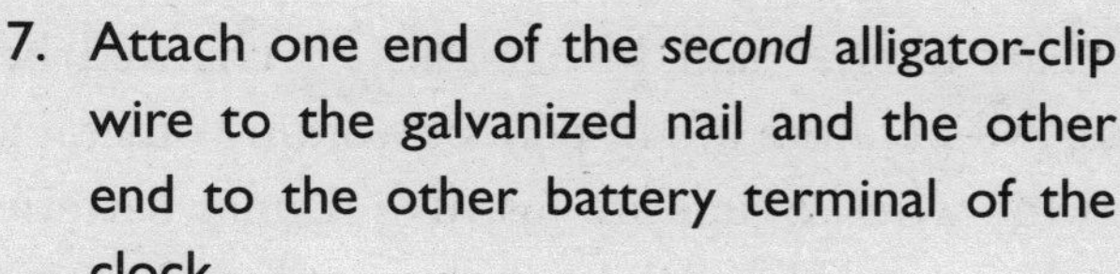

7. **Attach one end of the *second* alligator-clip wire to the galvanized nail and the other end to the other battery terminal of the clock.**
8. **Take the *last* alligator-clip wire and attach one end to the nail of one potato and the other end to the penny of the other potato.**
9. **Set the time!**

"*Potatoes* are going to make the clocks tick?" said Flossy Parmigiano skeptically.

"You got it," said Mr. Sparks. "Spuds are jam-packed with electrolytes, which means they're an excellent energy source."

"Kind of like potato chip fat?" said Thomas Warchowski.

"Actually, Thomas, spud clocks function differently. But let's talk about that after our timekeepers are up and running. Now break into groups, grab your goggles, and get started. First one with a fully functional potato clock can activate the Franklin Sparks pinwheel of honor."

That was all the incentive the class needed to split up and dash off to the table where Mr. Sparks had set out supplies.

But initial enthusiasm soon subsided.

"Hey, this isn't working," Lumpkin complained. "My potato must be busted."

"Not likely," said Mr. Sparks. "I checked before class. All potatoes are in perfect working order. Fiddle with the wires. Spuds are just like regular batteries. If you don't use the right positive and negative electrodes, the juice won't flow."

"Ours got going for a second or two," Thomas Warchowski called out, "but then it stopped."

"Keep trying," Mr. Sparks said. "Remember what Einstein said about mistakes."

The class continued to tinker with the potatoes and pennies, the nails and clips. Here and there students got their clocks going, but only for a short while.

"Eureka!"

Everyone turned toward P.W., who was smiling from ear to ear.

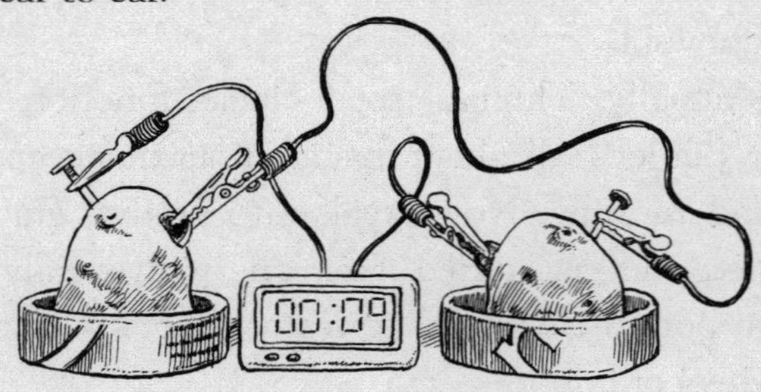

Mr. Sparks walked over his bench. "Let's see what you've got," he said. After a brief inspection, Mr. Sparks said, "Nice job," and reached into his pocket. He pulled out a remote and handed it to P.W. "Go ahead. Give it a whirl."

P.W. aimed the clicker and squeezed. Suddenly the

pinwheel at the front of the room began to spin and shed sparks.

Once the fireworks had died down, Mr. Sparks reclaimed the remote and asked P.W. to explain how he started his potato clock.

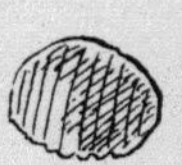

"I did the same thing I do whenever my Game Boy won't work," said P.W. "I licked the ends of the batteries."

Sparks nodded approvingly. "I never cease to marvel at the virtues of human saliva. It is, without a doubt, the most versatile non-Newtonian semisolid known to man—except, possibly, for ketchup."

"Really?" P.W. said excitedly.

"Really," said Mr. Sparks. "You can see for yourselves how well spit conducts energy. Remove the clips from your digital clocks and very gently touch them to your tongues. Do *not* squeeze open the alligator clip."

Flossy Parmigiano was the first to register a reaction. "I feel a tingle!" she called out.

"Me, too!" cried Thomas Warchowski.

"Yup!" said Leon. "I feel it. Kind of a zappy sensation?"

"Well, that zappy sensation," said Mr. Sparks, "is the movement of electrons. It's the same thing that lights up a football stadium, that sends astronauts to the moon, and that keeps potato chips rolling off an assembly line."

Leon raised his hand. "Are you telling us human spit *powers* the potato clock?"

"Not exactly," said Mr. Sparks. "Spit *helps* the process, but it's the potato, acting as a battery, that keeps the spud ticking. The potato is key to changing *chemical* energy into the *electrical* energy."

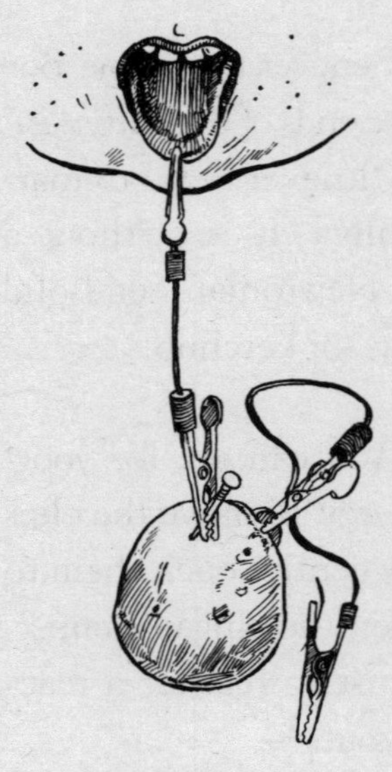

"OOOOWWWWWW!"

An ear-piercing scream interrupted the lesson.

Everyone turned toward Lumpkin, who was suddenly running around the lab with a potato dangling from his tongue like a Christmas tree ornament.

Leon shouldn't have snickered—but he did. And what's worse, Lumpkin saw him.

"No, Henry!" cried Mr. Sparks. "You weren't supposed to *clamp* the clip to your tongue—just gently *touch* it." He caught up with Lumpkin near the fish tank and administered first aid before sending him off to the nurse.

"So," said Mr. Sparks after things settled down. "Did all of you feel a tingle?"

"Yes!" the fifth graders shouted, with three in particular shouting louder than the rest.

SEVENTEEN

Thnickering and Thuffering

Immediately following the potato clock lab, P.W. and Lily-Matisse rushed over to Leon.

"Did you hear what Sparks said about spit?" P.W. exclaimed. "How it's an incredible energy source?"

"Hold it," said Lily-Matisse. "That's *not* what he said. All he said was spit *helps* the process along. It's those electrolyte thingies in the potatoes that power the clock."

"I think Lily-Matisse is right," said Leon.

"Still," said P.W. "Without the right spit, Fathead will never become operational."

"Hello! Earth to P.W.," said Lily-Matisse. "Weren't you listening? We're still missing the 'battery' that'll make the doll work."

"Action figure," P.W. corrected irritably.

The three argued about spit and spuds all the way through pickup.

"Spit's the key," said P.W.

"No, the potato is," countered Lily-Matisse.

"Spit!"

"Potato!"

"THEITHEL!"

Out of nowhere Lumpkin appeared. "I heard you thnickering," he said, clamping down on Leon's wrist.

"I didn't snicker," said Leon.

Lumpkin ignored the denial and tightened his grip.

"Hey, knock it off," said Lily-Matisse. "It's not his fault you clipped a potato to your tongue."

"If Lumpkin thuffers, Theithel thuffers," Lumpkin said. He eyed a nearby brick wall.

P.W. put two and two together. "Not the Howlitzer!" he cried.

Lumpkin's mouth stretched into a nasty grin, made all the more hideous by the flecks of caked blood. With his free hand, he grabbed Leon by the waist and prepared to hurl him against the side of the school.

Leon braced himself. But moments before he was to be turned into a human crash-test dummy, Mr. Groot, the shop teacher, emerged from the school.

Lumpkin had no choice but to suspend the maneuver. Leon tried to wiggle free, only to discover that he was still being held. By his underpants. He tried to protest, but protest was impossible. He tried to resist, but resistance was futile.

"One . . . two . . . *fwee*!"

Leon felt a quick, sharp, squeezing sensation as Lumpkin yanked upward on the waistband. Had it not been for the honk of a taxi horn, the attack might have continued.

"Tell anyone, Theithel—anyone at all—and I'll *really* knock the thtuffing out of you!" Lumpkin threatened before he let go.

"So," said Napoleon, "how is the mood of Monsieur Leon on this fine afternoon?"

Leon refused to answer. He fiddled with his underwear and hugged his backpack like a shield. No number on the moodometer was low enough to measure post-wedgie gloom.

Halfway to the hotel, Leon unzipped his pack and reached inside. He loosened the drawstring of the purple pouch and spent the remainder of the ride doing to Fathead what Lumpkin had done to him. Retaliation, however, failed to make him feel any better. He was still in a funk when the taxi reached the hotel. In fact, he barely grunted good-bye to Napoleon before dragging himself into the lobby. He trudged over to the reception desk, where his mom was busy taping up a sign that said ALL SHEEP *MUST* WEAR DIAPERS!

Normally a posting of that kind would have intrigued Leon. Not today.

"You're looking as crummy as a bag of crushed potato chips," said Emma Zeisel.

"Ha-ha!" Leon responded peevishly.

Emma Zeisel ignored her son's mood. "Chore time,

sweetie. Here's the new VIP list. After you've updated the signboard, there's a guest in five-oh-four who needs to be walked. Once that's done, go find Maria."

"*Why?*" Leon demanded testily.

"Because, sourpuss, she's got something that'll cheer you up."

Leon carried the wooden letter box and VIP list into the lobby and rearranged the signboard to say:

He lined up the letters unenthusiastically before returning to the reception desk. He grabbed a thin, retractable leash off a hook near the key rack.

"I'd go with something sturdier," Emma Zeisel advised. "That guest in five-oh-four is awfully rambunctious."

"Geez," Leon snapped. "Can't I choose my own darn leash!"

"Fine, be my guest!" said Emma Zeisel. "After all, everyone else here is."

Leon rang the door chime of Room 504.

"Hold on," a man called out over the sound of

bleating. The door opened. "You the fella who'll be walking Rambo?" asked the guest.

"Yup," said Leon.

"Well, howdy. Name's Roy. Rambo will surely be happy to see *you*! How are you around animals?"

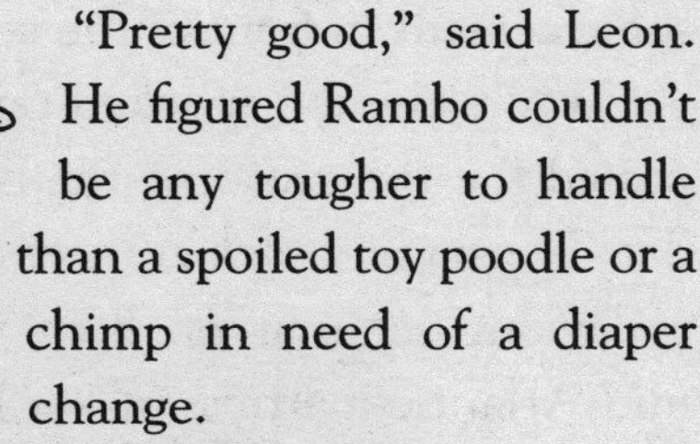

"Pretty good," said Leon. He figured Rambo couldn't be any tougher to handle than a spoiled toy poodle or a chimp in need of a diaper change.

"Well, we'll find out soon enough," said Roy.

Leon noticed bits of plastic sprinkled over the carpeting. "Sorry about the shower curtain," said Roy as he turned to unlock the bathroom. "Rambo got a—"

"Wow!" Leon exclaimed the moment his charge charged into the room. "That's one big sheep."

"Rambo ain't no sheep," said Roy. "He's a pure-blood prizewinning pedigreed Welsh mountain ram."

Rambo banged his pedigreed horns against the door. "And as you can see, he's hankering to stretch his legs."

"I'll take him out straightaway," said Leon. As he was clipping on the leash, he noticed Rambo wasn't wearing a diaper. Rule or no rule, he said to himself, there's no way I'm going anywhere near either end of *this* guest!

Out in front of the hotel, Leon tried to convince Rambo to answer the call of nature as quickly as possible. Unfortunately for Leon, Rambo had other plans. The beast dragged him down the block and across the street to a tempting patch of weeds poking through some cement in front of the convention center.

While Rambo snacked on sidewalk sprouts, Leon passed the time reading the convention center calendar. There was a sock congress coming up. Followed by a daylong seminar on floor waxes. Followed by the mid-Atlantic mattress maker meeting, followed by—

A poster caught his attention.

Leon couldn't believe his eyes. A snack food extravaganza was coming to town!

He smiled at the thought of all those potato chip professionals filling the convention center. It was a safe bet a bunch of them would be staying at Trimore Towers. That meant his chip collection was sure to grow!

Leon turned to a more pressing matter—getting Rambo to pee. He decided to try something Maria had told him worked wonders. He inched toward the front of the ram and covered its nostrils, keeping as far away from the horns as possible.

Less than a minute later, the task complete, Leon began the tug-of-war back to the hotel. Each time he pulled one way, Rambo pulled the other. By the time the leash was back on the hook near the key rack, Leon had blisters on every finger of his left hand. He headed down to Housekeeping.

"Hey, Maria, the nose trick is great."

"We do that with llamas all the time, Leonito."

"Mom said you've got something for me. Did a guest leave behind a bag of Rhode Island chips?"

Maria shook her head. "But maybe I have something for you just as good." She pulled a box from the broom closet. The words "FRAGILE!" and "BREAKABLE!" were stenciled on the sides in big block letters.

"The new shipment from the Chip of the Month Club!" Leon exclaimed.

"*Sí.* It just arrived this morning."

Leon tore open the package.

"So, Leonito? Any cheeps from the Rhode Islands?"

"Nah. But there's a real nifty Wyoming I've been wanting."

Leon took the chips to his room and spent the evening munching and cataloging—adding the names of new specimens to his checklist, slipping the emptied bags into protective sleeves, pinning flags into his map of the world.

Not bad, Leon said to himself, surveying the markers. He decided, in the interest of science, to donate two unopened duplicates to Mr. Sparks.

Preparing for bed, he was feeling pretty cheery. The mood didn't last. While changing into his pajamas Leon discovered that the after-school wedgie had turned his shorts into longs. Worse still, the yanking motion had left a permanent mark that no quantity of Poop-B-Gone could remove.

Leon decided to destroy the incriminating evidence. As soon as he was in his PJs, he crumpled the soiled underpants into a ball and tossed them down the hallway garbage chute.

Back in bed, Leon tried to push Lumpkin from his thoughts. He couldn't. The curbside wedgie kept looping through his brain. It was as if every time he tried to hit the Erase button, he accidentally hit Replay instead. He worried that memories of the wedgie would be wedged in his head forever.

Too bad they don't make something called Thoughts-B-Gone! he told himself. Or better still—Bully-B-Gone! Now there's a product worth inventing!

Be-e-e-eh! Be-e-e-eh! Pon! Pon!

Leon jumped out of bed to see what was up and, moments later, was on the phone to the reception desk.

"Mom? Rambo got loose, and he's grazing on the carpet across from our door."

"Thanks, sweetie, I'll handle it."

Emma Zeisel soon arrived with Roy. "Counting sheep is supposed to help folks fall asleep, not keep them awake," she scolded the guest.

"Rambo's not a sheep, Mom. He's a pure-blood pedigreed Welsh mountain ram."

"And prize-winning," Roy noted.

"It doesn't matter *what* Rambo is," said Emma Zeisel sternly. "My point is the same."

"I sure am sorry, ma'am," Roy said earnestly.

The apology softened Emma Zeisel. "No need to feel sheepish," she said. "But we will have to bill you for the cost of this rampage."

"Wouldn't have it any other way, ma'am," said Roy.

"And *please*," Emma Zeisel added, "keep Rambo properly diapered."

"Oh, I sure will," Roy promised.

Emma Zeisel took a break from the desk and tucked her son into bed. She flicked off his lamp and gave him a hug, which she noted was returned more forcefully than usual.

Leon felt okay as long as his mom was in the room, but once she left, his brain hit the Replay button. Lumpkin's parting threat circled through his thoughts: "Tell anyone, Theithel—anyone at all!—and I'll *really* knock the thtuffing out of you."

Leon groped about in the dark and found his backpack. He removed Fathead and gave him a squeeze. "Oh, yeah?" he said bitterly. "Well, maybe I'll knock the thtuffing out of *you*!"

All at once Leon froze in place. His head cleared. His hands began to shake. And soon he started to laugh.

"Eureka!" he cried out in the dark. "Eureka! Eureka! Eureka!"

EIGHTEEN

A Key Variable

Leon had to wait until after gym to announce his discovery to P.W. and Lily-Matisse. "I know what's wrong with Fathead," he told his two best friends.

"What?" said Lily-Matisse.

"Yeah," said P.W. "Spill the beans."

"It's not beans that need spilling," Leon said excitedly. "It's stuffing."

"What are you talking about?" said Lily-Matisse.

"Fathead's stuffing—*that's* what's causing the problems."

"No way," said P.W. "I checked the measurements. They're perfect."

"You don't get it," said Leon. "It's not the amount of stuffing, it's what the stuffing's made of."

"Huh?" said P.W.

"Eh?" said Lily-Matisse.

"It's simple," said Leon. "Spitting images need more than special spit. They need special stuffing, too.

Think about it. If the Hag doll used Miss Hagmeyer's panty hose, it only makes sense that Fathead has to be stuffed with—"

"Something that comes from Lumpkin!" Lily-Matisse exclaimed.

"Yup," said Leon.

"We've been total morons!" said P.W. "How did you figure it out?"

"That's the funny thing," said Leon. "Lumpkin told me."

"Lumpkin?" said P.W.

Leon nodded. "It was after school, when he threatened to knock the *thtuffing* out of me."

"The stuffing must be the energy source," said Lily-Matisse. "It acts like the potato battery that makes the clock tick."

"And spit is the conductor!" added P.W.

"Bingo," said Leon.

"Question," said Lily-Matisse. "How are we supposed to get hold of a pair of Lumpkin's underwear?"

"I've been thinking about that," said Leon. "I'm figuring that the stuffing doesn't have to be underwear. It just has to be a piece of clothing that comes from the person you're trying to control. So here's the question: What piece of clothing do you guys think of when you think of Henry Lumpkin?"

"The army jacket!" P.W. and Lily-Matisse both shouted.

"Jinx!" they both shouted again.

"Exactly," said Leon. "If we get our hands on his jacket, we'll be all set."

"And how are we going to do that?" said Lily-Matisse.

"We could steal it," P.W. suggested. "We stole the coach's spit when we needed it last year."

"That's a really dumb idea, even for you," said Lily-Matisse. "When have you ever seen Lumpkin not wearing his jacket?"

"I suppose you have a better suggestion," P.W. said testily.

"Yes, as a matter of fact."

"Okay, then," said P.W. "Let's hear it."

"Fine," said Lily-Matisse. "My plan is simple. We wait. After all, the jacket is already supertight on him. Eventually he'll have to shed it like a snake sheds its skin."

"You want us to wait around for Lumpkin to *grow*?" said P.W.

"Like I said, it's already tight on him."

"And how are we going to *get* the skin once he *sheds* it?" P.W. demanded. "You think he's going to leave his jacket behind for us to pick up?"

"Guys," Leon interjected. "Can we be practical about this? We can't go stealing Lumpkin's army jacket, and we can't wait for him to grow out of it either."

"All I know is we better act fast," said P.W. "It's just a matter of time before he tests out his Howlitzer."

"Agreed," said Leon. "But there's only one way to get that jacket. Lumpkin has to give it to us—willingly."

"He'll never do that," said P.W. "Not in a gazillion years."

"He will if we've got something he wants even more than the jacket," said Leon.

"You mean a swap?" said P.W.

"Yup."

"What do we have that Lumpkin would want?" asked Lily-Matisse.

"That's the part I haven't figured out," Leon admitted. "We have to figure out what Lumpkin is into."

"Hmm, let's see." P.W. began counting on his fingers. "There's military stuff. Beating kids to a pulp. Sloppy joes. What else? Hot fudge sundaes. Beating kids to a pulp and—hmm, anything else?—oh, yeah, beating kids to a pulp."

"How about an autographed picture of some famous war hero?" Lily-Matisse suggested.

"Not good enough," said Leon. "The jacket is way too important. We need something one-hundred-percent irresistible."

"Wait a minute!" P.W. cried out. "I got it. The perfect bait."

"What?" said Lily-Matisse skeptically.

"Let me do some checking first," said P.W. "I'll supply the details tomorrow."

* * *

The next day P.W. came to school looking like he'd won the lottery. "I know how we'll get Lumpkin to shed his army jacket. Take a look-see." He pulled a printout from his binder. "I found this online."

Leon and Lily-Matisse glanced down.

"Another army jacket?" said Leon.

"Not just *any* army jacket," P.W. said. "We're talking a vintage World War II M42HBT. Check out the special pockets and the anti-gas flap."

Lily-Matisse tittered.

"Get serious," said P.W. "It doesn't protect against *that* kind of gas. Anyway, this is what I'm thinking. Suppose Leon comes to school wearing one of these babies, say in an extra-extra-extra-large?"

Leon caught on immediately. "Lumpkin would flip!"

"He *might* consider a swap," Lily-Matisse allowed.

"*Consider* a swap?" said P.W. "Are you kidding? He'd *force* Leon to swap."

"Where can we get one of these jackets?" Leon asked.

"The address is at the bottom of the printout," said P.W. "Captain Frank's Army and Navy Surplus. It's the only place in town that sells the M42HBT. I called Captain Frank and had him put one aside."

"Excellent," said Leon.

"Uh, P.W.?" said Lily-Matisse.

"Yeah?"

"Question." Lily-Matisse tapped the printout. "Did you notice the price?"

"Geez!" Leon exclaimed. "A hundred and fifty-nine ninety-nine! Where are we going to get that kind of money?"

"Hey," P.W. snapped. "I can't come up with *all* the answers. At least we know what we need."

"Knowing what we need is one thing," said Leon. "Getting it is something else."

"How much do you have saved?" P.W. asked.

"Nothing," said Leon.

"Ditto," said Lily-Matisse.

"Double ditto," P.W. said. "What's your allowance?"

"I get ten dollars every two weeks," said Leon.

"I get three bucks a week, when I remember to take out the restaurant garbage," P.W. said.

"My mom doesn't believe in allowance," Lily-Matisse said irritably. "But sometimes she pays me when I help out around the art studio."

"If we pool all our allowance money starting right now, I guesstimate it'll take us about . . ." P.W. paused, "twenty weeks to save up for the jacket, give or take a couple of days."

"Twenty weeks of noogies?" Leon moaned. "Twenty weeks of Lumpkin Dunkin's, blood bracelets, and wedgies? No way! I'll never survive."

"Then we'll just have to speed things up," said Lily-Matisse.

That very afternoon the three fifth graders told their parents they were available for odd jobs, so long as the odd jobs paid cash.

P.W. helped out in the kitchen of the Curried Elephant, his parents' restaurant. He wrapped spring rolls, chopped lemongrass, and folded napkins in the shape of swans.

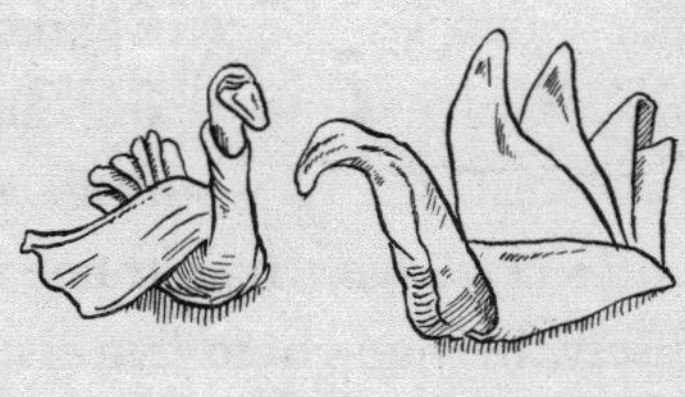

Lily-Matisse did her part by cleaning up around the school art studio. She scraped clay off the pottery wheel, washed brushes, and reorganized the crayon cart.

Leon's odd jobs were the oddest of all. He restocked the diaper shelf, fed the piranhas in 302, and took Rambo out for his daily constitutional (but only on a sturdy, short leash).

And when their parents asked why they needed the extra pocket money, the three fifth graders stuck to the same brief but satisfactory story.

"It's for an after-school science project."

NINETEEN

All-Chips-All-the-Time

Over the next few months, Mr. Sparks had his fifth graders burning chips and boiling chips, measuring, magnifying, and mashing chips. He even had them *flying* chips—or more precisely, he had them flying chip *bags*. After an aerodynamics workshop that focused on the design of foil kites, he took his students to the park and gave them a four-word assignment:

"Go fly a kite!"

For the following lab, he brought in an old shoebox. "I played with these when I was your age," he said, giving the box a shake. He made the class guess the contents and, after a dozen wrong answers, he removed the items, one by one: a plastic nose . . . a hand . . . a foot . . . *another* hand.

"It's a Mr. Potato Head!" Flossy Parmigiano cried out.

"Excellent deduction," said Mr. Sparks.

"Nanny got *me* the special anniversary version," Antoinette Brede informed the class.

"How very fortunate you are," said Mr. Sparks while he took out some plastic accessories. When the

shoebox was empty, Henry Lumpkin said, "Hey, news flash, Mr. Sparks. Someone swiped the head."

"News flash, Henry. Mr. Potato Head didn't come with a head when I was a kid. The toy maker expected us to supply our own."

Mr. Sparks reached into his satchel and produced a very large baking potato. "Observe," he said, jabbing some face parts into the spud.

"What do you think?" he asked the class.

The response was unanimous: *Booooorrrring!*

Mr. Sparks inspected the potato head. "Maybe you're right," he admitted. After careful deliberation, he applied a black wig. "How's this?"

"Now it looks like Miss Hagmeyer," said P.W.

The entire class cracked up—all except Flossy Parmigiano. "I don't get it," she said.

"Neither do I," said Mr. Sparks.

"That's because you two weren't here last year," said Antoinette Brede.

"And you don't know what we know," added Thomas Warchowski.

"*What* don't we know?" Flossy Parmigiano demanded.

"That the Hag wears fake hair!" hollered Henry Lumpkin.

"Henry!" said Mr. Sparks. "Her name is Miss Hagmeyer. And what scientific proof do you have to back up this ridiculous hypothesis?"

"She pulled her wig off in class," said Thomas Warchowski.

"All of us saw it!" said Lumpkin. "Talk about gruesome!"

"It's attached with Velcro," said Antoinette Brede. "Three strips, all in a row."

"Well, perhaps we should forgo the wig," Mr. Sparks said judiciously.

Leon, P.W., and Lily-Matisse remained unusually quiet on the subject of Miss Hagmeyer and her removable hair. They knew what the others did not: that their fourth-grade teacher had flashed her scalp in class because of the spitting image Leon had controlled.

"How about this?" said Mr. Sparks, after adding a pipe and glasses.

The whole class approved.

"This fellow does look thoughtful," said Mr. Sparks. "Very much the scientist. We'll call him Professor Spud."

"What's Professor Spud supposed to be teaching us about?" asked Antoinette Brede.

"Rot and mold," said Mr. Sparks as he placed the potato on the filing cabinet beside his desk. "Plus, I hope the Professor will help develop your skills in data collection. I want all of you to keep a photographic record of the changes he undergoes during the next few months."

"I don't have a camera," P.W. pointed out.

"Me neither," said Thomas Warchowski.

"I do," said Antoinette Brede. "Nanny got me one with all sorts of special lenses."

"That's dandy, Antoinette. But don't bother bringing it to class. You won't need it."

"Why not?"

"Ah," Mr. Sparks said with a smirk. "I'm delighted you asked." He held up an empty potato chip can. "Time to study optics."

For the remainder of the lab, Mr. Sparks demonstrated how to turn empty potato chip cans into fully functioning pinhole cameras, explaining as he went along how the upside-down backward image on the bottom of the can resembled the image that hit the back of the eye. "Today's project will also come in handy during our field trip next week," Mr. Sparks said at the end of class.

"Where are we going?" asked Lily-Matisse. "It's not mentioned on any of the handouts."

"To a research center specializing in *globuli solaniani*," Mr. Sparks replied.

"Globuli *what*?" sputtered Lumpkin.

Mr. Sparks sidestepped the question. "For those of you who haven't given me trip waivers, tell your folks to bring them in on Parents' Night."

"When's that?"

Mr. Sparks sighed. "Next Tuesday," he said, his voice turning curiously glum.

"You don't sound all that psyched to see our parents," said Flossy Parmigiano. "Not that I can blame you."

"Let's just say I prefer fifth graders to the parents of fifth graders," Mr. Sparks confessed.

Everyone knew the field trip involved potato chips. But *how*? That question drove Leon, P.W., and Lily-Matisse nuts. They were determined to discover the meaning of *globuli solaniani* before they boarded the school bus.

"Remember at carnival last year, how they had curly fries at the banquet?" said P.W.

"What about it?" said Lily-Matisse.

"They called them something funny."

"Solana tuberosa in modo crispus fricta," said Leon.

Lily-Matisse and P.W. both gave him funny looks.

"Hey, what can I say?" said Leon. "I know my chips and fries."

They went to the library and looked up the phrase in various dictionaries. None referred to *globuli solaniani*.

"Maybe I should check with my mom," said Lily-Matisse. "She could've heard something in the teachers' lounge."

The next day, at recess, Lily-Matisse updated Leon and P.W. on the results of her inquiry. "Mom was useless, field trip-wise," she said. "But she did have some dirt about Sparks. He's in trouble. People are complaining about the chip experiments."

"What people?" Leon said angrily.

"Well, the cook, for starters. Mom told me he's bummed that the fifth graders keep asking him for chips, chips, and more chips. Mom says he's used to his curly fries getting all the attention."

"That is *so* lame," said Leon.

"Well, it's not just the cook. The janitor's also peeved."

"Cranky Hankey?" P.W. rolled his eyes. "He's *always* peeved."

"Maybe," said Lily-Matisse. "But just so you know, he's grumbling about crumbs and chip bags littering the halls."

P.W. frowned. "That's totally bogus. We used the bags for kites."

"And for book covers on our lab journals," Leon noted.

"Plus," said P.W., "Sparks had us turn the empty chip cans into pinhole cameras."

"Hey, you don't have to convince me," said Lily-Matisse. "I'm just telling you what my mom said. Besides, the cook and Cranky aren't the real problem. The real problem is the parents."

"There's a surprise," said P.W.

"A bunch of parents think the all-chips-all-the-time experiments are a total joke," said Lily-Matisse.

"Bull chips!" exclaimed P.W.

"You think that's bad," said Lily-Matisse. "It gets worse. Birdwhistle called Sparks into her office."

"Sparks got Birdcaged?" said Leon.

Lily-Matisse nodded gravely. "Mom thinks he might be on some kind of probation. Birdwhistle will be checking out how he does during Parents' Night."

"That's why he looked so miserable when he mentioned it in class," said Leon.

"I feel sorry for Sparks," said P.W.

"Ditto," said Lily-Matisse.

"Double ditto," said Leon.

Twenty

Parents' Night

Mr. Sparks sat on the edge of his desk. He smiled at the parents as they filed into the lab. Only a few of them smiled back. Some even squinted and scowled, treating the science teacher like some toxic slide sample stuck under the lens of a microscope.

Lily-Matisse's mom stopped by to give him some professional advice. "Stand tough," whispered Regina Jasprow. "If you don't, these parents will devour you like snack food."

The feeding frenzy the art teacher predicted started before Mr. Sparks even had a chance to make an introduction.

"Po*tah*to chips?" a matronly figure queried harshly. She had a very large bosom festooned with a fat rope of pearls and a diamond brooch shaped in a *B*.

Mr. Sparks felt as if he'd been caught eating peas with a knife. "Mrs. Brede, is it?"

"It most certainly is," the woman

affirmed. "Tell us, Mr. Sparks. How on earth can po*tah*to chips educate my Antoinette?"

"Yeah, Teach!" a burly man with a crew cut chimed in. "Henry Lumpkin, Sr., here. Answer the lady. What's the deal with the junk food?"

Mrs. Brede glowered. She had no patience for interruptions, even when they confirmed her own views. "As I was *attempting* to say, Mr. Sparks, how can you justify an entire year devoted to a substance of such questionable nutritional value?"

"Potato chips are *not* nutritionally questionable—as long as they feed the curiosity of your children," said Mr. Sparks.

Mrs. Brede winced. "Oh, *puh-leese*."

"Yeah, gimme a break," echoed Lumpkin, Sr.

Mr. Sparks shot a desperate look at Regina Jasprow.

"Potato chips can be wholesome if you choose the right brand," the art teacher improvised.

"Wrong!" a parent blurted out.

"What makes you such an expert?" said Emma Zeisel.

"Dr. Joseph Parmigiano, D.D.S. And in case anyone's wondering, those three letters at the end of my name indicate I'm a dentist. *That's* what makes me an expert. You can take my word for it—potato chips are dental time bombs. They're worse than candy, which is why I refuse to let my Flossy eat them."

"Bottom line, Teach," barked Lumpkin, Sr. "We

don't need some ponytailed loon in green sneakers forcing our kids to eat chips. Hank, Jr., eats plenty all on his own."

Mr. Sparks struggled to keep his cool. "Okay, Mr. Lumpkin. I get it. You don't approve of my clothing or my educational methods. It's true, I don't wear a crisp white lab coat or sensible lace-ups. And I don't make your children memorize the life cycle of the frog or the parts of the flowering plant. But if the school had wanted that kind of science teacher, they wouldn't have hired me."

A lethal silence spread through the lab. Parents shifted in their seats as the battle lines were drawn between the pro- and anti-potato chip factions.

This was *not* how Mr. Sparks had hoped to start things off. He had planned to demonstrate the principles of combustion using a rocket fuel he had brewed out of potato chips, sugar, yeast, and warm water. But he abandoned the Parents' Night experiment when he realized that Mrs. Brede, Lumpkin, Sr., and Dr. Joseph Parmigiano, D.D.S., were doing a fine job triggering an explosion all by themselves.

A late arrival only made matters worse.

"Don't mind me," said Principal Birdwhistle as she tiptoed across the lab and took a seat near the inflated python.

"We were just discussing the value of the potato chip curriculum," said Mr. Sparks.

"Value indeed," huffed Mrs. Brede.

Mr. Sparks looked to Principal Birdwhistle for some guidance, but she responded with a wishy-washy shrug that said, You're on your own.

Fortunately he wasn't.

"I don't know why everyone's getting twisted into pretzels about a silly snack food," said Emma Zeisel. "Think about *last* year. Remember Miss Hagmeyer? The woman forced our kids to sew cloth animals stuffed with her old panty hose. I don't recall anyone complaining about *her* kooky teaching methods. Frankly I'll take potato chips over panty hose any day of the week."

Murmurs of agreement spread through the room.

"Sorry, toots," said Lumpkin, Sr. "Potato chips are a lot worse than underwear for one obvious reason." He patted his sizable paunch.

"I must concur," said Mrs. Brede.

"Plus let's not forget about cavities, bacteria, and plaque," Dr. Parmigiano noted.

"And while we are on the topic of undergarments," said Mrs. Brede, "there is something I have been meaning to ask you, Mr. Sparks."

"Fire away."

"My Antoinette tells me you remove your clothing during class. Is that true?"

"It is," said Mr. Sparks. "But strictly for educational purposes," he quickly added. "Here, let me show you." He undid his button-down and revealed a T-shirt that said:

**"WE KNOW NOTHING AT ALL.
ALL OUR KNOWLEDGE IS BUT THE
KNOWLEDGE OF SCHOOLCHILDREN."**
—ALBERT EINSTEIN

"Tough to argue with a Nobel Prize winner," said Emma Zeisel.

"Especially a Nobel Prize winner who, your kids may have told you, was born on March fourteenth."

"What's so special about March fourteenth?" said Lumpkin, Sr.

"It just happens to be National Potato Chip Day," said Emma Zeisel.

"Your point, Mr. Sparks?" Mrs. Brede demanded imperiously.

"My point is simple. The fifth graders aren't just learning *about* potato chips. They're learning *from* potato chips. And I might add I am learning from them."

Principal Birdwhistle looked up from her clipboard. "Do you mean, Franklin, that you learn from the potato chips or from the students?"

"From both," said Mr. Sparks. "I learn from both."

The response appeared to satisfy his boss.

An Asian woman with long black hair raised her hand.

"Ms. Dhabanandana?" said Mr. Sparks.

"Your potato chip experiments are very good. I've never seen my P.W. so excited about science. He even is helping in our restaurant, to earn extra money for a research project."

"Leon's doing the same thing," said Emma Zeisel.

"And Lily-Matisse has been extraordinarily helpful around the art studio," Regina Jasprow interjected.

"Nevertheless," said Mrs. Brede. "It is absurd to treat po*tah*to chips like precious diamonds."

"I agree," said Mr. Sparks. "Potato chips are much more valuable."

"*Well!*" huffed Mrs. Brede, clutching her gem-encrusted B-shaped brooch.

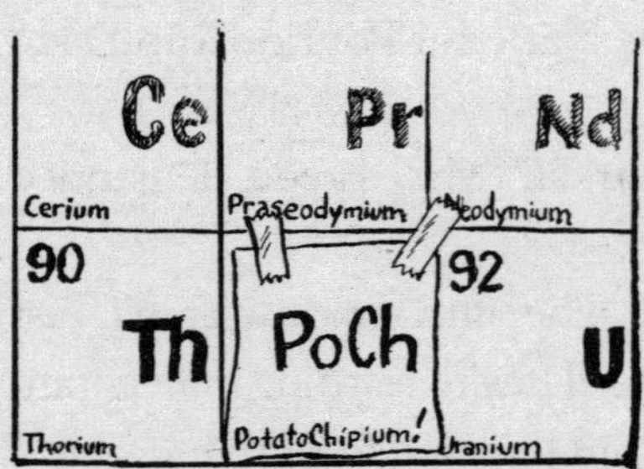

"Look around you at the room," said Mr. Sparks. "Can diamonds teach your kids about the conservation of energy? About timekeeping? About aerodynamics? About dichotomous classification? About the growth of *Peronospora infestans?*"

"What the heck is *that*, Teach?"

"Potato rot," said Mr. Sparks, pointing to the tuber standing on the filing cabinet. "Professor Spud is part of a long-term unit on optics and data collection. We've been documenting his decay using pinhole cameras made from recycled potato chip cans. Here, take a look. I think they're pretty nifty."

While the parents inspected the chip can cameras,

Mr. Sparks went around the lab with an open bag of chips. He quickly realized that the bag of chips was much more than a snack. It was a barometer of support. The parents who accepted his offer did so to endorse the all-chips-all-the-time curriculum. The parents who declined were rejecting his methods.

It came as no surprise that Mrs. Brede, Lumpkin, Sr., and Dr. Parmigiano, D.D.S., said no. But the reaction Mr. Sparks knew mattered most was that of Principal Birdwhistle.

She reached inside the bag.

That was a good sign—one that prompted Mr. Sparks to breathe a sigh of relief. But just when he thought he was off the hook, he noticed that the principal removed her hand without a chip.

Mr. Sparks put on a brave face. "Oh, darn," he said. "Look at the hour." He pointed at a wall of wired potatoes, thankful it was time to wrap things up. "I guess we got sidetracked by the lively discussion."

As the parents began to leave the lab, Mr. Sparks said, "Oh, and a quick reminder. My co-researchers and I will be taking a field trip next week, so please make sure to hand in their trip waivers."

"The form says the class is traveling to a *research center*," Mrs. Brede said suspiciously.

"That's right," said Mr. Sparks. "We'll be studying *globuli solaniani*."

Mrs. Brede frowned. "Nothing dangerous, I trust."

“Entirely harmless,” said Mr. Sparks.

“I don’t know, Teach,” said Lumpkin, Sr. “This *globuli* stuff—it sounds like a mouthful.”

“It is,” said Mr. Sparks. “But nothing your kids can’t handle.”

Twenty-One

The Bus Ride

At the start of the field trip, the fifth graders *still* didn't know where they were headed. They waited impatiently outside the school, fidgeting with their can cameras and angling their science journals to catch the sunlight. Normally lab notebooks don't reflect light. But normally lab notebooks aren't covered in foil chip bags, as most of these were, thanks to an art class taught by Lily-Matisse's mom.

"Did you bring Fathead?" P.W. asked Leon.

"Of course. You know what Sparks says. The scientist always prepares for inspiration to strike."

"The only thing I'm worrying might strike is Lumpkin," said Lily-Matisse.

"We've got to get our hands on that jacket," said P.W. "Where are we money-wise?"

Lily-Matisse, who was acting as the treasurer for the jacket fund, said, "We're up to thirty-one dollars and fifty cents. Plus four dollars that my mom still owes me for filling glue pots."

"That brings us to thirty-five fifty," said P.W. "One-fifty-nine ninety-nine minus thirty-five fifty equals . . . let's see, that's the same as one-sixty minus thirty-five fifty equals . . . one-twenty-four fifty, take away a penny equals . . . one-twenty-four forty-nine. If we keep doing extra chores, we'll have the jacket by—"

The arrival of the school bus, and the crush it caused, prevented P.W. from completing his guesstimation.

Mr. Sparks stood inside the bus and called through the glass, "What's the secret password?"

"*Globuli solaniani!*" the fifth graders shouted.

Mr. Sparks stepped back and pulled on a long metal handle. His students piled in.

"Time to tell you what we're up to," said Mr. Sparks excitedly as his students hustled for seats close to the front. "Despite what you may have heard, *globuli solaniani* is *not* a fatal disease that makes your limbs fall off at night. Nor is it a giant sea slug that lives on the ocean floor. Anyone figure out what it is?"

The class had no idea. Or rather, the class had tons of ideas, none of which were correct.

"It was actually Henry Lumpkin who came closest to unlocking the mystery."

All eyes focused on Lumpkin, who was as startled as the others to hear his name mentioned.

"Yes," said Mr. Sparks, "Henry Lumpkin—*senior*—pretty much nailed it at Parents' Night, when he said that *globuli solaniani* sounded like a mouthful."

The students giggled expectantly.

"Well, I won't keep you in suspense any longer. *Globuli solaniani* is the Latin phrase for a certain substance with which you all have some familiarity. Would anyone care to attempt a translation?"

"Potato chips!" the whole class hollered.

"You *are* a smart bunch," said Mr. Sparks. "But more to the point, the phrase has been promoted by a certain scientist named Furtles."

Leon immediately guessed what was up. "We're not going to the Furtles Potato Chip Factory, are we, Mr. Sparks?"

For an agonizing moment, the whole bus waited for an answer to that question.

"Yes," said Mr. Sparks at last. "We are."

Over the joyful shouts of his students, Mr. Sparks said, "I would contend that the coolest phrase in any language must be 'potato chips.' However, 'field trip' ranks a close second. And when you combine the two phrases? Well, I ask you, what could be cooler than that?"

Nothing, to judge from the cheering.

Mr. Sparks turned to Mr. Groot, the wood shop instructor who also took class pictures and drove the school bus. "Okay, Herman," he said. "Let's roll."

Mr. Groot released the parking brake and shifted into gear. But just as he was about to pull away, a distinct tapping sound intruded on the mobile merrymaking.

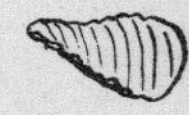

Thomas Warchowski was the first to locate the source of the tapping. "It's the Hag!" he exclaimed.

All at once the cheering stopped. Alarm spread through the bus like poison gas. Mr. Sparks gazed at the fourth-grade teacher through the window and made a show of pointing at his watch. "We're running late," he mouthed, tossing up his hands apologetically.

The tapping persisted.

"Herman," said Mr. Sparks, "cut the engine." He reached for the door handle and allowed Miss Hagmeyer to board.

She was wearing her usual getup: black cape, black lace-up boots, panty hose the color of cooked liver, a helmet of black hair that everyone on the bus (with the possible exception of Mr. Groot) knew to be fake. She had a clasp on her cape made from glass eyeballs—a reminder of her love of stuffed animiles. And in her bony fingers she gripped her tapper, a dagger-sized sewing needle designed as an instructional tool, but adapted by Miss Hagmeyer for disciplinary ends.

"Phyllis," said Mr. Sparks. "To what do we owe the pleasure?"

"Pleasure has nothing to do with my presence," Miss

Hagmeyer replied brusquely. "I'm here to chaperone."

"Surely Mr. Groot can provide the necessary backup, don't you think?"

"It really doesn't matter a stitch what *I* think," Miss Hagmeyer grumbled. "It's what Principal Birdwhistle thinks that counts. And *she* thinks you need me. So here I am." Miss Hagmeyer waved the sewing needle at her former students. "I tried to teach these ruffians last year. I know what they're capable of."

"I see," said Mr. Sparks. "I could use your help, of course, Phyllis. But I wouldn't dream of taking you away from your current fourth graders."

"Don't worry about them. They're working on their costumes for the medieval carnival. They'll be supervised until we get back."

"Oh," said Mr. Sparks, his voice all but disappearing.

Miss Hagmeyer wasted little time taking charge. "Okay, you troublemakers. You know the drill. Hop to it. I want to see everyone seated alphabetically by last name." She marched up the aisle, casting her eyes (and her needle) right and left. "Tighten that seatbelt, Miss Brede. Zip it, Miss Jasprow! Feet out of the aisle, Mr. Lumpkin! Is that bubblegum I see, Mr. Warchowski? Swallow it *now*."

When she reached the rear of the bus, her tone softened. "How's the new animile progressing, Leon?" she purred.

"Fine."

"Nearly finished?"

Leon shook his head and clutched his backpack. Special attention from Miss Hagmeyer was the last thing he wanted.

"Well, let me know when your animile is done."

"Okay," Leon whispered.

As soon as Miss Hagmeyer claimed her seat, Thomas Warchowski turned to Leon. "You really making an animile just for yourself?"

Leon noticed Lumpkin eavesdropping and quickly changed the subject. "Think the Hag's here to spy on Sparks?"

"Probably," Thomas Warchowski answered. "It's all over the school how ugly things got at Parents' Night."

"Pipe down!"

Leon cringed. He kept forgetting about Miss Hagmeyer's superpowerful hearing and equally powerful voice.

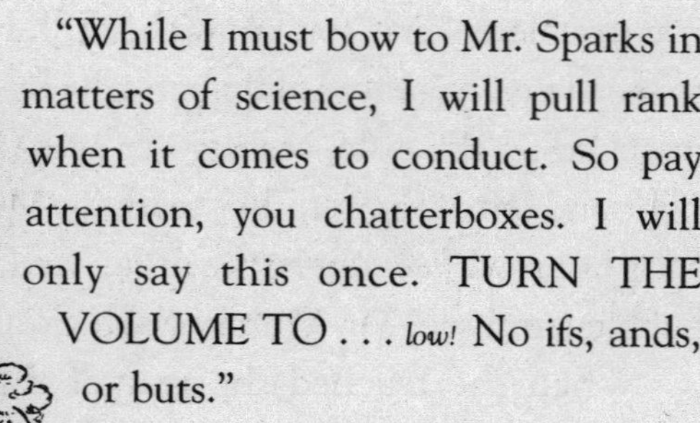

"While I must bow to Mr. Sparks in matters of science, I will pull rank when it comes to conduct. So pay attention, you chatterboxes. I will only say this once. TURN THE VOLUME TO . . . *low!* No ifs, ands, or buts."

Twenty-Two

Furtles

A very quiet hour later, the school bus passed through the wrought-iron gates of the Furtles Potato Chip Factory. A watchman emerged from a small wooden gatehouse and flagged down the bus.

Mr. Sparks cranked open the door. "Good morning!"

"You the group from Classical?" the watchman asked.

"We are," said Mr. Sparks.

"Been a bit of a hiccup in the plans. Mr. Furtles is sick with the influenza. So Mr. Furtles will be showing you around."

The statement confused Mr. Sparks, but before he could ask for an explanation, the watchman said, "Drive around the back. Mr. Furtles will meet you at the loading dock."

"Because Mr. Furtles is out sick?" said Mr. Sparks.

"That's right," the watchman confirmed.

The class assembled on the loading dock, underneath a sign that said FURTLES . . . FRIED WITH PRIDE ON THE LOWER EAST SIDE.

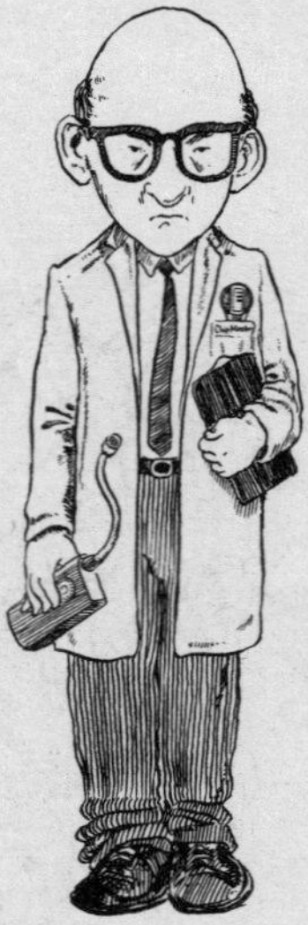

Leon spotted a short man in a crisp white lab coat approaching. "Geez, get a load of that guy."

"His head's almost as big as Professor Spud's," said P.W.

Lily-Matisse laughed. "All that's missing is the pipe."

"That's enough out of you three," Miss Hagmeyer warned.

The man with the big head approached Mr. Sparks. "Idaho Furtles," he said gruffly. "Vice president in charge of quality control." He patted the pocket of his lab coat, which had the words "Chip Master" stitched in yellow thread.

"Franklin Sparks. Science teacher in charge of fifth graders. And these are Miss Hagmeyer, Mr. Groot, and my eighteen chip-loving co-researchers."

Idaho Furtles scowled. "I'll tell you right off the bat, I'm not supposed to be showing you around. My brother, Russet, was the one who gave the okay—which, if you ask me, he should never, ever have done. But did Russet ask my opinion? Of course not. Never has, never will. And since Russet is the *president* of the company and I'm only the *vice* president, what he says goes. Now follow me."

As Idaho Furtles turned toward the entrance, Leon heard Mr. Sparks whisper to Miss Hagmeyer, "Seems

our Mr. Furtles has a chip on his shoulder."

"Very amusing," said Miss Hagmeyer, clearly not all that amused.

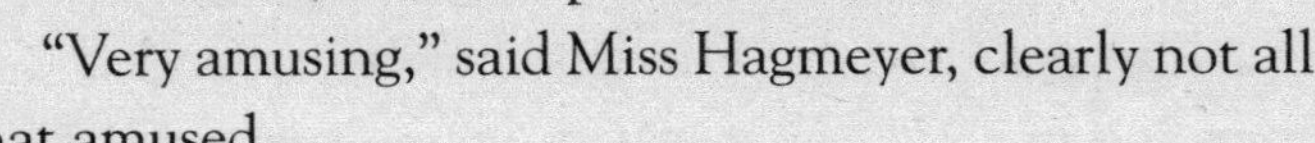

Idaho Furtles moved everyone up a metal staircase and down a long corridor. As the smell of chips grew stronger, so did the group's excitement.

"Where to first?" Mr. Sparks asked. "The peelers? The kettles? Maybe the salting station?"

"We will visit the factory floor in due course," said Idaho Furtles. "I think it advisable to begin the tour where all the most important work takes place—my testing room."

"That sounds promising!" said Mr. Sparks. "I could do with a little snack."

"Then you had better leave and go to the store," Idaho Furtles said curtly. "We haven't stayed in business for over eighty years by giving away free samples." He guided the group to a door that said TASTING ROOM. Only someone had crossed out the letter "a" and replaced it with an "e."

The testing room was a vast space filled with racks of trays containing thousands of chips. All along the wall, a variety of signs issued exclamatory warnings. ALL TESTERS MUST WEAR HAIRNETS! said one. NO UNAUTHORIZED CHIP CONSUMPTION! said another.

"What a rip!" Lumpkin protested.

Idaho Furtles ignored the complaint and launched

into a brief history of his family-owned business.

"My grandfather, Flinders Furtles, founded our company in 1921. That was the same year two of our Pennsylvania competitors started their operations. But whereas those two enterprises grew greedy, sacrificing quality to quantity, we here at Furtles have stuck true to our kettle-cooked roots. We started small and we've stayed small. Why? Because no bag of Furtles gets sold beyond the city limits. Why? To maintain quality control. How? By making sure every batch of Furtles gets tested and inspected by yours truly. Now come with me and I will show you how that happens."

Idaho Furtles took the class to a workbench that ran across one entire wall of the testing room.

"Man oh man, look at all this stuff," P.W. marveled.

"This *stuff*, young man, is the finest chip-testing equipment available. Much of it I designed or modified myself. So at the risk of stating the obvious, *do not touch*!"

"Did you hear that, you would-be vandals?" Miss Hagmeyer said.

"Tasting chips all day? That's my kind of job!" said Lumpkin.

"I do not *taste* chips," sneered Idaho Furtles. "I test them."

"What's the big diff?" said Henry Lumpkin.

"The 'big diff' is this: *Tasting* is at best a mere hobby, whereas *testing* is a hard science."

"Can't be that hard," Mr. Sparks joked.

"You are mistaken," said Idaho Furtles sourly.

Mr. Sparks ignored the tone. "That's some microscope," he said. "What's its maximum magnification?"

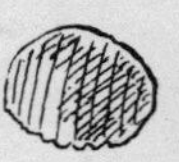

"It can enlarge things four hundred times."

"Impressive," said Mr. Sparks. He leaned toward the microscope. "May I?"

Idaho Furtles gave a reluctant nod.

Mr. Sparks peered through the eyepiece. "Amazing," he said. "What kind of potato chip am I looking at?"

"That's not a chip," said Idaho Furtles. "Frying destroys the integrity of the starch granules that infiltrate the tissue."

"So you're saying it's just raw potato?"

"Not just any raw potato, Mr. Sparks. It's a patented Furtles hybrid, one of the many reasons our chips are as crunchy as they are."

Mr. Sparks adjusted the focus. "Wow, my students have to see this. Would you mind?"

Idaho Furtles hesitated. "I'm not sure that's a good idea."

Mr. Sparks looked up. "Please," he said. "These students will never appreciate the true beauty of the potato chip unless they are given the chance to gaze at starch granules magnified four hundred times."

"I suppose you're right," said Idaho Furtles. "Just make sure they don't bump the slide."

While the fifth graders stared at potato tissue,

Idaho Furtles snapped on a pair of rubber gloves and prepared a few chips for testing.

"Now pay close attention," he said once everyone had had a turn with the microscope. He lifted a chip from a small paper boat.

"Why the boat?" asked Thomas Warchowski.

"For transport and protection," said Idaho Furtles.

"And the gloves?" said Flossy Parmigiano.

"To avoid contamination during chipometric analysis."

"Chipometric analysis?" said Mr. Sparks.

This was the first question of the day that prompted Idaho Furtles to smile. "Came up with the phrase myself," he boasted. "Chipometry—the science of potato chip evaluation—is the only way to maintain our standards."

"Don't you ever *eat* chips?" P.W. asked.

"Never," said Idaho Furtles. "Now if I may continue . . . where was I?"

"Chipometry," said Lily-Matisse.

"Thank you. Chipometry begins with a thorough visual inspection of the chip. That means studying the surface texture. Assessing roughness, particulate density, patina, and glow. In my job as Chip Master, I must make sure our chips are never too oily and never too dry."

Idaho Furtles removed a gadget from the wall. "This hydrometer is specially designed to register the moisture levels of our chips." He touched the sensor to the surface of his sample. "One-point-five percent. Just where it should be," he said approvingly.

"Next I evaluate the chip's color. For that I rely on a digital color wheel." He reached for another gizmo. "This unit can match 762 different shades of potato chip, from the lightest yellow to the darkest brown."

"What about Furtles Shamrocks?" said Leon.

Idaho Furtles frowned. "I see we have an *expert* in our midst. The boy is correct. We do produce a green chip for St. Patrick's Day. But the Shamrock is a dyed seasonal, and thus exempt from color analysis. Now if I might continue *uninterrupted*."

Miss Hagmeyer waved her needle at Leon, but Mr. Sparks softened the rebuke with a sly, conspiratorial wink.

"After I have checked for texture, moisture, and color," said Idaho Furtles, "I submit the chip to a smell test." He reached for an aluminum case.

"What's in there?" said Flossy Parmigiano.

"This," said Idaho Furtles, opening the case and removing a device that looked like a walkie-talkie, "is the Nose-It-All 3000. Top of the line. State of the art. Furtles is the only family-run chip lab in the country that uses an electronic nose to evaluate potato chips." He touched the "snout" to the surface of the sample. "The sensor helps maintain batch-to-batch consistency."

"Can't you just smell the chips?" Leon asked.

"Not with the accuracy of the Nose-It-All 3000. And unlike the human nose, this electronic sniffer never comes down with a cold or sinus infection.

"After I have evaluated texture, moisture, color, and smell, I must still measure the thickness of the sample. Most brands have an average width of zero-point-zero-five inches. That's about the thickness of a dime. But here at Furtles, we batch cook our chips in kettles filled with only the finest premium cold-pressed virgin peanut oil. It is one reason our chips are twenty percent thicker than the chips sold by our competitors."

Idaho Furtles reached into the breast pocket of his lab coat and pulled out yet another gizmo. "My Darhansoff external caliper gauge," he said. "I carry it everywhere. Accurate to point-zero-zero-zero-four inches." He pinched the sample chip between the crablike pincers of the device. "Point zero-zero-six-five inches. Perfect, right where it should be." He scribbled the results on a preprinted form.

"Um, Mr. Furtles?" said Leon.

"You again?" The Chip Master looked around for Miss Hagmeyer, clearly hoping she would intervene. Unfortunately for Idaho Furtles, Miss Hagmeyer had disappeared. "What is it?" he said.

"How about Furtles Double Crunchers? Aren't they a lot thicker?"

"I see you are acquainted with our complete line," Idaho Furtles sneered.

"Mister," said P.W. "Leon is more than just *acquainted.*"

"Oh, really?" said Idaho Furtles condescendingly.

"*Really!*" said Lily-Matisse. "Go ahead. Test him."

"Very well," said the Chip Master. He pulled a chip from a nearby sample tray. "Let's see if you can identify this without tasting it."

"Why would I want to do that?" Leon asked.

"Just as I thought," said Idaho Furtles, returning the chip to the tray. "Amateurs," he muttered under his breath.

"No, hold on," said Leon. "I'll give it a shot."

He looked the chip over for a few moments. He gave it a sniff. "Salt and vinegar?"

"Yes, *of course* it's salt and vinegar," said Idaho Furtles. "But what *brand* of salt and vinegar?"

"Huh?" said Leon. "I can't tell you that. It's impossible!"

"Oh, is it?" Idaho Furtles said with a self-satisfied smirk. He grabbed four paper boats, each containing a chip. To the untrained eye, the four chips looked identical. "The brand name of each specimen is marked on the bottom of its boat," he said. "Shuffle the boats while I turn away."

P.W. mixed up the boats. "Ready," he announced.

All eyes were on Idaho Furtles as he faced the rearranged fleet. Using each tool in turn, he completed his chipometric analysis in under two minutes.

"Starting from left to right," he said confidently, "Furtles Plain, Cousin Ray's Low-fat Kosher Dill Pickle Delights, Willie Winkle Salt 'n' Vinegar, and Okee-Dokey Plain."

Leon capsized the boats.

The first one was marked FRTLS-P.

The second was marked CR-LFKDPD.

The third was marked WW-SNV.

The fourth was marked OD-P.

"Yow!" Leon exclaimed. It was a sentiment shared by the rest of the class.

"You see," said Idaho Furtles. "The proper use of the proper tools allows the true professional to identify a potato chip without ever taking a bite. Taste is highly unscientific, and in the end—"

"DROP IT!"

The shrill command so startled Idaho Furtles that he dropped his thickness gauge on the floor.

Everyone turned and faced Miss Hagmeyer, who stood before a rack of chips, her needle aimed at Lumpkin.

Idaho Furtles scurried over.

"Caught him helping himself to an unauthorized mid-morning snack," Miss Hagmeyer said indignantly.

Idaho Furtles inspected the ransacked tray. "It's almost empty!" he fumed. "Don't they teach you to read at your school?" He pointed to a sign that said POSITIVELY NO SAMPLING!

"What's the biggie?" said Lumpkin defiantly. "I just helped myself to a few rejects."

"Those were *not* rejects!" Idaho Furtles raged.

Lumpkin plucked a chip off the tray—or rather he took two chips fused together in the shape of a butterfly. "You call this normal?" he said.

"That's exactly the point!" Idaho Furtles cried. "You have been eating off the specials tray!"

"The *what?*" said Lumpkin.

"The tray reserved for candidate chips."

"Candidates for what?"

"For the Furtles Potato Chip Museum."

"Oops. In that case, sorry," Lumpkin said unconvincingly.

Miss Hagmeyer tapped her needle on his shoulder. "You are hereby put on notice, Mr. Lumpkin. One more misstep, and you will end up someplace where that army jacket might come in handy."

"She means military school," P.W. whispered to his friends.

"That's exactly what I mean," said Miss Hagmeyer.

Lumpkin answered the threat with an insolent shrug.

The unlawful snacking ended the visit to the testing room and made Idaho Furtles extremely grumpy. Without a word, he marched everyone down a long corridor and onto an iron catwalk that overlooked the factory floor. The cavernous space was filled with noisy, creaky machines, most of which were linked together by ancient drive belts and conveyors that whirred and wheezed, sputtered and spat.

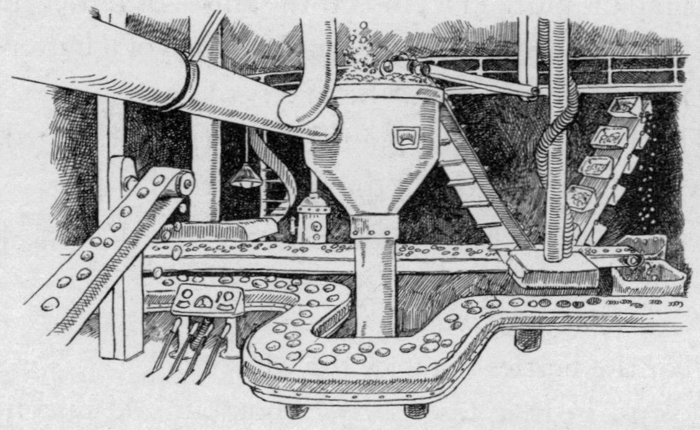

"It's like a giant potato roller-coaster," P.W. shouted as a piston valve hissed overhead.

"Seems like the only microchips in this place are the ones that get salted and bagged," said Mr. Sparks.

"If you're suggesting we could use new equipment, talk to my pigheaded brother," said Idaho Furtles. "I've been pushing to computerize the kettles and switch to a synthetic cooking oil, but he keeps saying no."

Mr. Sparks took a keen interest in a thick leather drive belt that looped around the axle of a very powerful motor. The top of the belt ran ten feet overhead and the bottom disappeared through two wide ovals cut into the floor. He was about to ask about the belt when a worker in overalls pushed his way to the front of the group.

"Mr. Furtles!" the worker said urgently. "We got problems."

"Let me guess," said Idaho Furtles. "The salting station?"

The worker nodded anxiously. "The tumbler is going haywire again!"

Idaho Furtles turned to Mr. Sparks. "I'm afraid we'll have to end the tour here."

The groans of the students competed with the clatter of the machines.

"Mr. Furtles, what if I were to guide the class through the rest of the factory?" Mr. Sparks proposed.

"Don't be absurd."

"But we have traveled all this way. It'd be a shame to come back. That would mean bothering you *twice*."

Idaho Furtles hesitated. The prospect of a make-up tour clearly did not please him.

"*Mr. Furtles?*" said the man in overalls. "The tumbler has already ruined two batches of Double Crunchers."

"Tend to your tumbler," Mr. Sparks advised.

"I don't know . . ."

"Go on, shoo. We'll be fine on our own."

Idaho Furtles relented. "Oh, very well," he said. "Follow the conveyor belts, and I will rejoin the group farther down the line."

"Excellent," said Mr. Sparks. "Don't worry about us."

"I *do* worry," said Idaho Furtles. "But a haywire

tumbler is more troublesome than a group of nosy fifth graders."

"Don't be so sure," Miss Hagmeyer muttered as Idaho Furtles and the worker disappeared behind a giant vat of premium cold-pressed virgin peanut oil.

Twenty-Three

A Hair-Raising Tour

"Okay," said Mr. Sparks, guiding the class down a spiral staircase to the factory floor. "Let's continue the tour."

"Don't you mean *start* it?" P.W. said.

Mr. Sparks didn't respond. He was too busy inspecting the belt-driven motor that had attracted his attention before Idaho Furtles was called away. He jumped over a chain to get a closer look.

"Mr. Sparks, do you think that advisable?" Miss Hagmeyer questioned.

"Remember what you said on the bus, Phyllis? You concern yourself with misconduct—let me tend to the science. This area is perfectly safe." He turned to his students and said, "What do you think would happen if I stood under that drive belt?" He pointed to the whirring loop of leather.

No one had a clue.

"The effect," said Mr. Sparks as he did just that, "should be hair-raising. Observe."

All at once his ponytail shot straight up!

The whole class broke into hysterics. Even Miss Hagmeyer found it hard to keep from laughing.

"Okay," said Mr. Sparks. "Maybe one of my co-researchers can tell me why my hair is dancing? Any guesses—excuse me, hypotheses?"

"Air currents?" P.W. postulated.

"Nope."

"Suction?" Flossy Parmigiano proposed.

"Guess again."

"A vacuum?" Thomas Warchowski wondered.

"Ix-nay," said Mr. Sparks. "The cause is electricity."

"Like the potato clocks?" asked Antoinette Brede.

"No," said Mr. Sparks. "The potato clocks rely on *current* electricity. Their movement is generated by a steady flow of electrons traveling in a circuit. But the belt is generating *static* electricity, and that's a whole different kettle of chips. Static electricity doesn't loop. It works by noncircular attraction and repulsion. Can anyone give me an analogy?"

P.W. leaned over to Leon and whispered, "how about, we're *attracted* to Lumpkin's army jacket, and we're *repulsed* by Lumpkin?"

"*Shhh!*" Miss Hagmeyer scolded.

"When I get a shock on the doorknob?" said Lily-Matisse.

"That's right," said Mr. Sparks. He held out his hand. "Come on in," he urged. "There's nothing to worry about."

Cautiously Lily-Matisse climbed over the chain and joined Mr. Sparks below the belt. Now the two of them had hair dancing on end.

"Well?" said Mr. Sparks. "What are the rest of you waiting for?"

Within seconds the whole class was lined up under the leather loop, laughing uncontrollably at the spectacle of all that dancing hair.

"Miss Hagmeyer," P.W. hollered. "Join us!"

"I shall pass, thank you very much," she replied firmly.

"Come on in!" Thomas Warchowski said. "It's a blast!"

"Trust me, Phyllis," said Mr. Sparks, "you'll get a charge out of it."

"Oh, why not," Miss Hagmeyer said at last, joining the others under the fast-moving drive belt. All at once, her hair began to shimmy. And soon after that, so did Miss Hagmeyer. For a few minutes, the whole group hopped about and giggled.

Sccritchh!

Leon heard a strange but familiar sound he couldn't quite place.

Sccritchh!

There it was again.

He looked about, searching for the source of the noise, which was hard to pinpoint over all the shouts, giggles, and mechanical clangs. He wasn't the only one who heard the strange sound. P.W. picked up on it, too, as did Lily-Matisse.

But it was Antoinette Brede who isolated the cause of the *sccritchh*ing. "Miss Hagmeyer!" she screamed. "Your hair!"

All at once the fourth-grade teacher reached up and caught hold of her wig, just moments before it separated completely from her scalp. She patted the fake hair more or less in place and swiftly removed herself from the path of the belt.

"Shoot!" P.W. said, barely able to contain his disappointment.

"Maybe we should move on," Mr. Sparks wisely suggested. He guided the group to the mechanical potato peeler. "Technically speaking," he said, "this contraption doesn't peel the potatoes. It *sands* them clean. If you look closely, you'll see that those rollers are covered with grit."

As the group was gazing at the peeler, Leon felt the weight of his backpack suddenly get lighter.

"So what the heck's in there, anyway?" Lumpkin whispered. "I saw you holding it like a baby when the Hag was talking to you on the bus."

Leon tried to pull away but found himself pinned against a handrail.

"Relax," said Lumpkin. "You're not going anywhere." He waited until the others were out of view before yanking on the pack.

Leon did his best to hold on, but the tug-of-war was brief and ended with Lumpkin heaving the pack over his head, like a prize-fighter displaying a championship belt. "Show-and-tell time, Zit-sel," he said, lowering the pack to the floor. "Let's see this animile that has the Hag so excited."

Lumpkin fumbled with the zipper. It jammed. He jiggered the metal tab, but it wouldn't budge. "Shoot!"

Leon could see that the zipper teeth had caught a piece of orange yarn. "Give me back my pack before the Hag catches us. You heard what she said about military school."

Lumpkin ignored the warning.

"Come on!" begged Leon, pulling on a shoulder strap. "Drop it."

Lumpkin stopped fiddling. "You sure you want me to *drop* it?"

"Yeah," said Leon. "I'm sure."

"Okay, then," said Lumpkin. "I'll drop it." He dangled the pack over the handrail, directly above a conveyor belt.

"Don't!" Leon yelled.

"But you *said* you wanted me to drop it. Sure wish you'd make up your mind."

"Please!"

"This little piggy went to market. . . ."

"No!"

"This little piggy stayed home. . . ."

"Stop!"

"This little piggy had potato chips, and this little piggy had—"

Lumpkin released his grip before completing the rhyme. The pack landed with a thud on a moving belt of peeled potatoes.

"Oops."

Leon scrambled down a spiral staircase and ran after his pack. He raced alongside the path of the conveyor until the pack dropped into a bucket elevator linked to a conveyor aimed at the mouth of a tunnel. The pack disappeared inside. On the other end of the tunnel, yet another conveyor carried its cargo toward a device that resembled a very large car tire—except that the "hole" of the tire was crisscrossed with razor-sharp blades.

Leon froze. Not the potato chipper! He watched for his pack to exit the far side of the tunnel. A minute passed, and the pack had yet to reemerge.

"Mr. Zeisel!" Miss Hagmeyer scolded. "Stop dawdling!" With a swift swipe of her needle, the fourth-grade teacher beckoned Leon back to the group. He made a beeline for his two buddies and told them about the ambush.

"We should let Sparks know," said Lily-Matisse.

"No way," said Leon.

"You're sure you didn't see the pack leave the tunnel?" P.W. asked.

"Positive," said Leon.

"Then it must be stuck in a catch bin that separates out all the non-potato stuff. False teeth, eyeglasses, that kind of thing."

"Swell!" Leon said miserably. "Fathead is stuck in a tunnel thirty feet off the ground. You'd have to be Spider-Man to reach him."

"Or a gymnast," said Lily-Matisse.

It took a second for her comment to sink in.

"You're not serious," said Leon.

Lily-Matisse eyed the pipes, ladders, and walkways that crisscrossed the factory. "I can do it," she said.

"Are you sure?" said Leon.

"Positive."

"Excellent," said P.W.

"If she's going up there," said Leon, "We'll need a diversion—something to keep Sparks and the Hag distracted."

"Leave that to me," said P.W.

"What do you have in mind?" asked Lily-Matisse.

"I don't know yet," said P.W. "I'll have to improvise, so I want you guys to be ready to roll."

Lily-Matisse, Leon, and P.W. rejoined their classmates not far from a giant copper kettle filled with boiling peanut oil. They stayed close together as Mr. Sparks advanced the group from the cooking area to an inspection platform, where four men in hairnets plucked potato chips off a conveyor. Their speed was impressive. Using long-handled rubber-tipped grabbers, they picked up and set aside individual chips as they rolled along the conveyor.

"What are you fellows doing?" Mr. Sparks asked one of the men.

"I an' I," said the picker.

"Identification and Isolation," another picker explained. "We're the guys who catch most of the specials that end up in the museum. Tommy over there found a Madonna just last week."

"That's nothing," said Tommy. "A few months back, Timmy found two Italys on the same day."

"Impressive," said Mr. Sparks. He guided the class to the haywire salt tumbler that had called away Idaho Furtles.

Mr. Sparks looked around. "Mr. Furtles?"

"In here."

"Where?" said Mr. Sparks, unable to isolate the echoey response.

"Franklin," said Miss Hagmeyer.

"Yes?"

The fourth-grade teacher pointed her instructional needle at a pair of salted shoes sticking out from an open drum that resembled an oversized clothes dryer.

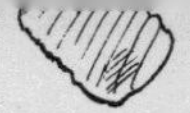

Mr. Sparks peered inside. "Mr. Furtles? Are you okay?"

"Better than this machine, I'll tell you that much."

"Should we wait for you?"

"No," said Idaho Furtles. "I still have to adjust the regulator and regulate the adjuster." He wiggled out of the tumbler with a monkey wrench in his hand. He was covered, head to toe, in salt. "See that exit beyond the bagging machine?" he said, pointing the wrench at a pair of swinging doors.

"I do," said Mr. Sparks.

"Well, meet me on the other side—at the entrance to the museum. Now if you'll excuse me." Idaho Furtles crawled back into the tumbler.

As the fifth graders passed the bagging station, Leon sidled up to P.W. "Where's that commotion you promised?" he asked anxiously.

"It's coming," said P.W. "Be patient. I've figured out what to do."

"The Hag's watching us like a hawk," Lily-Matisse warned.

"Don't worry about the Hag," P.W. reassured her. "She'll be busy soon enough."

* * *

Idaho Furtles (now salt-free) rejoined the group at the entrance of the museum. "I don't know why Russet insists I show all visitors our special holdings," he complained. He unlocked the curved doors to a vast circular room shaped like an old-fashioned potato chip tin.

Leon glanced about, but with none of his usual intensity. The upcoming disruption made it impossible to give the museum the attention it deserved. Still, he did manage to take in a few of the highlights. A time line marking milestones in the history of potato chips, from ancient potato harvests in Peru to the most recent advances in chipometrics. A collection of vintage potato chip tins. Photographs of smiling movie stars clutching bags of Furtles. A pair of mint-in-box 1932 shock absorbers, designed to minimize chip breakage during transport. And everywhere else—cabinets.

Two dozen wooden display cases housed a world-class collection of potato chip wonders painstakingly mounted like the insects exhibited at the Museum of Natural History. One cabinet contained chips in the shape of household objects (cup, stapler, telephone receiver). Another cabinet displayed chips shaped like animals (angelfish, cat, giraffe). Still another cabinet gathered together potato chip vehicles (rocket ship, car, snowmobile).

But it was the cabinet at the very center of the room—the one with the special lighting and the independent humidity gauge—that earned pride of place.

"The Furtles Presidential Potato Chip Collection," Idaho Furtles declared proudly. "The only complete set in the world—not even the Smithsonian matches us when it comes to breadth and quality."

Leon resisted the impulse to look at the unique collection and instead stayed near the exit doors, ready to duck out quickly once P.W.'s diversion began. The tactic paid off. Ten minutes after Idaho Furtles opened the museum, Miss Hagmeyer unleashed a bloodcurdling caw.

"You mischievous, ill-mannered hooligan!" she shouted. "Get away from there!"

Leon would have given anything to see what P.W. had cooked up, but he knew the rescue operation was more important.

"Come on," he said, grabbing Lily-Matisse by the arm. "It's now or never."

The two of them dashed out of the museum and through the swinging doors onto the factory floor. They retraced their steps, zipping past the bagging machines, the salt tumbler, the kettle cooker, and the chipper. In no time flat, they were standing below the tunnel where the pack had disappeared.

Lily-Matisse surveyed the network of belts, ladders, and catwalks that crisscrossed the factory. Her nose wrinkled and her eyes narrowed as she considered how to proceed.

"You're sure you want to go through with this?" Leon asked nervously.

Lily-Matisse answered the question by taking a running jump over a waist-high chain and landing on the conveyor belt leading directly into the tunnel.

Leon's jaw dropped as he watched her ride the belt, hopping over two bars and ducking under a third before disappearing inside the tunnel opening.

After a minute Leon began to worry. What was taking so long?

Another minute passed. *Still* no Lily-Matisse!

Leon climbed over a chain to put himself closer to the action. He squinched and clucked. Come on, Lily-Matisse! Get out of there!

He opened his eyes and felt a surge of relief when he saw that Lily-Matisse's head had emerged on the far side of the tunnel. Slowly, methodically, she inched forward, hands and feet keeping to the edges of the machinery as an endless parade of potatoes rumbled beneath her.

From where Leon stood, Lily-Matisse appeared strange—deformed, almost.

She looks like a hunchback, Leon said to himself. Either that or—

"Way to go!" he exclaimed, once he realized that the hunchback was actually a hunch*pack*.

Lily-Matisse cleared the tunnel exit and pulled herself up, still balancing on either side of the belt that was rolling toward the razor-sharp blades of the chipping machine.

All of a sudden she hopped *onto* the conveyor.

"Lily-Matisse!" Leon cried in a panic.

Forty feet separated her from the chipper. Then thirty feet. Then twenty. Fifteen feet from the blades, Lily-Matisse crouched like a swimmer preparing to take a dive. Seven feet from the chipper, she sprang into action once more, jumping up and grabbing hold of a sprinkler pipe that crossed above the belt just a few feet away from the honeycomb of razor-sharp steel. Hand over hand, she carried herself along the pipe. She dangled for a moment high above the factory floor.

Leon cupped his hands. "Careful!" he shouted.

Lily-Matisse was much too focused on her next move to respond to the useless warning. She swung back and forth like a clock pendulum until her feet rose above her head. And then she let go. . . .

Lily-Matisse sailed through the air and landed on a catwalk with an *ooooof*! She scampered across the metal walkway, hopped over a chain, and reached out to a vertical length of pipe. Effortlessly she wrapped her legs around the pipe and rode it, like a firehouse pole, down to a platform some eight feet off the factory floor. She finished off the improvised routine with an aerial somersault that set her down a few feet away from Leon. She hit the ground slightly off balance but corrected herself quickly.

"Let's get out of here," she cried, out of breath but beaming.

The two hightailed it back to the museum, hoping their absence would go unnoticed.

They got lucky. Things were still in chaos when they rejoined their classmates.

Leon located P.W. near the wall of antique chip cans. "Lily-Matisse was amazing!" he gushed. "She could have taught Spider-Man a thing or two." He held his thumb and index finger an inch apart. "She came this close to being chippified."

"Gimme a break," said Lily-Matisse, blushing. "My dismount was totally sloppy."

"The important thing is you got Fathead," said P.W.

Leon nodded. "Safe and sound. The zipper on the pack is still jammed, but I can tell nothing got broken inside. What about Lumpkin?"

"*Not* safe and *not* sound," said P.W. with a smile. "The Hag dragged him back to the bus."

"Excellent," said Leon. "How'd you do it?"

"It was a snap," said P.W. "I started complaining to him about how it was so unfair that we didn't get any samples."

"I bet he agreed," said Lily-Matisse.

P.W. chuckled. "That's an understatement. Anyway, then I kind of dared him to take matters into his own hands."

"You're kidding," said Leon. "Here? In the museum?"

P.W. nodded.

"But there's nothing to sample," said Lily-Matisse.

"Oh, really?" said P.W. "Come with me." He walked Leon and Lily-Matisse to the spotlighted display cabinet. The glass top was now open.

Lily-Matisse cupped her mouth. "Oh. My. God!"

"He jimmied the lock with a pocketknife," P.W. said matter-of-factly. "You should've seen Furtles when he got a look at the damage!"

"Who can blame him!" said Leon. "Lumpkin ate his way through all the Founding Fathers."

"Not all," Lily-Matisse nitpicked. "He skipped the Adamses."

"Look!" said Leon. "He ate Lincoln!"

"And Kennedy," said P.W.

"I would never have eaten Kennedy," said Leon.

"I don't think we'll have to worry about Lumpkin at recess," said Lily-Matisse.

"Yeah," said Leon. "I'm guessing he'll be Birdcaged all the way through seventh grade."

"That's assuming he isn't shipped off before then," said P.W.

"Now if we can just raise enough money to buy that army jacket, we'll be all set for the swap," said Leon.

"I think I've got that covered, too," said P.W. "Check this out. I found it posted on a bulletin board near the water fountain." He unfolded a bright yellow flyer that said:

THE ALL-STATE
POTATO CHIP ASSOCIATION™
SIXTEENTH ANNUAL CHIPAPALOOZA! CHIP-OFF
TEST YOUR TASTE BUDS AND YOUR BRAIN!
WHERE: THE CONVENTION CENTER
WHEN: MARCH 12
GRAND PRIZE: $1000

"Leon!" Lily-Matisse blurted out. "The convention center is right across the street from your hotel!"

"Yeah, so?" said Leon, though he knew perfectly well where all this was heading.

"*So*," said P.W. "You are going to enter the Chip-Off and, what's more, you are going to win. And with that prize money, you are going to buy a certain vintage army jacket that's going to get us a certain missing ingredient needed to activate a certain Fathead that will control a certain bully."

"You're off your rocker," said Leon. "How do you expect me to win against someone like Furtles?"

"By practicing," said Lily-Matisse.

"Exactly," said P.W.

"But—"

"No ifs, ands, or buts," P.W. said, doing a pretty good impression of Miss Hagmeyer. "Training starts as soon as school lets out."

Twenty-Four

Zero. Zip. Zilch.

Miss Hagmeyer was so outraged by Lumpkin's unpatriotic cannibalism in the Furtles Potato Chip Museum that she forgot to seat the students alphabetically as they filed onto the bus. That slip gave Leon, Lily-Matisse, and P.W. a chance to hash out their next move during the ride back to school.

"We'll go to the convention center straight after the bell," said P.W.

Leon renewed his earlier concern: "What if I don't win the potato chip contest? I mean, think about it, the Chip-Off is going to be packed with potato chip professionals."

"You'll win," P.W. said confidently.

"Okay, supposing I *do* win," Leon allowed. "We still don't know for sure that Lumpkin will want to swap."

"For a vintage army jacket that fits him?" said P.W. "Are you kidding me? He'll swap all right."

"Fine. Say I *do* win and say he *does* swap, what happens if the fixed-up, restuffed Fathead still misfires?"

P.W. finally lost it. "You're worse than she is," he said, nodding at Lily-Matisse.

"Hey, don't get on my case!" Lily-Matisse shot back. "I think Leon's a shoo-in, too."

"See," P.W. told Leon. "Even Miss Skeptical says you should enter."

"But—"

"Stop!" P.W. commanded. "Get it into your head. You're competing. We've got nothing to lose! Zero. Zip. Zilch."

P.W. stood firm. When the bell rang, he made sure to approach Napoleon before Leon had a chance to argue or escape.

"Bonjour, Monsieur Pay Dooble-vay," said the taxi driver.

"Bonjour to you, too, Napoleon," said P.W. "Listen, can you take us over to the convention center? Leon here needs to enter a potato chip contest."

"*Bien sûr!*" said Napoleon, not batting an eye. "You have received the necessary permissions, I assume?"

"No," said Leon, thinking that might get him off the hook.

P.W. gave Lily-Matisse a meaningful nod.

"Hold on," she said. "Be back in a sec." She disappeared into the school and returned moments later. "All set," she announced. "Mom's making the calls."

"In that case," said Napoleon, hopping out of his

cab to open the door. "My potato cheep chariot is at your service."

"You heard him," said P.W.

At the convention center, Leon trudged in and trudged out while Lily-Matisse and P.W. waited in the cab.

"Mission accomplished?" P.W. asked the reluctant competitor.

"Nope."

"Why not?" Lily-Matisse demanded.

"There's a ten-dollar entry fee," said Leon. "I tried to argue, but it's no use, so I guess that's that."

"Whaddaya mean 'that's that'?" said P.W.

"I thought the whole point of entering the Chip-Off was to *make* money—not spend it."

"Let's pay the ten dollars, Leon," said Lily-Matisse. "We can afford it."

"Besides," added P.W. "Competing in a potato chip contest? How cool is that?"

"Your friends are correct," said Napoleon. "You *must* enter."

"What's the point," Leon said. "I'll never win."

"Why not?" said P.W.

"Because it's a sure bet Furtles is competing. We're better off saving our money."

A ten-dollar bill suddenly fluttered into Lily-Matisse's lap.

"Are you sure, Monsieur Napoleon?" Lily-Matisse asked politely.

"*Allez!* Go on!"

Lily-Matisse handed Leon the money. "You heard Napoleon. *Allez!*"

"I'm afraid to ask," said P.W. when Leon returned the second time.

"Mission accomplished," Leon announced unenthusiastically. He held up an envelope. "The official contest guidelines. They're worse than I thought."

P.W. snatched the packet and read through the rules. "Says here the Chip-Off will be divided into two parts. Trivia, which you know cold, and flavor awareness."

"That's a fancy way of saying there's a taste test," Leon said miserably. "Which means I'm cooked."

Lily-Matisse gave him a gentle punch. "Hey, stop sounding so glum."

"Why shouldn't I sound glum?" said Leon. "You saw how I did back in the Furtles testing room. There's no way I can compete with the pros."

"Sure you can," said P.W.

"All it takes is practice," said Lily-Matisse.

"With what?" Leon shot back. "Where are we going to get all the different chips to practice with? Have you thought about *that*?"

"Worry no more, Monsieur Leon. Allow Napoleon to help."

"How?"

"Fasten your seat belts, my friends, and you shall see!"

* * *

For the next two hours, Napoleon's taxi crisscrossed the city, idling at shopping centers, corner grocery stores, gas stations, and gourmet shops just long enough for the three fifth graders to hop out and purchase training chips. By the time the buying expedition was complete, foil bags filled the trunk of the taxi.

Back at the hotel, Leon, Lily-Matisse, and P.W. resettled in the coffee shop to inventory their loot.

Frau Haffenreffer bustled over to greet her favorite customer and his favorite classmates. "Can I give you three some dough balls? They're just now out of the oven!"

"Thanks," said Lily-Matisse, "but I think we've got the snack situation pretty well covered."

P.W. dumped a shopping bag onto the tabletop.

"So many *kartoffel* chips!" Frau Haffenreffer exclaimed.

"And there are more under the table," said Lily-Matisse.

"Napoleon took us to just about every store we could find," P.W. added.

"Ach," said Frau Haffenreffer, clearly disappointed. "So no dough balls?"

"Sorry," P.W. apologized. "For the next few months Leon here is in training. We can't risk confusing his taste buds with the sweet stuff."

"Then I will leave you to it," said Frau Haffenreffer.

Lily-Matisse cleared the table while P.W. built a wall of menus. "Ready, willing, and able?" he said after solidifying the barrier with a couple of napkin dispensers.

"Just get on with it," Leon grumbled.

"Fine," said P.W. "Here comes the first mystery chip."

A familiar crinkling sound filled the air. Lily-Matisse passed a chip over the menu wall.

Leon reluctantly accepted it. He looked. He sniffed. He nibbled.

"Plain?" he said after some deliberation.

"Good!" said Lily-Matisse, a little too enthusiastically. "Now, can you tell what brand?"

"No way," said Leon.

"Well, can you tell if it's hand sliced?" P.W. asked.

Leon turned the chip over in his hands a few times. "Definitely hand sliced."

"Right!" said Lily-Matisse, again with too much encouragement.

"Stop babying me," Leon snapped.

P.W. ignored the outburst. "What else can you tell us about the chip?"

Leon could think of at least twelve brands of hand-sliced plain potato chips. But which one? "This is impossible!" he exclaimed at last, knocking down the menu wall in frustration.

"At least guess," said P.W.

"I can't!" Leon exclaimed. "I have *no* clue. Zero. Zip. Zilch. I'll never be able to ID chips without all that fancy stuff Furtles uses."

"Forget about Furtles and his stupid Nose-It-All 3000," said Lily-Matisse.

"She's right," said P.W. "You can't worry about Furtles. And besides, we've got our own knows-it-all."

"Oh, yeah?" said Leon. "Who?"

"Mr. Sparks," P.W. replied.

Twenty-Five

Common Sense

P.W., Lily-Matisse, and Leon stayed back after the next science class.

"Mr. Sparks?" said P.W., once the other fifth graders had left. "Leon here is entering a potato chip competition."

"That's splendid," said Mr. Sparks. "Science always benefits from work done outside the lab."

"I guess," said Leon.

"You don't seem too thrilled," said Mr. Sparks.

"He's not," said Lily-Matisse.

"He doesn't think he has a shot," added P.W.

"Nonsense," Mr. Sparks said. "I can't think of anyone, with the possible exception of Idaho Furtles, who knows more about chips than you, Leon."

"Yes and no," said P.W. "Here's the thing. Half the test is about potato chip trivia. Leon will ace that part for sure."

"And the other half?" Mr. Sparks asked.

"Flavor awareness," said Lily-Matisse. "Basically Leon has to be able to recognize mystery chips. Which is why we need your help. We started testing him yesterday and . . ." Lily-Matisse hesitated.

"Go on," said Mr. Sparks.

P.W. took over. "And let's just say the results weren't pretty."

"Of course they weren't," said Leon. "How could they be? I don't have any of Furtles's thingamabobs."

"You don't need them," said Mr. Sparks. "And in any case, Mr. Furtles's method works for Mr. Furtles. You must devise your own."

"That's why we came to you," P.W. said. "We need a foolproof trick for identifying chips."

Mr. Sparks scratched his beard for a moment. "I'm afraid there is no trick. All I can tell you is this. You need to combine scientific rigor with the passion you already possess."

"That's swell," said P.W. "But can you be a bit more specific?"

"Tell you what," said Mr. Sparks, "suppose I help you kick-start the process?"

"Now you're talking!" P.W. exclaimed.

"Why don't you three clean the test tubes in the sink, while I set things up? I'll let you know when I'm ready."

Five minutes later, Mr. Sparks called them back to his bench. "Okay," he said, "let's get started. As you can see, I've set out three petri dishes, each containing a chip."

"What are the index cards for?" asked Lily-Matisse.

"I've written the name of each chip on the

side that's facedown," Mr. Sparks explained. "Now Leon, I want you to analyze the chips using every one of your five senses."

"But—"

"No objections, no excuses," said Mr. Sparks. "Get to it."

Leon applied his five senses to the three chips. He looked. Smelled. Touched. Listened (by snapping the chips close to his ear). And, of course, he tasted.

"All I know is they're salt 'n' vinegars," he said at last.

"That's a fine start," said Mr. Sparks. "But I'm quite sure you can tell me more."

"Not without a thickness tester, or the other stuff Furtles uses."

"You don't need them, Leon, as long as you use common *sense*."

Leon gave Mr. Sparks a sideways glance. Why is he stressing the last word? he wondered.

Mr. Sparks started jingling some coins in his pocket. "*Penny* for your thoughts," he said with a smile.

And then, all of a sudden, Leon understood.

"Mr. Sparks," he blurted out. "Can I borrow some change?"

Lily-Matisse and P.W. gave Leon puzzled looks.

"Thought you'd never ask," said Mr. Sparks, slapping some coins on the top of the lab bench.

"What are you guys going on about?" said P.W.

Leon grabbed a penny and lined it up against the edge of a chip. He did the same with the nickel and the same with the dime. He repeated the comparisons on the other two chips.

"Got it," Lily-Matisse said giddily.

"Me, too," said P.W. "He's making common *cents* comparisons."

"Precisely," said Mr. Sparks.

It didn't take long for Leon to announce his results. "You see this chip here?" he said with newfound confidence, holding up the specimen from the middle dish. "This chip has the exact same thickness as a penny. And the chip to the right? It's thinner—closer to a dime. As for the last chip—it's the fattest of the three, and is almost as thick as a nickel. Definitely hand sliced. Which actually narrows things down. I may be wrong, but as far as I can recall, only the Palombo Brothers make a hand-sliced salt 'n' vinegar chip that is this thick."

"So you're saying that this chip, this one right

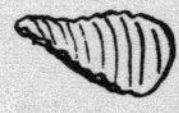

here"—Mr. Sparks aimed a finger at the sample in question—"is a Palombo Brothers Salt 'n' Vinegar?"

"Yes?" said Leon.

"That doesn't sound terribly confident," said Mr. Sparks.

"Yes," Leon repeated more forcefully.

Mr. Sparks turned over the index card. It said, PALOMBO SALT 'N' VINEGAR.

"That is too cool," P.W. declared. "All Leon has to do is match coin thickness to chip thickness and chart the results."

"Pretty nifty," said Lily-Matisse.

"Idaho Furtles may have his external caliper gauge, but you have something far more valuable," said Mr. Sparks.

"I'm not sure about that," said P.W., gazing down at the bench. "From the looks of it, Leon has sixteen cents."

Mr. Sparks chuckled. "I meant that his passion for chips is far more powerful than all of Mr. Furtles's gadgets combined. Now if there's nothing else, I've got to prepare for next week's experiment."

The coin trick was a real shot in the arm for Leon. It revived his confidence and enthusiasm. Back in his room, he stayed up until nearly midnight conducting thickness analyses, noting the results in his laboratory notebook. The following day he invited Lily-Matisse and P.W. back to the coffee shop for more tests.

"All set to try this new system of yours?" P.W. asked eagerly as he erected a menu wall.

"I wouldn't exactly call it a system," said Leon. "Not yet, anyway."

"Whatever," said P.W. "Are you ready?"

Leon gave a nod. "Go for it," he said.

Lily-Matisse passed him a mystery chip.

Leon measured it against the three coins and checked his thickness chart. He took a nibble, which confirmed his initial opinion. "It's a plain—probably a Goody Two-Chews or a Furtles. I can't tell which."

"A Goody Two-Chews," said Lily-Matisse.

"Nice get," P.W. said.

"Thanks," said Leon. "But there's still a lot more stuff to work out. Thickness tests are totally useless on crinkle cuts."

"So what are you going to do?" Lily-Matisse asked.

"What Sparks told me to do," Leon replied self-assuredly. "Approach the problem using science."

"And passion," said Lily-Matisse. "You can't forget that."

"I won't," Leon said.

Twenty-Six

The Zeisel Method

Although the three-coin test worked fine on conventional potato chips, it was useless on crinkle cuts. So Leon set out to overcome the limitation of the procedure. He studied every crinkle cut in his stockpile and ultimately identified three distinct profiles.

The most common kind of crinkle cut had perfectly even, zigzaggy ridges—like the saw blades in Mr. Groot's wood shop.

The second most common kind of crinkle cut had jagged, *un*even ridges—like the teeth of a great white shark.

The rarest kind of crinkle cut displayed edges that recalled the tops of castle towers, which Leon had learned (while studying the Middle Ages in fourth grade) to call "crenels."

Leon grabbed a pencil and sketched side views of the three basic profiles in his science notebook. Using the drawings as a guide, he then charted all of the crinkle cuts by profile type.

That covers thickness, Leon said to himself. What's next?

After taking a moment to look over his work, he drew up a list of potato chip properties that warranted further scientific study. He decided to tackle chip shape. But an hour of pattern analysis only established two basic groups: irregular "amoebas" and curvy, stackable "saddles."

Leon entered the data into his notebook and turned his attention to size. Nearly one hundred measurements later, he concluded that size was too iffy. He nixed that property and moved on.

Color came next. Leon realized very quickly that chip color presented a new headache. He could distinguish many shades of yellow and brown. The problem was he didn't know how to record those differences in his notebook. He tried using markers to make up a color chart. The results were lame. So Leon decided to seek out expert guidance. He ran to the phone and called Lily-Matisse. "Hey," he said.

"Hey," said Lily-Matisse.

"Is your mom around?"

"No, Leon. She just leaves me alone with a bag of chips for dinner. *Of course* she's around. Why?"

"I'm trying to color code potato chip brands, and I'm stumped. Your mom knows tons about colors, right?"

"She *is* an art teacher," said Lily-Matisse.

"Exactly," said Leon. "Do you think she can help?"

"Ask her yourself. Hold on."

Leon heard some talking, some laughter, followed by more talking.

"Hello, Leon?"

"Hi, Ms. Jasprow."

"My daughter tells me you're entering a potato chip competition."

"Yup."

"Sounds important. How can I help?"

"I was analyzing potato chip colors, and that made me think of you."

"It did?"

"Uh-huh. Remember on the field trip to that museum of the Middle Ages last year? We were looking at an old picture and you told us about a yellow paint made from cow pee?"

"That's right," said Ms. Jasprow. "Indian yellow used to be produced that way. Mango leaves would get fed to cattle to intensify the color of their urine, which was then collected, dried, and packed into small balls of pigment."

"That is really, really disgusting," Leon said approvingly. "Anyway, since you know so much about yellows, I was wondering if you could give me a list of all the different shades?"

"Sorry, Leon. You're out of luck. No such list exists."

"Darn."

"But I can make a suggestion. Do you have a hardware store near you?"

"Yeah," said Leon, thoroughly bewildered.

"Do they sell paint?"

"I guess."

"Go to the store and see if you can get some chips."

"I *have* the chips, Ms. Jasprow. It's a list of yellows I need."

"Not *potato* chips, Leon—*paint* chips."

"Oh."

"If it's a decent hardware store, they'll have sample cards for all kinds of paints in all kinds of colors."

"That's great," said Leon. But his excitement was cut short by a new concern. "How much do the sample cards cost?" he asked.

"They shouldn't cost a thing, Leon. Paint companies give them away."

"Super, Ms. J. Thanks."

"Glad to help," said Regina Jasprow.

The next day Leon asked his mom if he could make a run to the hardware store.

"If you promise to feed the piranhas in three-oh-two, " Emma Zeisel negotiated.

"No problem," Leon said before disappearing through the revolving door.

The local hardware store was a family business called Adler's that had a humongous black hammer mounted above the entrance. Leon wondered, as he passed underneath the hammer, if Adler had needed a second, even more humongous hammer to nail up the one overhead.

"Can I help you?" asked a tiny man wearing an apron that read "Fred."

"Do you have paint chips?" Leon asked.

"Adler's wouldn't be Adler's if Adler's didn't have chips," Fred said proudly. He pointed a wooden-handled screwdriver to the back of the store. "Take a right at the mousetraps, then your first left after the toilet plungers."

As soon as Leon passed the plungers, he knew he'd struck gold—and bronze and yellow.

Hundreds of paint chips covered the entire back wall of the hardware store. The bookmark-shaped samples, all arranged by color, made Leon think of a rainbow fed through a potato chipper. He dashed to the entrance and double-checked to make sure that the chips were free for the taking.

Fred confirmed what Regina Jasprow had said on the phone. "Grab as many as you like, sonny. Adler's wouldn't be Adler's if Adler's didn't give away chips."

Leon collected a complete set of yellows, a complete set of golds, plus a decent assortment of browns, light browns, reds, oranges, and purples to compare against various specialty chips.

The color harvest didn't take long. A half hour after he had begun his expedition, Leon was on his bed, dealing out paint chips like playing cards.

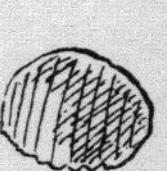

For a while he just stared.

Incredible! he said to himself. He never would have believed there could be so many shades of yellow—and each with its own special name. All at once Leon decided to classify the chips.

He began by isolating all yellows named after flowers: daffodil, dandelion, crocus, honeysuckle, marigold. He put them in a pile.

Next he grouped weather and time yellows: high noon, low sunrise, sun ray, sun spot, sun shower, sunshine, summer sunrise, sunny summer, summer solstice.

He stacked up a pile of golds: Venetian gold, Sutter's gold, nugget gold, yellow gold, fool's gold, Burmese gold, golden pond, golden fleece, mission gold, and golden fable.

He assembled a pile of yellows related to food and cooking: country kitchen yellow, dish glove yellow, cornmeal, corncake, butternut, curry spice, wildflower honey, citrus splash, mustard yellow, French mustard yellow, lemon sorbet, lemon soufflé, lemon drop, lemonade, pineapple soda, and Jell-O yellow.

He caged all the animal yellows: honey bird,

canary, chickadee, goldfinch, cheetah, lion's pelt, cat's eye, and goldfish.

He created a small atlas of place name yellows: African yellow, Indian yellow, Sumatran gold, Ceylonese gold, Sierra Madre, Panama beach, Jamaican dream, and yellow brick road.

Finally there were all those paint chips that resisted classification (and that served as a handy way to group them): straw hat, yellow submarine, kayak yellow, torch, ho-hum yellow, hello yellow, mellow yellow, and jolly good fellow yellow.

The only yellow Leon failed to find among the Adler's color samples was potato chip yellow.

That's nuts! he told himself. Potato chip yellow is probably the best-known yellow in the whole universe, except for (maybe) the sun. But as soon as Leon started trying to match edible chips to the paint chips on his bedspread, he understood why no color sample borrowed the name of the world's favorite snack food. There were too many different shades of potato chip. In fact, no two brands had exactly the same color. And that single fact was the key to Leon's potato chip/color chip comparison chart.

He lined all the paint samples face up on the rug and compared them to chips in his stockpile. Each time he found a perfect match, he would glue the paint chip into his notebook and write down the name of its potato chip partner.

There were some surprisingly logical matches. Byrd

brand chips matched canary yellow. Island brand chips matched Jamaican dream. But there were also pairs that didn't make sense. Wisdom chips matched fool's gold, and Furtles Double Crunchers corresponded to jolly good fellow yellow.

The paint company must not know Idaho Furtles, Leon said to himself.

After working through all the yellow potato chips, Leon took a break and went to feed the piranhas in 302. Then it was straight back to work, analyzing *non-*yellow brands. Incan treasure, a Peruvian chip Maria provided, matched a purple paint called plum. Miss Sippy River chips, a barbequed product from the South, paired perfectly with a paint called plantation brick. All in all, Leon ended up matching paint samples to ninety-eight brands of potato chip.

With color taken care of, Leon took a mental inventory. Thickness? . . . Check. Shape? . . . Check. Color? . . . Check. Sound?

Sound came next. Leon figured if bird-watchers could tell a robin from a wren by their chirps, he might be able to distinguish different brands of chip crunches. That was the idea, anyway. Leon picked up a Furtles Double Cruncher, shut his eyes, bit down, and *listened.*

Then, quick as he could, he grabbed a Wisdom chip and repeated the procedure.

The two brands sounded pretty much the same.

He tried again.

The second trial was no better.

After a few minutes of careful crunching, Leon felt soundly defeated and gave up. Only one item remained on his mental checklist—the one Idaho Furtles dismissed as useless and unscientific: taste.

Basic flavor distinctions were a snap for Leon. He had no trouble telling a barbeque chip from, say, a salt 'n' vinegar. But as Furtles had proven during the factory tour, distinguishing different brands of the *same* flavor was a whole lot tougher.

It took some doing, but Leon ultimately isolated three distinctive "chew factors" to help him tell apart similarly seasoned chips produced by different companies.

First of all, there was the way the chip broke apart at the *start* of munching. Second, there was the texture of the chip *during* munching. And third, there was the sensation that remained *after* the chip had been swallowed. Leon called these three factors: Crumbulosity, Mouthfeel, and Lingertaste.

For the better part of a Sunday, he refined his three-point guide to chew factors. When he was done, he flipped through his notebook. A full weekend's worth of research and writing had produced more than forty pages of chip analysis, an achievement that almost allowed Leon to forget *why* he had conducted his research.

Almost, but not quite.

Twenty-Seven

.500

Leon was more than chipper at the start of the next coffee shop training session. "Let's get crackin'!" he said, building the menu wall while Lily-Matisse and P.W. selected some test samples.

"That's what I like to hear," said P.W.

"Ready?" asked Lily-Matisse.

"Go for it," said Leon.

She passed a chip over the menu wall.

Leon inspected the specimen. Non-crinkle. Midway between a penny and a dime. He checked his notebook. There were twenty-seven chips in that range.

He turned to the color chart. The chip almost matched sunshine, but Leon knew better than to treat a near-match as a positive ID. Nevertheless, he was able to scratch ten chips off the candidate list.

"Well?" said P.W. impatiently.

"Don't rush him," said Lily-Matisse.

Leon took a nibble. Onion. He flipped through his notes some more. Onion narrowed the suspects to just six. He took another nibble, evaluated the chew factors, and again checked his data.

"I have it down to two," he said at last. "It's either a Wisdom Onion or a Furtles Onion."

"Not bad," said P.W. "It's a Wisdom."

"Ach, Leon!" exclaimed Frau Haffenreffer. "How can you do that?" She had been watching the analysis from behind the pastry case.

"Dichotomous classification," said P.W.

"We learned it in science," Lily-Matisse added.

Frau Haffenreffer shook her head in amazement. "This your mama must see." She bustled out to the lobby.

The testing resumed. Lily-Matisse handed Leon another potato chip, and another, and another, and another. After five trials P.W. announced the results. "Two out of five, Leon. That means you're batting four hundred!"

"That's not good enough," said Leon.

Just then Frau Haffenreffer returned, with Emma Zeisel and Maria in tow.

"I see we have an audience," said P.W. "Ready to show off your stuff, Leon?"

"Sure," said Leon.

Lily-Matisse presented a chip and, as he had five times before, Leon flipped through his logbook. He measured the thickness, checked the profile, and took a quick nibble. "Willie Winkle Krinkle Cut," he said.

"What flavor?" said Lily-Matisse.

"Cheddar, of course."

"That's a roger!" P.W. exclaimed, reaching over the menu wall to give Leon a high five.

"Way to go, Leonito!" cried Maria.

"Wow, sweetie, you sure bagged that one fast!" said Emma Zeisel.

"Ja," said Frau Haffenreffer. "All hail the *kartoffel* chip king!"

"It wasn't that tough," said Leon. "Shark tooths are a cinch to ID."

"Three for six," said P.W. "That brings your average to five hundred!"

"How much of the Chip-Off will be taste testing?" Emma Zeisel asked.

"Half," said Leon. "First there's a trivia round, then the taste tests."

"Leon will ace the trivia part for sure," P.W. said. "He probably knows more about chips than anyone alive."

"I wouldn't count on it," said Emma Zeisel. "From what Leon tells me, that Furtles fellow is one tough competitor."

"Your mother's right, Leonito," Maria said. "You better study *real* hard."

"But how can our little stinker study about chips?" asked Frau Haffenreffer.

The three women suddenly started giggling.

"Okay," said Leon. "What's up? What am I missing here?"

"Only this, sweetie." Emma Zeisel plunked a hefty package on the tabletop.

"A present?" said Leon.

"*Ja,*" said Frau Haffenreffer.

"*Sí,*" said Maria.

"Yes, sweetie," said Emma Zeisel.

The gift was wrapped in kraft paper and tied with the red string Frau Haffenreffer used to secure her pastry boxes. Leon dug into his pocket, pulled out the nifty knife ring he'd received for his tenth birthday, and cut through the wrapping.

"Holy guacamole!" said P.W.

"Sheesh!" said Lily-Matisse.

Leon read the cover out loud: "*The Official Potato Chip Encyclopedia* by Fergus O'Hare, Executive Director, All-State Potato Chip Association . . . This is *amazing*! I've heard about this book, but I've never seen it." He flipped to the back. "It's seven hundred and eighty-three pages long! And check out this index! It goes from Abalone Chips all the way to . . . Zarathustra Über Tubers!"

Leon gave each of the three women a hug. "Thanks! This must have cost a bundle."

"Don't worry, Leonito," said Maria.

"*Ja*, we all of us pitched in," said Frau Haffenreffer.

"We were going to wait until your birthday, but we figured you could use it for the Chip-Off," said Emma Zeisel.

"With this book, Leon, you'll be even more unstoppable," P.W. predicted.

"I hope you're right," said Lily-Matisse.

"*Of course* P.W.'s right," said Emma Zeisel. "It's in the bag."

Two weeks remained until *Chipapalooza!* During that time, Leon went to school, did his homework, practiced the flute, and tended to chores. But his mind focused on one thing and one thing only—potato chips.

He ate chips. He studied chips. He dreamed chips. He lived chips. He heard the sound of crunching everywhere. His eye was drawn to each and every chip bag that littered the city streets. When he wasn't refining the Zeisel Method, he was poring over the *Encyclopedia*. He crammed his brain with thousands of new facts relating to deep-fried tubers. The first potato chip. The biggest potato chip. The smallest potato chip. The biggest bag. The smallest bag. The most potato chips eaten in a single sitting. And with each passing day, his knowledge and self-assurance increased.

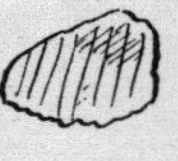

But all that changed one week before the big event.

Leon called P.W. with some grim news. "We've got problems," he said.

"What kind of problems?"

"I'm not going to win," Leon said gravely.

"What do you mean? You've got a batting average that's better than Babe Ruth's."

"Potato chips aren't baseball," said Leon.

"I only meant that—"

Leon cut him off. "Will you just listen for a sec!" He read a passage from the *Encyclopedia* into the phone:

> *"The highlight of* Chipapalooza! *is the Chip-Off, a battle of 'trivia and taste' that tests chip experts on their knowledge of the world's most popular snack food. Previous winners have included Idaho 'The Chip Master' Furtles and Alphonse 'The Chippopotamus' Cipollini."*

"Yeah? So?" said P.W. "We always knew Furtles was a hotshot. I *still* say you can take him."

"It's not Furtles that worries me," said Leon. "It's the other guy—Cipollini. He has his own entry. Listen to this." Leon flipped to the relevant page and again read a key passage into the phone:

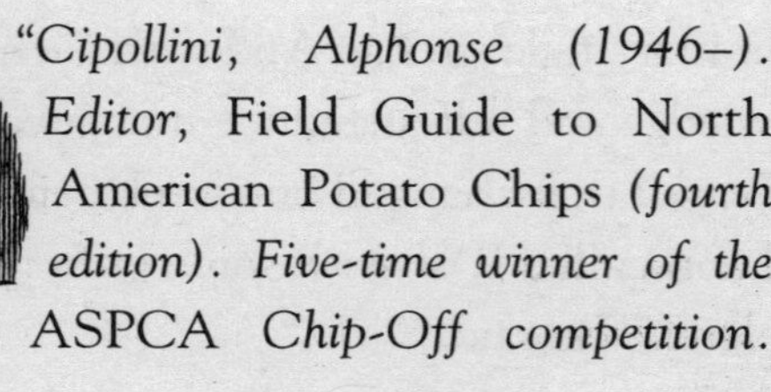

> *"Cipollini, Alphonse (1946–). Editor,* Field Guide to North American Potato Chips *(fourth edition). Five-time winner of the* ASPCA *Chip-Off competition.*

Known in snack circles as 'The Chippopotamus,' Mr. Cipollini [pronounced chip-oh-lee-nee] also holds the record for the most consecutive chip identifications, having correctly named twelve in a row during his first year of competition."

"Don't sweat it," said P.W. "That was then, this is now."

"I don't have a chance," said Leon.

"Look, if he had rookie's luck, why shouldn't you?"

"Even if—"

"No ifs, ands, or buts," said P.W. "You've got to stay positive. Remember what your mom said?"

"Yeah, yeah, I know," said Leon. "It's in the bag."

TWENTY-EIGHT

A Glitch

The big day finally arrived.

The competition was set to take place at noon. At nine that morning, Leon greeted his support crew in the hotel coffee shop, where Frau Haffenreffer was already handing out dough balls.

"Okay, one more, Frau H.," P.W. agreed, his mouth rimmed with powdered sugar.

"Not for me," said Lily-Matisse, her lips similarly coated.

Frau Haffenreffer knew better than to tempt Leon. "I know, I know," she said irritably. "You're in training."

"Sorry," said Leon. "It's been crazy. We must have thirty potato chip sales reps checked in. My taste buds are wiped out!"

Emma Zeisel and Maria both stopped by the coffee shop to wish Leon good luck.

"I'll try to make it over to the competition, sweetie, but it's going to be tough. There's a pair of koalas arriving any moment."

"Leonito doesn't need our help," said Maria. "I lit two candles on Sunday *and* bought an Axomama prayer card."

"What's Axomama?" asked Lily-Matisse.

"Not what," said Leon. "Who. She's the South American goddess of potatoes."

P.W. looked at his watch. "T minus two hours and forty-nine minutes to Chip-Off. We'd better head over."

"Holy mackerel!" P.W. yelled as they passed under a giant yellow banner that said FEAST WITHOUT FEAR.

"That's the motto of the ASPCA," Leon explained.

"Can't argue with that, can you?" said P.W.

"Nope," said Leon. "Time to be fearless." They pushed through the crowds and into an exhibition hall packed with booths promoting potato chips and potato chip-related products.

"Listen!" said P.W. "Have you ever heard so much crinkling and crunching?"

"And what about the smell!" said Lily-Matisse. "It's even more potato-chippy than the Furtles assembly line!"

"Yeah, only here, they give away free samples!" said

P.W., reaching for a chip. He stopped in mid-munch. "Guys," he said abruptly. "Do you hear that?"

"What?" said Leon.

"That *wocka-wocka-wocka*," said P.W. He dragged Lily-Matisse and Leon past a display of bagging machines to an electronic game called Snackman.

While P.W. tested the game, which required the Snackman to gobble his way through a maze of potato chips, Leon looked around the nearby booths.

He returned in panic before P.W. had finished playing.

"Let go of that joystick!" said Leon.

"What's the matter?" Lily-Matisse asked.

"I'll tell you what the matter is. I've seen at least three brands of potato chip I never knew about—and that means there must be others. What if the Chip-Off includes samples I haven't tested?"

P.W. released the joystick and looked at his watch. "Don't sweat it," he said. "We've got time." He ran over to an information booth and returned with some pamphlets. "Floor plans," he said. "I got one for each of us. They give the names and locations of all the chip makers in the hall." He handed a pamphlet to Leon. "Mark the brands you need to analyze."

Leon pulled a pencil from his backpack and scanned the list. The ground level of the convention center housed booths promoting American chips. The balcony was reserved for the international exhibitors.

"What's the count?" P.W. asked when Leon was done.

"Twelve Americans," said Leon. "Plus sixteen internationals. Here, take a look." He handed the pamphlet to P.W., who studied it like a four-star general preparing an invasion.

"Okay, here's what we'll do," P.W. said. "Lily-Matisse, you cover aisles one through five. I'll handle six through ten. That'll take care of the U.S. targets. Leon—think you can deal with the rest of the world?"

Leon took a long look at the balcony. "I'll give it a shot," he said.

"You'll do fine," P.W. reassured him. "We'll regroup at oh-ten-thirty in front of the information booth, then head back to the hotel. That'll give Leon a solid hour for chip analysis."

"Hold on," said Lily-Matisse. "How are we going to carry all the samples?"

"I know," Leon said almost at once. He dashed over to a trash can, yanked out the plastic liner, and looked inside. He waved Lily-Matisse and P.W. over. They arrived to find him pulling out three fresh garbage bags.

"How'd you know they'd be in there?" P.W. asked.

"Don't you remember the old housekeeping trick?" said Leon. "Maria always stashes spares in the bottom of the can."

With their garbage bags and floor plans, the three chip hunters darted off to their assigned sections of the exhibit hall.

* * *

Leon nabbed the first item on his checklist—Gondola Chips from Venice—in under a minute. The second and third items (from England and France) were also a snap to snag. The only European sample that proved elusive was the Struwweltater, a bratwurst-flavored *kartoffel* chip popular in Germany. Leon eventually hunted down a sample from a slovenly man with long fingernails and uncombed hair.

Leon took a nibble. Not bad, he said to himself.

With Europe checked off his list, Leon turned to Asia, where he nabbed squid, seaweed, and tofu chips in quick succession. But the collection process slowed to an irritating crawl at a booth promising Zen Chips. To get a sample, Leon had to listen to a man in a black robe recite a poem:

"One potato chip
Happy inside my tummy.
Is that not enough?"

No way! Leon said to himself. When at last he received a sample, he noticed that the bag was extraordinarily light. He pulled open the seams and peered inside. "Excuse me," he said. "There's only one chip in this bag."

"Yes," the man in the black robe replied calmly. "The Zen Chip teaches us to honor the one among the many."

Well, I'd rather honor the *many* among the many, Leon found himself thinking as he grabbed an extra sample bag and moved on to Africa. There he quickly located the two bags he needed—Tim Bucktooth Chips and Malagasy Munchies. He then made his way to Australia. He only needed one bag from there—or rather two, since every bag of Kangaroo Chips came in a flapped pouch containing a second package of chips.

Leon took a moment to tally his haul. Twelve down. Four to go. The remaining bags would all be found in the South America section.

The first of those four came easily enough. A man dressed in a leather vest and black hat sidled up to Leon, reached into a saddlebag, and presented him with some Macho Gaucho Nachos.

"*Gracias!*" said Leon.

Thirteen down! Three more to go!

Leon picked up some Chile Chili Chipotle Chips from a man dressed like a red pepper.

Fourteen down! Two left!

A woman wearing a bowler and a brightly woven poncho handed Leon a much-needed bag of Bolivars.

Fifteen down! One to go!

It was 10:15. Leon checked his floor plan. The last item on the list—Tierra del Fuego Chips—was supposed to be distributed from a booth near the back of the balcony. But when he reached the spot marked on the map, he found the area deserted. He asked around. No one seemed to know a thing about the absent exhibitor.

So having bagged fifteen of the sixteen chips, Leon rushed back to the rendezvous point, where he found P.W. and Lily-Matisse checking over their haul.

"We got all except one," Lily-Matisse announced. "The Rhode Island booth ran out of samples. How'd you do?"

"Same," said Leon. "All but one. Tierra del Fuego was a no-show."

"It's not the end of the world," said Lily-Matisse.

"No," said P.W. "Antarctica is."

"Very funny," said Leon.

"I still say twenty-four out of twenty-six is pretty good," said Lily-Matisse.

"Getting the final two would've been better," said Leon.

"Tell you what," P.W. said. "You guys head over to the hotel. I'll scout around here a little longer and try to snag the missing brands."

"Makes sense," said Leon.

Five minutes later Lily-Matisse and Leon were back in the Trimore Towers coffee shop, setting up a testing area on the tabletop of a corner booth.

Leon whipped out his notebook, coins, and a pencil. "How much time do we have?" he asked.

"If we leave here at eleven forty-five, you've got about an hour," said Lily-Matisse.

"With twenty-six different chips that means . . ." Leon made a quick calculation. "I've got about two minutes a chip."

"Plus a little," said Lily-Matisse.

"Okay, then," said Leon. "Here's what we'll do. You prescreen for doubles, group the bags by basic flavor, and keep me posted on the time."

"What about blind taste tests?"

Leon shook his head while reaching for a bag. "Not enough time."

The analysis started off pretty well. Leon completed the first five write-ups in under eight minutes.

"Keep going," said Lily-Matisse. "You're ahead of schedule."

But after twenty minutes of munching, Leon's taste buds began to play tricks on him. By the time P.W. arrived, Leon was clearly in trouble.

"So did you find the missing brands?" Lily-Matisse asked as P.W. scooted into the booth.

"That's a negative," he said.

Leon glanced up from an untested Macho Gaucho Nacho. "Who cares," he said despairingly. "I won't even be able to finish testing the chips I have."

"Sure you will," said P.W. "Take a breather from

tasting and chart the new crinkle cuts."

Leon took the advice and entered profile data on two saw blades, a shark tooth, and a crenel.

The break proved helpful. Leon got a second wind, and by eleven-thirty he was back up to speed. "Eighteen chips analyzed," he said. "Eight to go."

At 11:40 Lily-Matisse said, "Maybe we should start packing up."

"What's the rush?" said P.W. "We still have five minutes."

Leon kept tasting and scribbling.

At 11:43 Emma Zeisel came by to wish her son good luck one last time.

"He's doing some last-minute cramming," Lily-Matisse explained.

"So I can see," said Emma Zeisel.

"He's got six more chips to go," said P.W.

Emma Zeisel looked at the coffee shop cuckoo clock. "Shouldn't you guys skedaddle?"

Leon kept munching and scribbling.

An alarm buzzer beeped on P.W.'s wristwatch.

"Eleven forty-five," Lily-Matisse said urgently. "The Chip-Off starts in fifteen minutes."

Leon reached for another bag.

At 11:49 P.W. said, "T minus *eleven* minutes and counting. Okay, Leon. Time. Let's pack it in."

"Listen to P.W.," Lily-Matisse pleaded. "You'll be disqualified if you arrive late."

"Two more," Leon said. He continued to test, taste, and take notes.

"Eleven fifty-five," P.W. hollered. "Let's move it, Leon!"

Leon shook his head. "One more bag," he said stubbornly.

Emma Zeisel reached over and closed her son's bulging notebook just as he finished documenting the last chip. "Time's up, sweetie. Like it or not, you'll have to let the chips fall where they may."

Twenty-Nine

The Chip-Off (Round One)

Leon, Lily-Matisse, and P.W. raced through the lobby of Trimore Towers on their way to the Chip-Off just as a deliveryman was arriving with a large bundle of eucalyptus leaves.

Lily-Matisse and Leon both ducked to avoid the long leafy stems. P.W. wasn't so swift.

THWOMP!

Branches spilled across the hotel's shag carpeting like so many giant pickup sticks.

"You okay?" Lily-Matisse asked P.W., who lay sprawled out on the carpet.

"I'm fine," he grumbled, more annoyed than hurt by the fall.

Emma Zeisel arrived on the scene moments later. "Leave it," she said. "The koalas will be checking in soon. I'm sure they'll take care of it."

Leon hesitated.

"Vamoose," his mother commanded.

* * *

"T minus one minute and thirty-six seconds!" P.W. hollered as they bounded up the steps of the convention center. But they hit a bottleneck at the FEAST WITHOUT FEAR banner, where hundreds of new arrivals, grazing on free chips, blocked the way.

P.W. pulled out the floor plan and studied it intently. "Shazam!" he cried. "There's a faster route. Follow me!" He led the way through a fire door leading down a corridor that bypassed the convention floor. They were halfway to the auditorium when P.W.'s wristwatch started beeping. "Twelve o'clock high!" he yelled. "Activate turbochargers!"

"Twelve . . . oh . . . two," P.W. panted as he opened the door to the auditorium stage, ". . . and . . . thirty . . . four . . . seconds."

Leon rushed over to the sign-in desk.

"Too late," said the official handling registration. He reinforced the decision by snapping shut a thin yellow ledger.

Leon knew he needed to do something, and he needed to do it fast. He looked the official over while catching his breath. The man was short and round and clearly took more than a professional interest in potato chips. The official's name tag attracted Leon's attention.

"Are you *the* Fergus O'Hare?" he asked.

"Do you know *another* Fergus O'Hare?" the official said stiffly.

"Guys," said Leon. "This is *the* Fergus O'Hare."

"Yeah," said P.W. "We kind of got that."

"Mr. O'Hare," said Leon, "is the author of the *Official Potato Chip Encyclopedia.* He's like the William Shakespeare of potato chips."

"They should name a potato chip after you," said P.W.

"They really should," Lily-Matisse seconded.

Fergus O'Hare tried not to smile. "Now let's not exaggerate. You're just saying that because I am judging this year's Chip-Off."

"No, I'm not," Leon insisted. "You're a legend, Mr. O'Hare. Former chief of the Potato Division of the Department of Agriculture. Currently executive director of the Potato Chip Council *and* the All-State Potato Chip Association."

Fergus O'Hare's cheeks turned the color of a red-skinned potato. "I see you've done your homework."

"Of course he has," said Lily-Matisse.

"But you know what I remember most of all, Mr. O'Hare?" said Leon.

"No, what?"

"That you started the Worldwide Chip of the Month Club. That's what got me hooked on chips, and why I want to enter the Chip-Off—if you'll let me."

"Hmm." Fergus O'Hare began to waver. "I *suppose* an exception might be made." Leon remained silent, until at last the judge reopened his ledger. "Name?"

"Zeisel comma Leon," said Leon.

"Here you go, Zeisel comma Leon," said Fergus O'Hare, presenting him with a competitor's badge.

"Thank you very much," said Leon. He moved away from the sign-in desk before the judge could change his mind and headed for the front of the auditorium to inspect the stage. It was large and brightly lit, furnished with three rows of folding chairs and a podium, plus a microphone planted front and center. The only decoration was a circular ASPCA seal, which hung down from the ceiling.

"Hey," said P.W. "Check out the guy with the nose plug." He pointed at an enormous man.

"He makes Lumpkin look like a chopstick," said Lily-Matisse.

Leon shuddered when he saw that the man wore a competitor's badge. "That can only be one guy."

P.W.'s eyes widened. "You mean . . ."

"Yup," said Leon. "Alphonse Cipollini."

"The Chippopotamus?" said Lily-Matisse.

"In the flesh," said Leon.

"In the flesh is right," said P.W.

"Uh, guys," said Lily-Matisse. "Do you see who's standing behind him?"

Leon looked more closely. "Oh, super," he said when he spotted the crisp white lab coat.

Fergus O'Hare stepped up to the microphone and gave it a couple of taps. "Testing. Testing. One, two, three.

Would the Chip-Off contestants please take their places."

After Leon and the other entrants had seated themselves, and the audience had quieted down, Fergus O'Hare approached the podium and went over the rules. The Chip-Off would consist of two parts. The first part, an elimination round modeled on a spelling bee, would test the contestants' knowledge of potato chip facts. Once the field narrowed to three, there would be a brief intermission, followed by the Flavor Awareness Test—also known as the FAT round.

"Study guides, instruments of measure, and notes are only permitted in the FAT portion of the event," Fergus O'Hare noted. "So I ask that all contestants put such materials aside until *after* intermission. Now let's get started.

"Round one. First question. What are the three basic ingredients of the potato chip?"

Leon relaxed. He knew the answer cold.

The first contestant, a spice mixer from San Francisco, approached center stage and provided her answer succinctly: "Salt, oil, and potatoes."

"Correct," said Fergus O'Hare. "Please reclaim your seat. Question number two. Who is generally credited with inventing the potato chip?"

The second contestant, a chip bag manufacturer from Minneapolis, walked to the middle of the stage and said, "Crump."

Fergus O'Hare tapped a bell. *Bing!* "Incorrect. Please leave the stage. Will the next contestant answer the last question?"

Alphonse Cipollini heaved himself off two seats and lumbered up to the mic.

"The proper response to the query 'Who invented the potato chip?' is George *Crum*—not Crump. Often described as a Native American—though opinions regarding his ethnicity remain divided—Mr. Crum is said to have fried the world's very first potato chip in 1853, at Moon's Lake House, an elegant establishment located in Saratoga Springs, New York."

"That is correct, Mr. Cipollini," said Fergus O'Hare. "But I must ask that you keep your answers brief."

Alphonse Cipollini nodded and returned to his seats.

George Crum

Three more contestants approached the microphone before Leon got his shot. All three got stumped, and were thus eliminated, by the same question: "What is the Spanish term for 'potato chip'?"

"*Papas fritas*," Leon answered.

Fergus allowed himself to smile. "That is correct, Zeisel comma Leon."

* * *

By the end of the first packet of questions, the field had narrowed to fifteen. Four more competitors bit the dust during the second set. Another six got the *bing*! in the third.

That left only five survivors, and Leon was one of them.

The questions got tougher as the competition progressed. The first of the five remaining competitors—a potato farmer from Beaver Head—was eliminated after flubbing the question "In what country are curry, consommé, and soy sauce-flavored chips most popular?"

Leon was next up.

"Would the contestant like me to repeat the question?" asked Fergus O'Hare.

Leon nodded and used the time to consider the possibilities. Curry-flavored chips sell well in India, he told himself. Then again, soy sauce chips are a huge seller in Japan. Consommé chips—where are they eaten?

Leon couldn't remember.

"The contestant will please provide a response," Fergus O'Hare said formally.

Leon hesitated. Japan or India? . . . India or Japan?

Fergus O'Hare cleared his throat and reached for the elimination bell. His hand was poised above the plunger when Leon blurted out his answer.

"Japan?"

"Correct!" said Fergus O'Hare.

The crowd, led by two particularly feisty fifth graders, clapped loudly. The contest continued.

"Mr. Cipollini," said Fergus O'Hare. "Where is the world's biggest potato chip company headquartered?"

"What do you mean by *biggest?* Do you wish the location of the company that makes the *most* potato chips? Or the location of the company that makes the *biggest* chips?"

"The location of the company that makes the *most* chips," Fergus O'Hare specified.

"That would be Plano, Texas."

"Correct," said Fergus O'Hare.

Alphonse Cipollini returned to his seats.

"Mr. Furtles," said Fergus O'Hare. "You are up. Who is credited with inventing the mechanical potato peeler?"

"Herman Lay," said Idaho Furtles.

"Correct."

"Ms. Wilkenson," said Fergus O'Hare. "On what date do we celebrate National Potato Chip Day?"

Wanda Wilkenson, founder of the Snack Shaque chain of gourmet shops and treasurer-elect of the ASPCA, stared at the microphone for the better part of a minute.

"April fourteenth?" she said at last.

Bing! "That is *in*correct," said Fergus O'Hare. "Will the next contestant please answer the question."

Leon walked up to the mic. “Two days from now,” he said. “*March* fourteenth.”

“Correct!” said Fergus O’Hare. “We have our final three contestants!”

Over the applause of the audience, the judge said, “After a ten-minute break, Mr. Furtles, Mr. Cipollini, and Mr. Zeisel will be competing in the Flavor Awareness Test to determine the winner of this year’s Chip-Off!”

THIRTY

The Chip-Off (Round Two)

Leon hopped off the stage, happy and even proud to have survived the first round of the Chip-Off. Lily-Matisse and P.W. rushed up to him.

"You murderized the competition!" said P.W. "That thousand bucks is as good as ours!"

"Don't jinx things," said Lily-Matisse.

"Lily-Matisse is right," said Leon. "Furtles and the Chippo are going to be super tough to beat. Plus I got lucky during the first round. I almost blew that soy sauce question."

"But you didn't," said P.W.

"How'd you know about Potato Chip Day?" asked Lily-Matisse.

"That one was easy," said Leon. "Don't you remember what Sparks told us?"

"No," said Lily-Matisse.

"March fourteenth isn't just Potato Chip Day."

"It isn't?"

"Nope," said Leon. "It's also Einstein's birthday."

"Well, thank you, Albert Einstein!" P.W. exclaimed.

"And thank you, Mr. Sparks," said Leon.

While the crowd milled about, a pair of stagehands made preparations for round two. They removed all but four of the folding chairs—one for Idaho Furtles, one for Leon, and two for Alphonse Cipollini. They then set up three card tables and supplied each with a bottle of water, a scratch pad, and a pencil. Once that was done, the stagehands rolled out a heavy metal cabinet and positioned it next to the judge's podium.

"That must be where O'Hare stores the quiz chips," P.W. speculated.

"It is," said Leon. "I read about it in the *Encyclopedia*. It's a modified tool cabinet, like the kind mechanics use."

The stagehands positioned a large wooden partition around the cabinet and put a box of rubber gloves and a stack of paper chip boats on the judge's podium.

With that, the stage was set for round two.

"Will the three finalists please approach," said Fergus O'Hare.

To further applause, Leon, Alphonse Cipollini, and Idaho Furtles stepped up to the judge's podium.

"Draw a number," said Fergus O'Hare, holding out an open potato chip bag.

Alphonse Cipollini drew a plastic chip marked #3.

Leon picked #2. Idaho Furtles got #1.

"Looks like you'll be starting, Idaho," said Fergus O'Hare.

"Figures," the Chip Master grumbled before he marched away.

Leon sat down at his card table, laid out his things, and then sneaked a peek at the competition.

Alphonse Cipollini appeared unnaturally calm, his massive hands resting on his stomach like a pair of boiled hams. He gave Leon a friendly good-luck nod, which Leon felt honored to return. He did his best not to stare, but it was tough given the man's size (not to mention the swimmer's plug clamped on his nose).

Leon's other rival presented a very different picture. Idaho Furtles was anything but calm, and he certainly wasn't friendly. Dressed in his signature lab coat, the Chip Master focused all of his attention on the battery of testing tools arrayed before him.

"Let's begin," said Fergus O'Hare. He snapped a rubber glove onto one hand and stepped behind the wooden screen. Leon heard a metal drawer open, followed by the familiar sound of crinkling.

The judge reemerged holding a potato chip in the gloved hand and a stopwatch in the other. He placed the chip in a paper boat and walked it over to Idaho Furtles.

"You have ninety seconds starting . . . *now*."

Idaho Furtles reached for his external caliper gauge

and closed its claws against the top and bottom surfaces of the mystery chip. After marking down a measurement, he spun the dial on his digital color wheel until he found a match. He checked the moisture and the odor—the latter obtained by the Nose-It-All 3000—and consulted a binder. Less than a minute after receiving the chip, he was done.

"It is a Wisdom brand Sour Cream 'n' Chive," he said with obvious self-satisfaction.

"That is correct," Fergus O'Hare confirmed, peeling off the rubber glove. He put on a new one and ducked behind the screen. He reappeared soon after with the next mystery chip.

"Here you go, Mr. Zeisel," said Fergus O'Hare as he docked the paper boat.

Yes! Leon said to himself. A crinkle cut. I can skip the three-coin test and go straight to profile analysis.

He held up the chip and studied the edge. Saw blade, he concluded.

He checked the shape. Amoeba.

He took a nibble and determined the flavor. Plain.

He pored over his charts in search of a plain saw-blade amoeba. He found seven.

He checked the paint samples. Color allowed him to cut the list of suspects to three.

He tested the chew factors and . . . Bingo!

Only one of the three remaining candidates had the mystery chip's crumbulosity.

"Howdy Doody Ridglets?" said Leon.

"Correct!" declared Fergus O'Hare.

The audience erupted in cheers. P.W., sitting in the second row, jumped to his feet. "Man oh man!" he hollered. "The Zeisel Method rocks!"

"Shhh!" said Lily-Matisse, embarrassed by the outburst. "Sit back down."

"Excuse me," said a man wearing a potato chip-patterned bow tie seated directly behind them. "What, if I might ask, is the Zeisel Method?"

"My friend's superaccurate chip identification system," P.W. said over his shoulder. "It's what's going to help him obliterate the competition. You watch and see."

"Oh, I will," the man said keenly.

Up on stage Fergus O'Hare had already shipped off the next chip.

The Chippopotamus turned the sample around and around in his plump but delicate fingers. "Hmm," he said in a nasal voice. "The small size suggests an early harvest. And the dark speckling indicates a dangerous foray into sugary hybrids. We'll see soon enough if those risks were worth taking."

He removed his nose plug and took a whiff. "A perky, confident aroma of pepper and pears," he said approvingly, his voice now sounding less whiny. "I have a *very* good feeling about this chip."

He took a bite. A moment passed. "I *like* what I'm tasting," he said. "This chip is starting off *very* boldly."

He took another bite and chewed fussily. "Nice—*very* nice. A sturdy follow-through with delicious starch highlights."

He swallowed and smacked his lips. "Pow!" he exclaimed. "What a finish! The gorgeous afterglow could *only* be the handiwork of one man. Ulf Poppenheimer, the Tubermensch of Tübingen. Mr. O'Hare, I believe you have been kind enough to start me off with a Papa Poppenheimer Pepper Chip. Am I right?"

"You are indeed," said Fergus O'Hare.

Leon was amazed. So was everyone else in the room. It was instantly obvious why Alphonse Cipollini had won so many competitions. His ability to describe and identify potato chips was, like the man himself, HUGE.

The contest that followed was longer and fiercer than any Chip-Off on record. Each of the competitors was in top form. For nearly an hour, a fleet of chip boats voyaged across the stage. And with each correct answer, the applause of the audience grew louder.

"Zikes!" Alphonse Cipollini exclaimed. "I am surprised at you, Fergus! Is this a potato chip or a poison pill?"

"Contestants are reminded to restrict their remarks to matters of identification," warned Fergus O'Hare.

"Sorry," said Alphonse Cipollini. He held up the chip that had triggered the criticism. "With its texture of day-old Band-Aid and its aftertaste of pencil shavings, this can only be an Okee Dokey—and a stale one at that."

"Correct," said Fergus O'Hare. "Next."

"Chipometric analysis indicates this chip to be a Friar Greiermeier's Golden Fryer."

"Correct. Next."

"An Edvard's Munch Madness chip?"

"Absolutely right, Mr. Zeisel. Next."

"This chip is a charmer, Fergus. A pleasant follow-up to the Okee Dokey. The color reminds me of Rapunzel's golden hair, and the deep canola oil aroma, plus the salty grace notes, only compounds the fairy tale qualities. I would be very surprised if this weren't a Bratwurst Struwweltater."

"Is that your answer?" asked Fergus O'Hare.

"It is," said Alphonse Cipollini.

"Correct," said Fergus O'Hare. "Next."

"The smell print is a perfect match for Miss Sippy River Chip. That is, therefore, my answer."

"Correct, Mr. Furtles."

"Golden Flake Cheeseburger-Flavored Potato Chips?"

"Yes, Leon, good for you."

After some forty chips had been tested, tasted, and correctly identified, Fergus O'Hare was forced to suspend the competition.

"I've been cleaned out," he said. "The chip cabinet is completely empty! We will have to take a five-minute break while we restock."

After a stagehand was dispatched to round up more potato chips, Alphonse Cipollini heaved himself off his seats and took a stroll around the stage. "So, Idaho, we meet again," he said to his lab-coated competitor.

Idaho Furtles harrumphed.

"I see you've lost none of your conversational skills," said Alphonse Cipollini.

"Do you *mind?*" said Idaho Furtles.

Alphonse Cipollini lumbered over to Leon. "I would just like to say, you are a most formidable opponent. I am honored to compete against you."

"Thanks," said Leon.

The stagehand returned carrying a very large box. Fergus O'Hare whisked him behind his screen and shortly thereafter asked everyone to sit back down. "I believe it is your turn, Idaho," he said, quickly docking a newly provisioned chip ship.

After a minute or so, Idaho Furtles started muttering to himself. It was clear he was having a tough time identifying the chip.

Leon could pick up parts of the babble: ". . . moisture content point-oh-one-nine . . . digital color wheel reading three-one-seven . . . thickness point-oh-six-one . . . texturometer . . . smell print . . ."

Idaho Furtles eventually looked up. "I believe you have given me a Cousin Ray's Low-Fat Kosher Dill Pickle Delight," he said unsteadily.

Bing!

A wave of gasps spread through the audience.

"That is not correct," said Fergus O'Hare.

"Maybe you didn't hear me," said Idaho Furtles. "I *said* Cousin Ray's Low-Fat Kosher Dill Pickle Delight."

"I heard you perfectly," said Fergus O'Hare. "That is not the chip I gave you."

"But the chip *has* to be a Cousin Ray's Low-Fat Kosher Dill Pickle Delight. My Nose-It-All 3000 *smelled* it! My digital color wheel *matched* it. My external caliper gauge *measured* it!"

"To repeat," Fergus O'Hare said firmly, "it is *not* a Cousin Ray's."

Idaho Furtles banged his fist on the table. Only then did he notice that the snout on his electronic nose had fallen off. He quickly replaced it with a spare.

"Mr. O'Hare, I had an equipment failure. I require another chip and another chance."

"Sorry, Idaho. You know the rules. Second guesses are not allowed."

"I protest!"

"Hey, Furtles! Didn't you hear the judge?" P.W. yelled from his seat. "NO DO-OVERS!"

"Quiet in the audience," Fergus O'Hare admonished before turning back to Idaho Furtles. "Please sit down and allow the competition to continue."

Idaho Furtles refused. He stormed off the stage in a huff, only to return a moment later to reclaim his tools and storm off in an even greater huff.

That left Alphonse Cipollini and Leon.

Fergus O'Hare allowed the room to settle down and presented Leon with a chip from the same bag that had stumped Idaho Furtles.

No way, Leon said to himself. It can't be.

Despite a strong hunch, he performed the coin test and flipped through the paint chips. He found a perfect color match: jolly good fellow yellow.

"Ohmygosh!" he said out loud, before laughter overtook him.

"Leon?" said Fergus O'Hare. "Are you okay?"

"Fine," Leon replied, struggling to suppress the giggles. Even though he had a positive ID, he double-checked his data by analyzing the chew factors. He

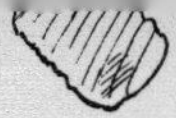

took a nibble. The crumbulosity was exactly what he'd expected. Likewise, the mouthfeel and lingertaste.

Leon now *knew* he had it nailed.

"The contestant will please identify the chip," said Fergus O'Hare.

Leon shook his head in disbelief. "Furtles," he said. "The chip is a Furtles Double Cruncher."

"Correct," said Fergus O'Hare.

Everyone suddenly understood the reason for Leon's behavior. Furtles had been stumped by a Furtles!

An explosion of guffaws (the most powerful of which came from Alphonse Cipollini) filled the auditorium.

Bing! Bing! Bing! Bing! Bing! Bing! Fergus O'Hare banged on the elimination bell to bring the crowd to order. "Could everyone quiet down! The Chip-Off is already running late."

Once calm returned, the chip boats again traveled from cabinet to podium and from podium to table. Only now, of course, there were just two ports of call.

"A delectable dry-rub style offering from the Billy Bob line of barbeque chips."

"Correct."

"Wall Street Blue Chips?"

"Correct."

"This chip, with its chestnut color and robust crunch, must be a Saul T. Sam's Sweet Russet Gourmet."

"Correct."

"Gondola Chips?"

"Correct."

"Ahhh! The ruffled texture and shipshape citrus highlights tell me I have just received a Wavy Navy Sub Lime Chip."

"Correct."

The testing continued until Fergus O'Hare was forced to call yet another time-out. "I have used up all the chip boats and testing gloves," he announced apologetically before sending a stagehand scrambling.

This time, however, the problem was resolved less successfully. The stagehand returned with a tube of paper drinking cups and a box of ordinary dish gloves.

"I doubt these substitutions will meet the approval of the governing board," said Fergus O'Hare. He placed an emergency call to the headquarters of the All-State Potato Chip Association. Following lengthy deliberations, the ASPCA directors okayed the cups and gloves, and the contest resumed.

Four chips after the second interruption, Leon received a sample that caught him off guard. It was blistered and hand-sliced, which allowed him to eliminate most of the chips in his notebook. Yet when he checked the color of the sample against the paint chips, he failed to find a match.

With color resisting the Method, Leon turned his attention to the chip's chew factors. There, too, the sample proved confounding. Its crumbulosity,

mouthfeel, and lingertaste were unlike any he had recorded.

Leon closed his notebook and made a mental list of all the chips he had heard of but never had tasted.

There weren't many.

Then Leon realized the obvious. Since Fergus O'Hare had received all the recent chips from the convention floor, it only made sense that the killer chip had come from one of the display booths in the hall. Leon pulled out the floor plan, zipped through the list of exhibitors, and quickly determined that the chip in his hand must be one of the two brands that had eluded capture.

It's either a Rhode Island Monk Chip, he told himself. Or it's a Tierra del Fuego.

Leon grabbed the testing dime and placed it on his thumbnail.

Heads Tierra del Fuego, tails Rhode Island, he said to himself.

He gave the dime a flick. It spun in the air, hit the table, and clattered out of reach.

Not a good sign, Leon thought.

"Time," said Fergus O'Hare.

Leon quickly repeated the gesture with his nickel.

Heads Tierra del Fuego, tails Rhode Island.

This time he caught the coin in midair and slapped it flat on his arm.

Everyone sat on the edge of his seat—except for Alphonse Cipollini, who sat on the edge of two seats.

Leon squinched and clucked.

"Time," Fergus O'Hare repeated. He reached for the bell just as Leon lifted his hand.

The nickel had landed faceup.

"Tierra del Fuego!" Leon blurted out.

A long moment separated his response from the judge's.

Correct is what Leon wanted to hear. If he didn't hear that word that would mean . . .

Bing.

Groans of disappointment spread through the auditorium.

"I am so sorry," said Fergus O'Hare. "That is not the right answer."

Still, the competition was not over. To clinch the title, Alphonse Cipollini had to identify the chip that had stumped Leon.

Fergus O'Hare delivered a fresh sample to Alphonse Cipollini, who turned it over in his hands like a jeweler inspecting a gem.

"The thickness tells me at once that it is hand sliced," he said, "and the blistering suggests a commitment to the higher cooking temperatures." He removed his nose plug and inhaled deeply. "Hmm. Italian grape-seed oil. A first pressing, if I'm not mistaken." He took a swig of water and gargled, a procedure he hadn't found necessary during previous tastings.

After gargling, Alphonse Cipollini took a small bite out of the chip. He chewed slowly and thoughtfully, pausing for a long while before taking another deliberate bite.

"Give up?" P.W. shouted hopefully.

Fergus O'Hare tapped his microphone. "Quiet, please!"

Alphonse Cipollini closed his eyes and tilted his head back. All at once a smile spread over his face. "It took me a while," he said as he leaned forward in his chairs, "but I think I have a match. Could the sample in question be a hand-sliced, kettle-cooked chip, bagged by an order of clerics living in a monastery outside Little Compton, Rhode Island, and sold under the Monk Chips label?"

Leon hoped—with all his might he hoped—to hear the *bing!* of the elimination bell. But he knew, deep down, no *bing!* would sound.

"Correct," Fergus O'Hare was obliged to say. "We have a winner. A round of applause for Alphonse Cipollini on his *sixth* ASPCA Chip-Off victory."

Suddenly a number of things happened all at once, and none of them involved Leon. Alphonse Cipollini let out a fittingly hippopotamic bellow of joy. The giant ASPCA seal hanging overhead exploded, showering the auditorium with potato chip confetti. And a television reporter wearing a yellow flak jacket jumped up onstage and planted himself directly in front of Leon's table.

"Yell-*ow* everybody!" the reporter intoned. "This is Thomas 'Spud' McSorley of the *Chipping News*, bringing you live exclusive coverage from the stage of the convention center, where Alphonse Cipollini—alias the Chippopotamus—has just *devoured* Idaho Furtles and newcomer Leon Zeisel to gobble up his sixth ASPCA-sponsored Chip-Off victory. In a ferocious feat of two-fisted feasting, the Lance Armstrong of the potato chip world displayed Herculean stamina by—"

Leon tuned out.

No thousand bucks, he said to himself.

No vintage army jacket.

No swap.

No transfusion for Fathead.

No payback.

No hope of surviving Lumpkin.

Fergus O'Hare approached the runner-up. "Tough luck, kid. I thought you had him beat."

"I might have, if I'd gotten hold of some Monk Chips before the competition."

"Well, if the ASPCA can ever be of assistance, you be sure to let me know," said Fergus O'Hare.

"I will," said Leon. His friends rushed over.

"You did great!" said Lily-Matisse.

"Yeah, right," Leon said glumly.

"You did," said P.W. "Think about Furtles. He messed up on a *Furtles* chip! How lame is that?"

"Not as lame as coming in second," Leon said dejectedly. "We *needed* that prize money."

"Hey, we've already got one hundred and two dollars and fifty cents," said Lily-Matisse. "We're almost there."

"Lily-Matisse is right," said P.W. "I figure we'll have the remaining fifty-seven forty-nine in three weeks and three days—give or take."

Leon sighed. "Wonderful," he said, unable to hide his despair.

The television reporter, having completed his intro, turned and stuck a microphone in Leon's face.

"Yell-*ow* there, Leon Zeisel. Thomas 'Spud' McSorley of the *Chipping News*. How's it feel to have placed second in your very first Chip-Off?"

Leon just shrugged.

"He's not feeling all that great," said P.W.

"Well, he should!" said Spud McSorely. "After all, nabbing the silver isn't exactly shabby. Tell me, what's your secret?"

"He's got a special method," said Lily-Matisse.

"A special method, eh? Mind telling me about it? No, wait, don't bother. I think the Chippo's ready for my exclusive. Good luck to you, Leon Zeisel!" And as quickly as he had intruded, Spud McSorley pulled away.

Lily-Matisse leaned over and whispered to P.W.,

"Don't look now, but the guy with the potato chip bow tie is listening in."

"I'm on it," said P.W.

But the eavesdropper beat him to the punch by presenting P.W. with a potato chip-shaped business card.

"*Russet* Furtles?" exclaimed P.W. "Idaho's brother?"

"Guilty as charged. Sorry your friend didn't win."

"Yeah, well, your brother wasn't all that lucky either."

"If you ask me," said Russet Furtles, "that know-it-all with the Nose-It-All got what he deserved. Anyway, I just wanted Leon to know I was mighty impressed by his achievement."

"Why don't you tell him yourself?" said Lily-Matisse. "He could use cheering up."

"Hey, Leon," said P.W. "Guess who this is! Russet Furtles—Idaho's brother."

"And in my spare time, I also run a potato chip company," said Russet Furtles.

"Hello," Leon managed unenergetically.

"I was just telling your friend here I was amazed by your skill. You beat the pants off my brother. I hear you have your own chip identification system. I'm always in the market for better ways of judging chips."

"It's all in his notebook," said Lily-Matisse.

"Is that a fact?" said Russet Furtles. "Well, I'd love to see what's in it."

P.W. had a sudden thought. "That could be arranged," he said.

Leon shot him a look.

P.W. ignored it. In fact, he grabbed the notebook and said, "Everything you want to know is right in here, Mr. Furtles. The whole entire patented Zeisel Method for potato chip identification."

Russet Furtles reached over to take a look.

"Wait a sec," said P.W., slipping the notebook under his arm. "I was just thinking, Mr. Furtles. Did you just say you were *'in the market'*?"

"I did."

"Well, usually you have to pay for stuff in markets, don't you?"

It didn't take Russet Furtles long to figure out where P.W. was taking the discussion. "How much?" he said abruptly.

"We'll let you have a look for fifty-seven dollars and forty-nine cents," said P.W.

The sum took Russet Furtles by surprise. "Fifty-seven dollars?" he said.

"*And* forty-nine cents," said Lily-Matisse.

"How about this?" Russet Furtles countered. "You kids let me flip through the chip notes. *If* I learn something new, I'll pay you the fifty-seven dollars."

"And forty-nine cents," said Leon, warming to the plan.

"*And* forty-nine cents," Russet Furtles confirmed.

The three fifth graders closed ranks and weighed the proposal. After considerable discussion, they came to a decision.

"Well," said Russet Furtles, "do we have a deal?"

"Deal," said P.W.

Russet Furtles propped himself on the table and leafed through the notebook. "The paint chip–potato chip comparison chart—did you come up with this yourself, Leon?"

"Pretty much."

"My mom helped," Lily-Matisse interjected.

"That's true," said Leon. "Ms. Jasprow was the one who told me to check out the paint chips at the hardware store."

"And the chew factors?" said Russet Furtles. "Who devised those?"

"I did," said Leon. "And no offense, Mr. Furtles, but I think your brother is wrong if he thinks you can judge a chip without tasting it."

"Don't get me started," said Russet Furtles. "What about the three-coin test?"

"That came from our science teacher," said Leon.

"Oh, yes, that would be Mr. Sparks. He's the one I spoke to on the phone. I'm sorry the flu kept me out the day your class came to the factory. If my brother has his way, yours will be the very last tour we give. I trust none of you ate our potato chip presidents."

"No way," Lily-Matisse assured him.

"Glad to hear it," said Russet Furtles as he shut the notebook.

"So?" said P.W. "Is Leon's book worth fifty-seven dollars and forty-seven cents?"

"No," said Russet Furtles.

"No?" said Lily-Matisse.

"No," Russet Furtles repeated. "A look at this notebook is worth a whole lot more than fifty-seven dollars and forty-seven cents." He reached into his wallet and handed Leon a crisp one-hundred-dollar bill.

"Hold on," said Lily-Matisse. "I think I have change." P.W. gave her a kick.

"That's okay," said Russet Furtles. "You keep it. Buy yourselves some Double Crunchers."

"All right!" said P.W.

"Thank you, Mr. Furtles," said Lily-Matisse.

"Yeah, thanks!" said Leon.

"I'm the one who should do the thanking," said Russet Furtles. "Best hundred dollars I've spent since . . . well, since I bought a mint-condition Clinton at last year's *Chipapalooza!*"

As soon as Russet Furtles was out of earshot, P.W. let out a victory roar that almost rivaled the Chippo's. "See, guys? Leon's mom was right. It *is* in the bag."

"Not yet it isn't," Lily-Matisse cautioned. "We still need the vintage jacket."

"Which we are about to get," said P.W. "Activate turbochargers. Next stop, Captain Frank's Army and Navy Surplus!"

Thirty-One

Captain Frank

As soon as the Chip-Off came to an end, the three fifth graders beat a path to the pay phones outside the convention center and placed a call to Napoleon.

"He'll be here in five minutes," Leon announced after he cradled the receiver.

The yellow cab pulled up to the curb right on time. "How was the Cheep-Off, Monsieur Leon?"

"You better point the dial on the moodometer to nine."

Napoleon flashed a silver-toothed smile. "You won?"

"Nope," said Leon.

"He came in second," said Lily-Matisse.

"And earned a hundred bucks!" P.W. added. "Show him."

Leon produced the crisp new bill.

"We must celebrate," said Napoleon.

"Absolutely," said P.W. "And I know just the place." He gave Napoleon Captain Frank's address.

"Monsieur Pay Dooble-vay, that is not in a great part of town."

"We won't be there long," said P.W.

"How long is that?" Napoleon asked.

"Just long enough to pick up something *special* for Leon," Lily-Matisse answered sweetly.

A half hour later, P.W. led Leon and Lily-Matisse into the courtyard of an old brick warehouse. "Must be over there," he said, pointing to a field cannon that flanked a distant doorway.

"You don't say," said Lily-Matisse. "How could you tell?"

A painted sign in the shape of a dog tag confirmed P.W.'s hypothesis.

They entered a cramped shop. It was filled, floor to ceiling, with military gear. There were khakis and canteens, face paint and battle flags, tents, hats, caps, and helmets, plus enough army boots to outfit a barefoot battalion.

"The place looks deserted," said Lily-Matisse.

Leon picked up a pair of handcuffs. "These could come in handy when Lumpkin returns to the playground."

"We won't need 'em once we get Fathead working," said P.W.

They walked past a pile of parachutes.

"Mmaaaaay shhuuu hannnnn mmme ghkajgdg!"

Lily-Matisse let out a yelp.

"It's only P.W.," said Leon. "Hey, P.W? We can't understand a word you're saying with that gas mask covering your face."

P.W. peeled off the mask. "I just said they should hand these out in the lunchroom when they're serving beans."

"Will you guys knock it off!" said Lily-Matisse.

"You heard her!" someone barked. "Knock it off!"

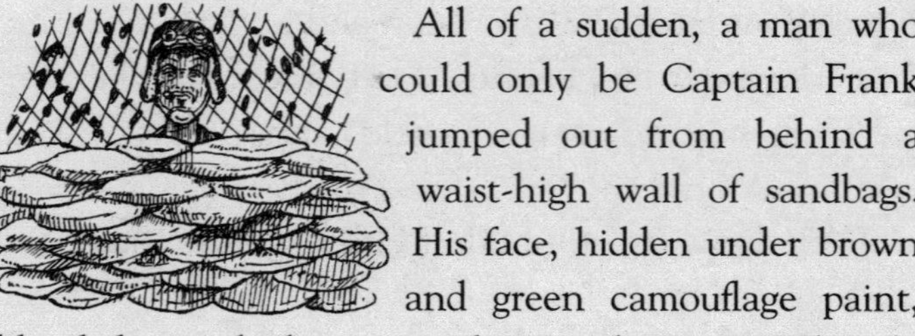

All of a sudden, a man who could only be Captain Frank jumped out from behind a waist-high wall of sandbags. His face, hidden under brown and green camouflage paint, blended in with the surrounding surplus gear. "What do you grunts want?" he snarled between chews on a cigar stub.

"I called a while back about a vintage army jacket," said P.W.

"The M42HBT in a large?"

"Yes," said P.W.

"Yes *what*?" growled Captain Frank.

"Yes, *sir*," said P.W.

"You positive about the size? All three of you pip-squeaks could fit into a large with room to spare."

"Can we see the jacket or not?" Lily-Matisse asked boldly.

"Lock the safety on that yap of yours, missy," Captain Frank commanded.

Lily-Matisse refused to back down. "Do you have the jacket or don't you?"

"I've got it," said Captain Frank defensively. He

ducked under some mosquito netting, disappeared through a tent flap, and returned a minute later. "Here you go," he said. "One vintage M42HBT, in the large."

"This is the jacket with the special pockets and the anti-gas flap, right?" said Leon.

"Check for yourself," Captain Frank said gruffly.

Leon and P.W. inspected the jacket.

"Looks okay to me," said P.W.

"Better try it on, Leon," Lily-Matisse advised.

Captain Frank let out a chortle when he saw Leon in the jacket. "Those sleeves go straight down to your knees!"

"That's good," said Lily-Matisse. "It'll fit our friend like a glove."

"Fine," said Captain Frank. "One fifty-nine ninety-nine plus tax. No refunds, no returns." He spat a fleck of cigar stub into an upturned helmet that doubled as a spittoon. "Cash only."

Lily-Matisse pulled out a fat roll of singles and fives. Leon added his crisp one-hundred-dollar bill. P.W. counted and re-counted the money and, after getting the okay from his friends, handed over the wad of cash.

"Do you want the jacket gift wrapped?" Captain Frank asked sarcastically.

"That's okay," said Leon, rolling up the sleeves. "I'll wear it home."

As they headed for the exit, something caught

P.W.'s eye. "Hold on," he said, surveying the contents of a display cabinet. "Hey, Captain Frank. How much for the sergeant stripes?"

"Why? Looking to give your friend a promotion?"

"*Maybe*," said P.W.

"In that case," said Captain Frank, "why settle for stripes? Ten bucks makes your buddy a general."

"Excellent!" said P.W.

"General Lumpkin?" said Lily-Matisse. "Now *that's* a scary thought."

Thirty-Two

The Swap

"General Zeisel reporting for duty!" Leon said, saluting his friends at the top of the school steps.

"That jacket looks ridiculous on you, Leon," said Lily-Matisse.

"Hey, show some respect to a superior officer," P.W. said. He pretended to polish a silver star pinned on Leon's shoulder.

"Tell you what," said Lily-Matisse. "I'll show respect *after* we've completed the swap."

Lumpkin first spotted the star-spangled jacket during homeroom. He tried to approach, but the bell rang before he could close in. During the classes that followed, Lumpkin's interest only intensified.

"He's watching," said Lily-Matisse at lunch.

"Like a shark circling his next meal," said P.W.

The circles got smaller and smaller as the day progressed. But it was only after school that Lumpkin took the bait.

"Hey, Leon! Wait up. Where'd you get the jacket?"

Leon was standing at the curb, with Lily-Matisse

and P.W. observing from a safe distance. "A guest left it in his room," he said.

"It's way too big on you," said Lumpkin.

"I guess," Leon responded, trying to sound casual.

"Kind of makes you look dorky."

"What does?"

"The jacket."

"I don't know," said Leon. "This anti-gas flap is kind of cool. And check out the stars." Keep calm, he told himself.

"Too bad for you your guest wasn't smaller," said Lumpkin.

"Yeah, well, what can you do?"

Lumpkin stared at the silver stars.

Come on, Leon said to himself. Say it. Say the magic word. . . .

"Wanna swap?" Lumpkin blurted out.

Bingo!

"Swap?" said Leon, as if the idea took him totally by surprise.

"Yeah," said Lumpkin. "See, this way, you get an army jacket that fits you, and I get an army jacket that fits me."

"I don't know," said Leon, pretending to hesitate. "My jacket has stars, plus—" He stopped himself in mid-sentence when he noticed Lumpkin's fingers starting to curl into fists. "Well, okay. I guess we can swap."

Lumpkin shucked off his jacket. "At the count of three?"

"Sure," said Leon, removing the M42HBT.

Lumpkin counted. "One, two, three!" He clamped onto the M42HBT and tossed his own jacket over Leon's head.

The stench knocked Leon for a loop. By the time he freed himself from the stink bomb, Lumpkin was long gone.

P.W. and Lily-Matisse approached.

"Don't get too close," Leon cautioned. "This jacket reeks worse than clam chips."

P.W. treated the warning as a challenge and leaned over to take a whiff.

"P.U.!" he exclaimed "That's worse than week-old gym sock soaked in month-old fish guts!"

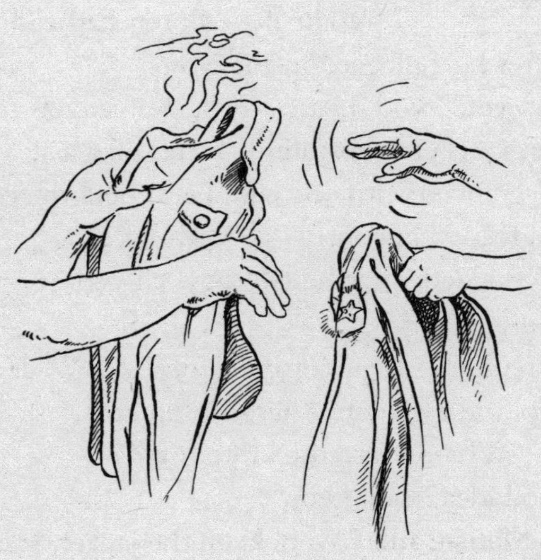

THIRTY-THREE

The Transfusion

An hour after the swap, Leon, P.W., and Lily-Matisse (plus one very smelly army jacket) were back at Trimore Towers. Leon chained the door to his apartment and prepared for yet another operation.

"Lily-Matisse, set out the towel. P.W., go fetch the bed lamp. I'll check over the repair tools."

"Want me to prep Fathead?" P.W. asked after he'd plugged in the lamp.

"Not yet," said Leon. "First we've got to turn Lumpkin's jacket into stuffing. Here, take a sleeve."

P.W. grabbed onto one cuff; Leon held the other.

"Ready?" said Leon.

P.W. nodded, and the two boys tugged in opposite directions.

"Man oh man, this cotton is tough," P.W. declared.

"You won't get anywhere doing that," said Lily-Matisse. "Why not use the knife ring?"

"Good idea," said Leon.

Lily-Matisse and P.W. held up the jacket, and Leon

attacked it like a half-crazed ninja. In a few minutes, he had reduced the sleeves to shreds.

"That must have been satisfying," said P.W.

"It was," Leon confirmed. "I just hope the material wads up okay."

"Why shouldn't it?" Lily-Matisse asked nervously.

"Because it's a lot thicker than panty hose," said Leon.

"It'll work fine," P.W. said. "Now let's get the operation over with."

"Hold on," said Leon. "There's one more thing to do before I start." He reached under his bed and pulled out a bag of Furtles Double Crunchers.

"What are those for?" asked Lily-Matisse.

"Don't you remember what Sparks said during the flameout experiment and the potato clock lab?"

"Remind us," said P.W.

Leon opened the bag and said, "Sparks told us potato chips are a first-rate energy source." He took a chip and ate it.

"Hey, give me some of that energy source!" P.W. demanded.

"And me," said Lily-Matisse.

The contents of the bag quickly vanished.

"*Now* can you operate?" P.W. asked.

"Yup," said Leon.

He reopened the seam running just above Fathead's scalp line. Panty hose popped out the moment he released the pressure.

Leon placed the gray matter to one side.

"He looks like a beady-eyed sock," said Lily-Matisse after the de-hosing.

"Fathead ain't Fathead no more," said P.W.

Leon adjusted the wire-hanger armature inside the emptied figure, then began the refilling process. He poked small wads of jacket cotton into the extremities with the eraser end of a pencil. The results proved disappointing. "The material keeps bunching up funny," he said as he removed the stuffing.

"Why don't you do what my mom does when she has her class make pincushions?" Lily-Matisse said.

"What's that?" said Leon.

Lily-Matisse picked up a strip of cotton and pulled at the individual threads until the fabric turned into fluff.

Leon rubbed the fluff between his fingers. "Not bad," he said. "It might work."

After an hour spent teasing apart the cotton, Leon said, "That ought to do it." He refilled the body with the fluff and closed the hairline seam. "He's still a bit lumpy, but the shape is a whole lot better than before."

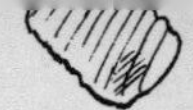

"We should double-check for biometric inconsistencies," P.W. said.

"You've got to be kidding," said Lily-Matisse.

"Do I look like I'm kidding?" P.W.'s expression made clear he was not. So Lily-Matisse and Leon waited while P.W. took measurements of the limbs, head, and body of the refilled spitting image and then compared them with the numbers on his graph paper chart.

"Perfect," P.W. declared.

"I can barely tell the difference between Fathead and this new guy," said Lily-Matisse.

"He's not as spongy," said Leon, "but I have to admit he looks pretty good."

"What are we calling this version?" Lily-Matisse asked.

"How about 'Refill'?" said P.W.

Leon shook his head. "Nah, that's kind of boring."

" 'Cottontail'?" said Lily-Matisse.

P.W. grimaced. "You can't be serious. That's way, *way* too girly. What about 'Pumpkinhead four-point-oh,' code name 'Army Boy'?"

"Forget it," said Lily-Matisse.

"How about 'Lumpy'?" Leon suggested.

"Lumpy isn't bad," Lily-Matisse allowed. "It's kind of a cross between bumpy and Lumpkin."

"Lumpy it is," said P.W.

"So when do we find out if Lumpy controls Lumpkin?" asked Lily-Matisse.

"The sooner the better," said P.W.

"No need to convince me," said Leon.

"How about tomorrow at oh-eight-hundred?" P.W. proposed.

"What's that in real time?" Lily-Matisse asked.

"Eight in the morning," said P.W.

"Sounds like a plan," said Leon.

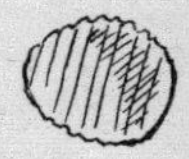

THIRTY-FOUR

The Third R

By 7:45 A.M. Leon and his two best friends had already posted themselves near the entrance to the school.

"This is it," said P.W. "Time for the third R."

"You're sounding awfully confident," said Lily-Matisse.

"Why not?"

"Let's just say I hope that this time the 'R' stands for reanimation instead of *re*ject, or *re*do, or *re*play, or—"

"*Re*lax," said P.W. "It'll work. We've swapped out the energy source, plus we've got a superconductor for starter fluid."

"You mean spit," said Lily-Matisse.

"Exactly," said P.W.

"Yeah, well, we'll see," said Lily-Matisse.

"What's your first move, Leon?" P.W. asked. "Still planning to give Lumpkin a turbowedgie?"

"Of course not," said Leon. "I'm planning to make Lumpkin give *himself* one."

"I take it a double backflip is out of the question?" said Lily-Matisse.

"Afraid so," said Leon. "There's some stiffness in Lumpy's left leg. Besides, I want to hold off on the fancy stuff."

"Enough gabbing," said P.W. "Let's get Lumpy primed."

Leon wasn't leaving anything to chance. He insisted on fresh starter fluid, which Lily-Matisse provided without complaint. Months of scientific research had made her less squeamish around saliva.

Once Lumpy was properly soaked, Leon bided his time by doing finger exercises—variations on the warm-up drills his flute teacher forced upon him.

Oh-eight-hundred came and went, and General Lumpkin hadn't showed.

"The bell's about to ring," Lily-Matisse warned.

"Bell or no bell, I'm waiting," said Leon.

"Me, too," said P.W.

Lily-Matisse was about to object when P.W. spotted Lumpkin turning the corner. "Visual contact established!" he announced giddily. "Target in sight. Repeat. Target in sight! Assume attack positions!"

He and Lily-Matisse planted themselves shoulder to shoulder, giving Leon a shielded post from which to work his magic. He pressed his palms against Lumpy's waist and gripped the figure's flexible arms between his own thumb and index finger. "Hey," he said urgently, "is Lumpkin a lefty or a righty?"

"Lefty," said Lily-Matisse.

"You sure?"

"Positive," said P.W. "He always noogies with his left."

"That's right," said Leon, wincing.

"Range . . . forty-five feet," P.W. announced.

"Forty," he said in a lower, but still excited voice. "Thirty-five!"

Lumpkin continued to climb the steps, unaware of the ambush.

"Target in range!" P.W. whispered urgently. "Repeat. Target in range!"

Using thumb and index finger, Leon bent Lumpy's left arm behind his back, cautiously curled his tiny fingers, and hooked them onto the elastic waistband of the figure's custom-made underpants.

"Bottoms up!" said Leon, giving the shorts a quick, firm yank.

Suddenly he detected a slight warmth in his fingers. He looked down at Lumpy and noticed his beady eyes seemed to be sparkling.

"Ohmygosh!" Lily-Matisse exclaimed.

"Eureka-roonie!" P.W. cried. "Mission Control, we have liftoff! Repeat. We have liftoff!"

And what a liftoff it was!

Henry Lumpkin managed (with the help of Leon and Lumpy) to reach around and pull up on his own underpants so energetically that they rose halfway up his back. More incredibly, he maintained that improbable grip from the bottom of the steps all the way to the doors of the school, at which point he moved out of range.

As soon as Lumpkin had disappeared, P.W. turned to give Leon a high five but settled for slapping Lumpy's palm, since Leon had his hands full.

"Talk about action figures!" said P.W.

"And if I know Leon, the action's just starting," said Lily-Matisse.

The next chance to test-drive Lumpy came during science lab. Leon grabbed a stool within range of Lumpkin, but far enough away that his hocus-pocus would escape detection.

"Henry, is anything the matter?" Mr. Sparks asked soon after class had begun.

"Uh, nah," Lumpkin answered unconvincingly. He wasn't about to admit that his underpants had taken on a life of their own.

"Well, try to control the squirming," said Mr. Sparks. "I've got something cool to show you. I'll need a volunteer."

Leon couldn't resist a little covert fingerwork. Lumpkin's arm suddenly shot up straight as a flagpole.

"H-Henry?" Mr. Sparks stuttered, as startled by the offer as Lumpkin was himself. "Well, well. This is a pleasant surprise. Come up to the front."

Lumpkin had no choice but to approach the teacher's bench.

"Right," said Mr. Sparks. "First things first. What kind of chips should we use for today's experiment? My stockpile currently contains garlic, plain, and peppercorn."

"Garlic, I guess," said Lumpkin.

"Fine choice," said Mr. Sparks. "While I retrieve the chips and chemicals, could you please fetch the stainless-steel mixing bowl and wooden spoon that I set beside the sink?"

With the chemicals and equipment assembled, Mr. Sparks put on a pair of heavy-duty gloves and safety glasses and made Lumpkin do the same.

"All set," said Mr. Sparks. "Let's get started." He handed Lumpkin the garlic chips. "Think you can pulverize these?"

"Yeah," said Lumpkin. "I'm good at crushing stuff."

"He sure is," said Flossy Parmigiano.

"Henry Lumpkin can crush up just about anything," Thomas Warchowski noted.

"And he usually does," P.W. whispered to Leon as Lumpkin effortlessly turned the garlic chips into garlic powder.

"That's perfect," said Mr. Sparks. He again faced the class. "You all recall I said I had something cool to show you. Here it is." Mr. Sparks reached for a special thermos and unscrewed the top.

A vapor cloud rose up and spilled onto the lab bench.

Everyone *oohed*.

"Nothing to worry about," chirped Mr. Sparks as he waved his students to the front of the room. "Liquid nitrogen. *Minus* three hundred and twenty degrees Fahrenheit. It's the science teacher's best friend—after potato chips, of course. Horror movies use this stuff by the tank-load for special effects."

The class gathered around Mr. Sparks as the fog was clearing.

"Are you ready, Henry?"

"I guess."

"Here's what I want you to do." Mr. Sparks tapped a flask containing a thick white fluid. "Pour this emulsion of fat globules and casein micelles into the bowl. Then add this glucose powder and stir the two together with the wooden spoon. While you're stirring, I will add the liquid nitrogen. Then, on my say-so, sprinkle in the potato chips. Whatever you do, Henry, *keep stirring*!"

"What the heck are we making?" Lumpkin demanded.

"You'll find out in about thirty seconds," said Mr. Sparks. "You can begin pouring and stirring. That's excellent, Henry. Now for some liquid nitrogen. Keep stirring, Henry. Good. Now add the chips. Keep that spoon moving until the fog disappears."

"What *is* that?" P.W. asked.

Mr. Sparks removed a packet of plastic spoons from

his satchel and spread them out on the bench. "Find out for yourselves!" he told the class.

"You mean we should *taste* that gunk?" said Antoinette Brede, unable to hide her terror.

"What's the matter?" said Mr. Sparks. "Don't you guys want to be the first to taste test instant garlic-flavored potato chip ice cream? If you do, you'd better hurry. This stuff melts a whole lot faster than your run-of-the-mill store-bought ice cream."

The fifth graders couldn't believe their ears. They couldn't believe their eyes. And soon they couldn't believe their taste buds.

But the fascination didn't last very long. Moments after nibbling the frozen concoction (and once their tongues began to thaw), they all rushed to the sink to rinse their mouths.

"I guess Ben and Jerry can sleep well tonight," said Mr. Sparks. He checked the thermos as the students reclaimed their places. "We still have some liquid nitrogen left. Might as well put it to good use. Any of you want to see a potato chip shatter like glass?"

The question prompted widespread cheering.

"I thought so," said Mr. Sparks as he poured the last of the frigid liquid into a Styrofoam cup. "Henry," he said. "Grab a pair of insulated tongs, pick up a potato chip, and dip it into the liquid nitrogen."

Leon was tempted to use Lumpy to make Lumpkin do something stupid, but Lumpkin beat him to it.

"Henry!" Mr. Sparks shouted. "Don't!"

Lumpkin ignored the warning and tried to eat the frozen chip. Instantly tongs and tongue bonded together, chip fused to lip, and Lumpkin began to yell—insofar as it's possible to yell with a potato chip and a pair of metal tongs frozen to separate parts of your mouth.

The whole class watched in stunned silence as Mr. Sparks rushed to the sink, filled a beaker with warm water, and splashed it on Lumpkin's face.

Eventually chip fell from lip, tongue and tongs parted company, and Lumpkin slunk back to his stool.

"Henry," said Mr. Sparks. "Go and see the nurse."

"Yeth, Mithter Thparkth."

THIRTY-FIVE

The Human Hot Fudge Sundae

Finally! After five years of hurt and humiliation—half a lifetime of noogies, wedgies, and less common schoolyard maneuvers—Leon had a chance to even the score.

The next morning he waited on the school steps, with Lumpy by his side. For the first time ever, he *wanted* to see Lumpkin.

The bully failed to appear by the time the first bell rang.

"Must be out because of the tongue injury," Lily-Matisse speculated.

"Maybe," said Leon disappointedly.

Lumpkin was a no-show at homeroom, and at first-period math class, at second-period English, and at third-period social studies.

Things took a turn for the better at lunch. Strategically seated at a table that had views of the lunch line, sundae bar, and cleanup area, the trio watched and waited. Their surveillance eventually paid off.

"There," cried Lily-Matisse. "He just cut the line."

"Figures," said P.W. "I bet you he hits someone before he has dessert."

"You're on," said Lily-Matisse.

P.W. won the wager moments later, at the tray station.

Leon reached for his pouch.

"Sure that's wise with so many people around?" asked Lily-Matisse.

"Get real," said P.W. "After all these years of Lumpkin being Lumpkin?"

"P.W.'s right," said Leon. He began working Lumpy's legs just as Lumpkin was about to take some pizza.

"Not so fast," Leon said in his best teacher voice. "Where are your manners, Mr. Lumpkin?"

The whole lunchroom watched in amazement as the bully marched himself to the very back of the line.

"Much better, Mr. Lumpkin," Leon intoned. "You are learning."

Each time a student got on line, Leon made Lumpkin bow and give the new arrival frontsies.

"This is like having our very own move-back-three-spaces card," P.W. marveled. "Do not pass Go. Do not collect your lunch!"

"Now, now," said Lily-Matisse, warming to the possibilities. "Growing boys *do* have to eat."

"You know, Miss Jasprow, you have a point," said Leon. "What do you propose we serve Henry?"

"Not pizza," said P.W.

"Certainly not," Lily-Matisse agreed. "Pizza is hardly nutritious enough. Still, we cannot allow him to starve."

"Actually, starvation sounds kind of tempting," said P.W.

Leon looked around until he found the perfect substitute for pizza. "Might we consider brussels sprouts?" he asked primly.

Lily-Matisse suppressed a giggle. "Brussels sprouts *are* nutritious."

"Very," said P.W. as he turned to Leon. "Maestro, if you please?"

Leon worked Lumpy's legs so that Lumpkin moved straight to a steam table piled high with brussels sprouts.

"Do remember," said Lily-Matisse, "the school has a strict 'take all you want, eat all you take' policy."

"As well it should," said P.W.

Leon worked Lumpy's arms. "Hmm," he said. "I'm feeling a little resistance."

"Is that a problem?" asked Lily-Matisse.

"I don't think so," said Leon. After five minutes of diligent manipulation, he managed to devise a move—a tricky wrist flick and leg-lunge combination—that dispatched Lumpkin with a plateful of brussels spouts.

"He's heading toward the garbage bins," Lily-Matisse warned moments later.

"Not for long," said Leon. A bit more finger work seated the reluctant vegetarian next to Mr. Groot.

"That should fix him," said P.W. "Now he's *got* to eat those suckers!"

Lumpkin tried his best to ignore the food on his plate, but Leon wouldn't let him.

"Time to take your medicine," he said, handling Lumpy's arms like an expert crane operator.

"That's one," said Lily-Matisse gleefully as Lumpkin shoved a brussels sprout into his mouth.

"That's two!" said P.W.

"Three!" said Lily-Matisse.

"Four!" said P.W.

Leon kept at it until every sprout was gone.

"Phew," he said, after he'd finished the forced feeding. "That was rough!"

"I bet it was rougher for Lumpkin," said Lily-Matisse. "Look at the way he's slumped over."

"You know what might just improve his mood?" P.W. said with a sly grin.

"Oh, boy, here it comes," said Lily-Matisse.

"A food fight," P.W. said. "I mean, after all, it's practically a tradition." He recalled the goopy cafeteria clash he had set off the previous year, soon after gaining control of Miss Hagmeyer.

"That was different," Lily-Matisse pointed out.

"Leon had the teachers start it. None of us got into trouble."

"She has a point," said Leon. "And anyway, somehow Lumpkin throwing food is too—I don't know—*Lumpkinian.*"

"Plus it's a waste," Lily-Matisse noted. "There's got to be a better way to teach Lumpkin a lesson."

"There is," said Leon.

"What do you have in mind?" said P.W.

"Take a look at where Lumpkin is heading."

"The sundae bar?" said Lily-Matisse.

"Yup," said Leon.

"You're kidding, right?" said P.W.

"Why not?" said Leon.

"What am I missing?" said Lily-Matisse.

"Simple," said Leon. "You're about to see Henry Lumpkin make himself a hot fudge sundae."

Lily-Matisse's eyes widened.

P.W. licked his lips. "Well, this should be sweet!"

It's too bad the judges from the *Guinness Book of Records* weren't on hand for Leon's next maneuver. Had they been, they could have confirmed a new entry for their record book: "Biggest human hot fudge sundae."

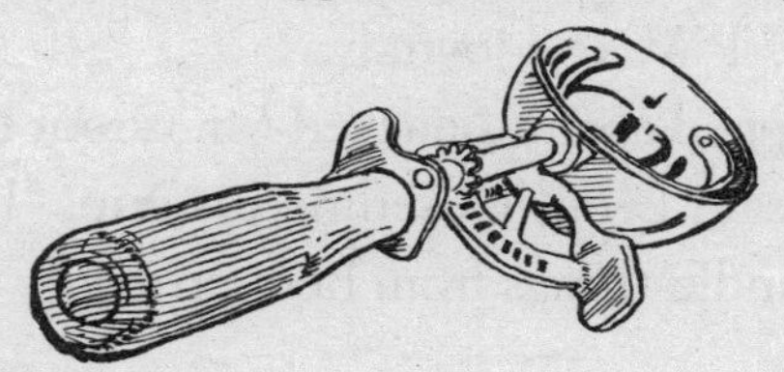

Leon began his dessert making with three scoops of vanilla ice cream—one scoop for each shoulder (easily targeted, thanks to the silver stars) and a third scoop applied to the head.

Next came the hot fudge. Using Lumpy, Leon forced Lumpkin to ladle a generous amount of the sauce on each of the three scoops of ice cream.

"What about his face?" said P.W.

"Don't!" cried Lily-Matisse. "You might burn him."

"Relax," said Leon. "I'm done with the hot fudge."

"Don't be a wuss," said P.W.

"I'm not being a wuss," said Leon. "I'm saving the face for the whipped cream."

"Oh," said P.W. "Sorry."

"You better hurry up," said Lily-Matisse. "Groot is heading over there."

Leon swiftly worked Lumpy's hands so that Lumpkin would grab hold of the whipped cream. A few quick jiggles of the tiny forearm prompted Lumpkin to shake the can.

"Here goes," said Leon. He made Lumpkin shoot off a thick stream of whipped cream.

"Ohmygosh!" said Lily-Matisse.

"Misfire!" P.W. said joyfully.

The whipped cream smacked Mr. Groot in the eye.

"Yikes," said Leon, loosening his grip. "I think I'll let Groot handle things from here on out."

Thirty-Six

Bad News

Two days later, much to everyone's surprise, Lumpkin was released from the Birdcage. His recess detention was over. High atop the jungle gym, underneath the basketball hoop, from the free throw line to the handball wall—all fifth-grade eyes focused on the large, lone figure shuffling into the yard.

There was no way to know what Lumpkin would try next, but given his recent behavior, everyone assumed it would be weird.

After all, he had fused a frozen potato chip to his lip. That was weird.

He had given *frontsies* to third graders. That was weird.

He had eaten twenty-three brussels sprouts. That may not have been weird, but it was certainly disgusting.

And he had made himself a hot fudge sundae. That was *very* weird.

As Lumpkin approached, students backed away. They all knew the law of the jungle gym—the savage beast is far more deadly when wounded.

Lily-Matisse, Leon, and P.W. monitored Lumpkin from behind the giant maple.

"Something's different," said Lily-Matisse. "He looks smaller—tiny, almost."

"'Tiny' is not a word I think of when I think of Lumpkin," said P.W.

"Must be that he's not wearing an army jacket," said Leon.

"Probably in the wash," P.W. suggested. "Hot fudge must be tough to get out."

"Remind me to bring some Poop-B-Gone to school," said Leon.

The joking stopped abruptly when Lumpkin's target became clear.

"He's heading over!" said Lily-Matisse.

"Quick," cried P.W. "Grab Lumpy!"

"I can't!" said Leon. "He's in my locker."

"Why'd you leave him there?" Lily-Matisse said anxiously.

"How was I supposed to know Lumpkin would get released? After the—"

"*Shh!*" Lily-Matisse hissed. "Here he comes!"

It was clear from the glower and the clenched fists that Lumpkin wanted to make up for lost time.

P.W. bravely stepped forward and faced the bully

head-on. "So what's it going to be today?" he said fearlessly. "A noogie? A purple nurple? A blood bracelet? No, I know. You're going to test out your patented Howlitzer."

"Nah," said Lumpkin, cracking his knuckles. "Gotta be on my best behavior—at least for a while." He glanced up at the principal's office. "Just thought you guys would want to know, seeing how you're all charter members of the Franklin Sparks Fan Club . . ." Lumpkin smiled maliciously.

"Know what?" Leon demanded.

"That your favorite teacher is toast," Lumpkin revealed.

"What are you talking about?" said Lily-Matisse.

"Let's just say I'm not the only one who's been Birdcaged. Take a look for yourselves."

Lumpkin pointed toward the principal's office. Sure enough, Mr. Sparks was standing in the window, his back to the playground.

Lumpkin snickered. "Birdwhistle wasn't too happy when she found out I got a fat lip in science class."

"But you did that to yourself!" Lily-Matisse said angrily.

"Maybe," Lumpkin admitted. "But when Birdwhistle kicked me out to grill Sparks, I heard her say, 'It's good-bye chips, mister!' She said it twice, and she said it mean."

Leon had heard enough. "Come on!" he said.

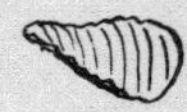

Joined by Lily-Matisse and P.W., he hightailed it out of the playground and up the stairs. When they got close enough to view Mr. Sparks and the principal through a large plate-glass window, they ducked down and took turns peeking in.

"Boy, they're really going at it," said P.W.

"Can you hear what they're saying?" asked Lily-Matisse.

P.W. shook his head. "The darn glass is too thick. Can either of you make out what's on that piece of paper Birdwhistle is waving at Sparks?"

Leon inched up to get a better look. "Well, whatever it is, it's not good. The big fat Confidential stamp at the top always, *always* means trouble."

"We'll just have to swipe it," P.W. said.

"Are you crazy?" exclaimed Lily-Matisse. "We can't just walk in there and take it."

"We don't have to walk in there," said P.W.

Lily-Matisse made a face. "What are you talking about?"

"He's talking about using Lumpy," Leon said as he rose to his feet. The three fifth graders rushed back to Leon's locker, retrieved Lumpy, and dashed out to the playground, where Lumpkin had reclaimed his favorite spot at the top of the jungle gym.

Leon took up his position behind the maple and used Lumpy to lower Lumpkin from his perch. By the time he had guided the bully into the building and up the stairs, the Birdcage was empty.

"How should we do this?" P.W. asked.

"One of you has to be lookout," said Leon. "The other has to be the reader. I'll be way too busy with Lumpy to handle anything else."

P.W. posted himself at the end of the hall. Once he gave the all-clear signal, Leon sent Lumpkin into the Birdcage.

"Which sheet should I get him to grab?" Leon asked Lily-Matisse. She scanned the interior of the principal's office.

"I can't tell," she said. "I've got to get a closer look." As she moved toward the plate-glass window, she accidentally hit Leon's arm and triggered a chain reaction. Leon jerked Lumpy. Lumpy jerked Lumpkin. And a large stack of files toppled off the principal's desk.

Leon panicked as he struggled to get Lumpkin to retrieve the scattered papers.

"Hold it!" said Lily-Matisse. "Make him lift up the sheets one at a time before he puts them back."

Leon worked Lumpy's arm. The effect was instantaneous—Lumpkin, entranced by the power of his spitting image, pressed a document against the plate-glass window.

"Nope, that's not it," said Lily-Matisse. "That's a

memo about sword safety during the medieval carnival. Next . . . Nope. This one's a requisition for mops. Next . . . Next . . . Nope . . . Ix-nay . . . Next . . .

Leon (and Lumpy and Lumpkin) repeated the robotic pickup procedure nearly a dozen times before Lily-Matisse hit pay dirt.

"Bingo!" she exclaimed.

Out of the corner of his eye, Leon could see the blood-red Confidential stamp. "What's it say?" he demanded.

"Ohmygosh!" said Lily-Matisse. "Listen to this." She read the key passage out loud:

> ". . . Nimble fingers make nimble minds, Mr. Sparks, but not when those fingers are forever handling potato chips. I am sorry to report that complaints have only intensified since your Parents' Night presentation. Certain members of the Classical School community believe you have been feeding the fifth graders the mental equivalent of junk food, and frankly I am hard-pressed to dispute that charge. Unless I can offer our parents concrete proof that your unconventional methods benefit our children *educationally*, I will have no choice but to release you from your duties following the science fair at the end of the year."

THIRTY-SEVEN

A Hypothesis

The campaign to save Mr. Sparks and the all-chips-all-the-time science curriculum began the very next day. Leon pulled aside a few classmates and told them to meet at the playground maple during recess. There he made his pitch simply and directly.

"Okay, here's the thing," he said. "Sparks is in trouble. A bunch of parents are trying to get him fired."

"That's just wrong!" protested Flossy Parmigiano.

"What do you expect?" said P.W. "Parents tend to be a little thick."

A murmur of agreement spread through the ranks.

"Anyway," Leon continued, "there are barely two months of school left. Which means from now on, every chance we get, we've got to bring up potato chips and show how they're worthwhile."

"How do you expect to pull *that* off?" Antoinette Brede asked skeptically.

"You'll see," said Leon. "I've got a few ideas."

The first of those ideas was presented at the start of the next math class. Leon, P.W., and Lily-Matisse snuck in five minutes early and scribbled three word problems on the blackboard:

Question 1. If the world consumes 1.8 billion pounds of potato chips each year, and there are on average two hundred chips per pound, how many chips get eaten?

Question 2. EXTRA CREDIT: Using the answer for Question 1, if potato chips have an average length of two inches, how many linear feet of potato chips get eaten each year worldwide?

Question 3. SUPER-DUPER EXTRA CREDIT: Using the answer for Question 2, calculate if it's possible for a "yellow chip road" to stretch from the earth to the moon. (HINT: figure that the average distance between the earth and moon is about 250,000 miles.)

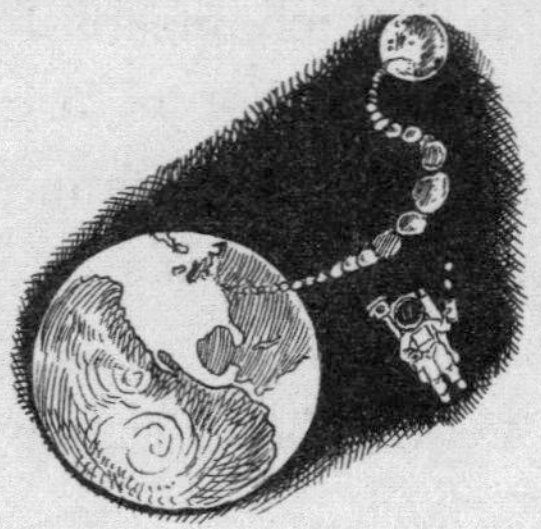

Principal Birdwhistle caught wind of the scheme and handed out a word problem of her own.

THE CLASSICAL SCHOOL

"Where Nimble Fingers Make for Nimble Minds"

Office of the Principal

To the fifth-grade class,

If 18 students disrupt a math class with word problems about potato chips, and each student receives 4 hours of detention, how many total hours of detention will the students receive?

Yours,
Hortensia Birdwhistle
Principal

That put a stop to potato chip math problems, but it did not put a stop to Leon. He expanded his campaign to include English class, where the fifth graders were studying haikus, a seventeen-syllable poem invented in Japan. Leon stood up and recited the following original haiku:

> "A *hypothesis.*
> *Potato chips can teach us*
> *All science matters.*"

P.W. stood up next and performed a hip-hop haiku:

"Yo! Don't spill that bag!
Wasting potato chips is
Not a good idea."

Lily-Matisse went third, offering a more gentle recitation:

"Be considerate.
Potato chip littering
Makes our world crummy."

After that, everyone wanted to get into the act—even Lumpkin:

"Crunch! Crunch! Crunch! Crunch! Crunch!
Are those chips you hear? Or just
Me, *Henry Lumpkin?"*

Probably the most heartfelt potato chip haiku came from Flossy Parmigiano:

"Dad sniffs my fingers.
They smell like potato chips.
I am so *busted!"*

Unfortunately Flossy Parmigiano wasn't the only

one who got busted. When Principal Birdwhistle learned about the single-subject verse, she used the PA system to broadcast a haiku of her own:

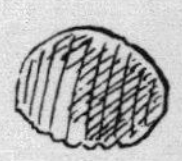

"No more chip poems.
They make fifth graders forget
The important stuff."

Leon disagreed. He called another maple tree pow-wow to figure out what to do next.

"Birdwhistle is totally against potato chips," Thomas Warchowski complained.

"Birdwhistle's not the real problem," said Flossy Parmigiano. "The real problem is the parents. Trust me, I know. You should hear my dad going on about dental time bombs."

"Then we'll have to work on the parents," said Leon.

"How?" said Antoinette Brede.

"Glad you asked," said Leon. "I've been giving this a lot of thought. The science fair is one month away, right? Since tons of parents will be there, it makes sense to use the fair to prove, once and for all, that Sparks is a first-rate teacher and that potato chips rule."

Leon spelled out the scheme to his classmates. All those present, including Antoinette, agreed to join in.

"Remember," said Leon. "No one can talk about this."

"Yeah," said Thomas Warchowski. "Anyone who rats gets sliced up and deep-fried in boiling hot peanut oil. Agreed?"

"Agreed!" everyone pledged.

Pffut! P.W. was the first to seal the oath of silence by spitting on the ground. And all the others followed suit with differing degrees of enthusiasm: *Pffut! Pffut! Pffut!* . . . . . *Pffut!* . . . . *Pffut!*

Editor's note: Answers to word problems on page 288. Question 1) 360 billion chips. Question 2) 60 billion feet. Question 3) Yes. A yellow chip road could travel from the earth to the moon and back nearly twenty-three times.

THIRTY-EIGHT

Crunch Time!

The oath held. No one did rat. During the weeks that followed, the fifth graders who had entered the potato chip pact all kept their mouths shut—except, of course, when research required munching.

The science fair was scheduled to start at one P.M. in the school gym. Exhibitors were given the morning to set up their projects. Leon arrived early and distributed Trimore Towers bedsheets to each of his co-conspirators.

"What's the sheet for?" asked Thomas Warchowski.

"To hide your project," said Leon. "We don't want Birdwhistle or Sparks or the parents seeing anything before we make our presentations."

Mr. Hankey, the janitor, had prepped the gym by lining up folding tables around the edge of the basketball court. He dispensed a stern warning before he left the fifth graders to their own devices. "You pests better keep things neat and tidy," he grumbled. "That means no explosions, no spills, no stains, no bubblegum, and no crumbs. You read me?"

"Loud and clear," said P.W.

When one o'clock arrived, the doors opened and visitors entered a gymnasium filled with glassware, plant life, poster board, and six experiments covered by bedsheets bearing the Trimore Towers logo.

Attendance was better than expected. In addition to parents, siblings, and grandparents (and stepparents, step-siblings, and step-grandparents), countless friends showed up for the event. Leon's supporters were particularly numerous. His mother and Maria came, as did Napoleon and Frau Haffenreffer. (The baker arrived with a very large pastry box.)

There was one other visitor in attendance because of Leon—a short, round man clutching an official-looking briefcase.

A whistle blast silenced the crowd.

"Okay, all you Edisons and Einsteins!" yelled Coach Kasperitis. "Settle down and listen up! And that goes for the rest of you, too. Principal Birdwhistle wants to say a few words."

The visitors gathered around the principal, who stood at center court, nervously clutching an index card.

"Welcome to the Classical School science fair," she read stiffly. "Before we begin, I wish to *mention* that it is my *contention* that this *invention convention* will prompt some *reflection*."

A few guests chuckled.

Emma Zeisel leaned over to Regina Jasprow and whispered, "Someone deserves *detention* for that *intervention.*"

"So to avoid any more *tension,*" the principal continued, "please give your *attention* to Franklin W. Sparks."

The fifth graders all cheered. The reception from their parents was more mixed.

"Hello, one and all," said Mr. Sparks. "Thanks for coming. Here's how the science fair will work. Exhibitors should stand next to their projects, while the rest of us make our way around the gym. Principal Birdwhistle and I will be looking for three things today. First of all, there's the matter of scientific rigor. We will be asking ourselves—and the exhibitors—has the experiment been thoroughly researched, accurately undertaken, precisely performed, and clearly explained?

"Second, we will evaluate the elegance of the exhibit. Just because someone spends a ton of money on fancy gizmos doesn't guarantee brilliance. Remember, all Isaac Newton needed was an apple.

"Finally—and this is a biggie—we'll be assessing the Wow! Factor—the originality of the project and its broader contribution to the world in which we live. Well, enough squawking out of me. Let's see what my co-researchers have cooked up."

And with that, Mr. Sparks, accompanied by Principal Birdwhistle and the visitors, advanced to the first folding table.

"Tell everyone your name and what you've put together," said Mr. Sparks.

"Antoinette Brede," replied Antoinette Brede. "And what I've put together is an analysis of pH levels in various everyday foods."

"Fascinating," said Mr. Sparks. "Go on."

"Okay. Well, as you've taught us, Mr. Sparks, pH levels tell us how acidy stuff is." Antoinette held up a fat softcover book. "This government report lists the pHs of over three thousand foods," she said. "Name a food, any food, Principal Birdwhistle."

"Graham crackers," the Principal said blandly.

Antoinette scanned the Gs. "It says here graham crackers have a pH level between seven-point-one and seven-point-nine-two. Anyone else?"

"Boiled tongue!" said Emma Zeisel. (She had a soft spot for tongue sandwiches.)

Antoinette flipped back to the Ts. "The pH of tongue is six-point-two."

"What about caviar, darling?"

Antoinette rolled her eyes before turning to C. "Caviar has a pH of five-point-seven, Mother."

"Well, perhaps the child has learned *some*thing useful after all," said Mrs. Brede, a taut smile stretching from one diamond-studded ear to the other.

"How about potato chips?" asked the short, round man carrying the briefcase.

"*Potahto* chips?" sniffed Mrs. Brede. "Must we bring *that* up again?"

"Mother, please," said Antoinette Brede. "I am perfectly happy to answer that question." She flipped to the P's. "Hey, what do you know," she said. "The government forgot about potato chips!"

"Really?" said Mr. Sparks.

"Really," said Antoinette. "Here, take a look."

Mr. Sparks scanned the Ps. "You're right," he said. "No potato chips."

"Which is why," said Antoinette Brede, "I took matters into my own hands."

She pulled off the bedsheet to reveal a poster that said THE pH OF POTATO CHIPS and dishes of test samples.

"Oh, good grief!" exclaimed Mrs. Brede before shooting a stern look at Mr. Sparks.

"Hey, Teach, did you put the kid up to this?"

"I assure you, Mr. Lumpkin, I did not."

"It's true," said Antoinette. "Mr. Sparks had nothing to do with my project."

"Perhaps we should all quiet down and allow the girl to make her presentation," said the short, round man standing off to the side. "I, for one, would like to learn about the pH of potato chips."

"Me, too," said Ms. Dhabanandana.

"*Moi aussi!*" Napoleon added.

Principal Birdwhistle raised her hand to halt the outbursts. "Go on, Antoinette."

"Okay," said Antoinette Brede. "Here's what I did. First I crushed up different brands of chips. Then I mixed them into a paste of saliva."

"How revolting!" said Mrs. Brede.

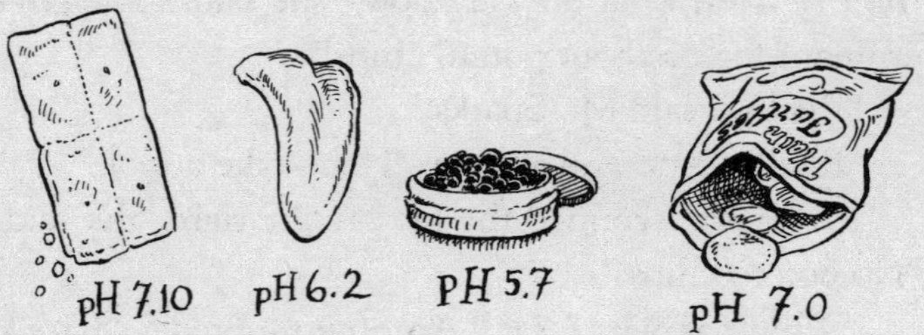

Antoinette Brede pushed on. "I tested each solution using a pH strip and found that the average *plain* potato chip solution has a pH that's as neutral as water—meaning a seven. Seasoned chips, however, are a whole different story."

She tapped a chart on her poster. "As you can see, the salt 'n' vinegar chip solution registered a pH of four-point-five."

"That's about the same acid level as acetic acid," sputtered Dr. Parmigiano. "And people wonder if potato chips are dangerous."

"Lemons have a similar pH," Antoinette Brede countered. "If you're thinking of banning potato chips, you'll have to ban lemons and limes, too."

"Let's not be hasty," Mrs. Brede cut in. "I can't

imagine my recipe for lobster à la Brede without a splash of lemon juice."

Mr. Sparks surveyed the exhibit. "Zesty work, Antoinette. You—and your mother—should be very proud."

"Yes, well, I suppose," Mrs. Brede allowed.

With that small but unexpected endorsement, Mr. Sparks quickly moved on, pleased that one parent, at least, was mildly less critical of potato chips and even, perhaps, of him.

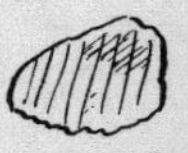

THIRTY-NINE

Cantennas, Spud Guns, and Dresses Made of Foil

Not all the science fair projects made use of potato chips. But the ones that didn't—the baking soda volcano (Lumpkin's contribution to the study of the natural world), the tin foil solar system, the kidney bean plantings born inside Baggies—received a lot less attention than the exhibits that incorporated thin-sliced deep-fried tubers.

"Whatcha got for us, Thomas?" Mr. Sparks asked, eyeing the second bedsheet-covered exhibit.

"Well," said Thomas Warchowski, "I decided to investigate the science of resonance. That's the study of sympathetic vibrations."

"Could you put that more simply, Thomas?" asked Principal Birdwhistle.

"Sure thing. I built an antenna to extend the wireless signal on my mom's laptop. Antennas can cost more than a hundred dollars at the store. But using stuff I found around the house, I made my cantenna for six dollars and forty-five cents."

"What a clever boy," said Mrs. Brede.

"Not bad," said Lumpkin, Sr.

"Now that's more like it," said Dr. Parmigiano. "A science project that is practical, economical, and wholesome."

Thomas Warchowski's parents looked on proudly as sympathetic vibrations of a non-acoustical variety spread throughout the gym.

"Excuse me, Thomas," said Principal Birdwhistle. "Did I hear you correctly? Did you say *can*tenna?"

"Yup."

"What is the difference between an *an*tenna and a *can*tenna?" asked Dr. Parmigiano.

"Well," said Thomas Warchowski, "let me show you." He whipped off the bedsheet to reveal his homemade frequency extender.

"You got to be kidding me!" exclaimed Lumpkin, Sr. "*More* potato chips!"

"No," said Thomas Warchowski. "I didn't use potato chips. I used a potato chip *can*."

"Who's responsible for this?" Dr. Parmigiano demanded angrily.

"Thomas is," said Mr. Sparks.

"And if you pipe down, we might all find out how his invention works," said the short, round man with the briefcase.

The rebuke silenced the dentist.

"Thanks," said Thomas Warchowski. He returned

his attention to the exhibit. "As we learned from Mr. Sparks, metal is an excellent conductor. If you look closely at this chip can cross section, you'll see the metal coating on the inside of the tube wall. That coating touches the metal on the bottom of the can and forms a supereffective reflector.

"Using a few locknuts, six inches of aluminum tubing, some copper wire, and a bunch of other stuff—including a potato chip can—I was able to build a cantenna that hooks up to the wireless port of any computer. When properly adjusted"—Thomas Warchowski fiddled with the position of the can—"my cantenna can extend the range of a wireless frequency by more than five hundred feet."

"What does that mean in practical terms, Thomas?" Mr. Sparks asked.

"It means that if I point my cantenna just the right way, I can link this laptop to the school's internal computer network."

"You had better not," Principal Birdwhistle said firmly. "I think we've seen enough."

"Very elegant, Thomas," said Mr. Sparks. "Truly first-rate."

"Florence Pontevecchio Parmigiano! How could you?"

A parental outburst drew attention to the adjacent table.

"I'm just trying to be *scientific*, Dad," Flossy Parmigiano told her father, who was shaking his finger angrily at a poster that said POTATO CHIPS AND TOOTH DECAY: MYTHS AND FACTS.

"You want facts, young lady?" sputtered Dr. Parmigiano. "Fact: Potato chips are carbohydrates. Fact: Carbohydrates stick to teeth! Fact: Foot particles rot teeth! Fact: Tooth decay is the most widespread noncontagious disease in the whole entire world!"

"Sorry, Dad, but that's not exactly true. Check out my research." Flossy Parmigiano pulled a Trimore Towers bedsheet off her exhibit and grabbed a big white plastic tooth wearing eyeglasses. "Let's hear what Mr. Molar the Wisdom Tooth has to say, Dad. Fact: Potato chips are a *non-sweet* carbohydrate. Fact: Non-sweet carbohydrates do not produce fermented sugars. Fact: Fermented sugars are the real dental time bombs—the number one cause of tooth decay."

Dr. Parmigiano's brow furrowed. He was clearly taken aback by his daughter's counterargument. "Where's your proof?" he challenged.

"Right here," said Flossy Parmigiano. She put down Mr. Molar and picked up two jars. One was labeled TOOTH IN SODA (AFTER TWO WEEKS). The other said TOOTH IN POTATO CHIP SOLUTION (AFTER TWO WEEKS).

"Where'd you get the teeth?" asked Dr. Parmigiano.

"Where d' you think?" his daughter answered, smiling broadly to reveal two gaps in an otherwise perfect set of choppers.

Dr. Parmigiano inspected the jars. The one filled with soda contained a tooth eroded beyond recognition.

"Looks like an olive pit," Maria remarked.

As for the jar filled with the potato chip solution, its tooth appeared to be perfectly intact.

"I must admit," said Dr. Parmigiano. "Mr. Molar the Wisdom Tooth does make a pretty convincing case."

Pleased by the turnaround, Mr. Sparks moved the group to the next table, where a formless shape was rustling underneath a Trimore Towers bedsheet. He bent over and whispered, "Lily-Matisse? Is that you under there?"

"Yes."

"Mind telling us what your project is?"

"I decided to study the benefits of recycling," came the muffled reply.

"How admirable," said Mr. Sparks. "But Lily-Matisse? We're all waiting to view your exhibit, so Ollie-ollie-oxen-free."

"Actually," said Lily-Matisse, "I'd like Principal Birdwhistle to unveil me."

The principal reluctantly grabbed a corner of the bedsheet and gave a yank.

"Oh, my goodness!" she exclaimed.

"Chip chip hooray!" cheered Emma Zeisel.

"Wow!" said Mr. Sparks.

"Oh, brother," said Lumpkin, Sr.

Lily-Matisse stood up on the table and spun around with gymnastic grace before hopping down.

"She made everything herself," said Regina Jasprow.

"Not completely, Mom." Lily-Matisse corrected her. "You showed me how to do the straps."

"True," said Regina Jasprow, "but you wove them on your own."

"That's the first time I've ever seen a student *wear* a science exhibit," said Principal Birdwhistle.

"It makes me hungry just looking at her," said Frau Haffenreffer.

Lily-Matisse was dressed, head to toe, in clothing made from recycled potato chip bags. She wore a foil dress and foil slippers and clutched a foil purse.

Mrs. Brede approached to scrutinize Lily-Matisse more closely. "Your use of Mylar is simply divine, and that purse! It's *ab*solutely *dar*ling!"

"Is it possible," said Emma Zeisel, "that these exhibits are chipping away at your objections?"

"Perhaps," said Mrs. Brede.

"I didn't make all this stuff to be divine or darling," said Lily-Matisse. "I did it to make a point about recycling. Guess how many dresses we could produce with all the tossed-away potato chip bags."

No one ventured a guess.

"Try *fifty* million!" said Lily-Matisse. "A billion potato chip bags are trashed every year, and it only took me twenty bags to make this dress."

"A billion divided by twenty is fifty million," Mr. Sparks explained for the less mathematical parents.

"You could dress every woman in Haiti!" said Napoleon.

"Plus every señorita in Peru!" said Maria.

"And all Fräuleins in Austria!" added Frau Haffenreffer.

"Hey, Mr. Sparks! Principal Birdwhistle!" P.W. shouted. "Want to see an exhibit that'll *really* blow you away?"

"Heaven help us," mumbled Principal Birdwhistle as she led the way. "I'm afraid to ask," she said, gazing down at the next bedsheet.

"No reason to be afraid," P.W. said cheerfully. He uncovered a wooden board on which he had mounted an apparatus fashioned from potato chip cans, black electrical tape, and white plastic plumbing pipe.

"What in heaven's name is *that*?" asked Principal Birdwhistle.

"This," said P.W. "is the crown prince of potato propulsion systems."

"A spud gun!" exclaimed Lumpkin, Sr., suddenly taking an interest in the fair.

"I prefer the term 'potato delivery apparatus,'" said P.W. "I call this particular model the Extermitater."

"The *exterminator*?" Principal Birdwhistle said with obvious concern.

"I believe the boy said Extermi-*tater*," said the short, round man.

The correction only heightened the principal's agitation, which Lumpkin, Sr., raised further still.

"Doesn't the school have rules about guns?" he asked.

"The Extermitater is *not* a gun," P.W. was quick to point out.

"It's not?" Principal Birdwhistle said dubiously.

"No," said P.W. "Guns use gunpowder. All the Extermitater requires is plain old hair spray." He pointed to a can of AquaNet.

"I'm not terribly convinced," said Principal Birdwhistle. "Please reassure us that your terminator is not charged."

"Of course it isn't," said P.W. "And it's pronounced 'ex-term-ih-tay-ter,'" he added patiently.

"Could you give us an overview of the apparatus?" Mr. Sparks asked.

"Glad to," said P.W. "Let's start with the muzzle—see how I have added a beveled ring of plastic? That allows the user to slice down oversized potatoes, making for a nice snug fit—not that potatoes are the only thing the Extermitater can deliver."

"Go on," Mr. Sparks prompted.

"After I've filled the Extermitater," P.W. continued,

"all I have to do is spray some aerosol into the ignition chamber and push this bright red button."

Napoleon raised his hand. "Tell us, Monsieur Pay Dooble-vay, what happens when the bright red button is pushed?"

P.W. smiled. "Same thing that happens at the end of the *Incredible Hulk,* volume one, number two-twenty-nine."

"I'm not familiar with that work," said Principal Birdwhistle.

"Allow me to demonstrate." P.W. cupped his hands around his mouth and shouted: "KA-BOOM!"

Principal Birdwhistle shook her head. "Would you mind telling us the scientific value of this extirpator?"

"Of course," said P.W., resisting the urge to correct her once more. "As we learned last year, while studying the Crusades, ammunition is generally made of stone, wood, or metal. Slingshots fling rocks. Bows launch wooden arrows. Guns use powder to shoot bullets. The beauty of the Extermitater is its versatility."

Mr. Sparks provided another prompt. "Can you explain?"

"Absolutely," said P.W. "Basically this apparatus will propel anything."

"Anything?" asked Lumpkin, Sr.

"Anything," P.W. confirmed. "Here, take a look." He turned to a poster board that included a data chart.

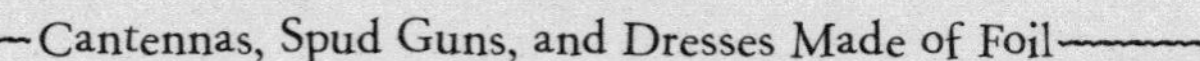

"Now I know where all those appetizers kept going!" said Mr. Dhabanandana.

"I don't think your sister would be happy if she knew about item two," added Ms. Dhabanandana.

"I have another concern," said Mr. Sparks. "The potato calculations at the bottom of your chart are not very precise."

"I know it," P.W. acknowledged. "But the potatoes flew so wicked far they whizzed off the roof and down into the street!"

"Are you saying you simply *eye-balled* the distance?" Principal Birdwhistle asked critically.

"Of course not," said P.W. "I calculated the distance based on trajectory and triangulation." He pointed to a set of figures at the bottom of the poster board.

Mr. Sparks double-checked the calculations on a piece of scratch paper.

"Well?" said Principal Birdwhistle.

"The final number may not be precise," said Mr. Sparks, "but the method he used to obtain it is flawless. Excellent work, P.W."

FORTY

The Four Domes of the Universe

The science fair was going as well as could be expected. Two of the most vocal critics of potato chips—Mrs. Brede and Dr. Parmigiano—were considerably less hostile to Mr. Sparks and his single-substance curriculum. Still, the battle wasn't over. Leon would have to pull a rabbit out of his hat to neutralize Lumpkin, Sr., and to win over Principal Birdwhistle.

He had set up at the last exhibit table, for tactical reasons. He now waited for his turn to fulfill the potato chip pact.

"So, Leon?" said Mr. Sparks when that fateful moment came. "What are you serving us?"

"I'm quite certain we all know what Leon is serving," said Principal Birdwhistle.

"I doubt it," said Leon. He pulled back his bedsheet to reveal four domed food warmers, on loan from the Trimore Towers coffee shop. "My science fair exhibit tells the history of the universe."

"Well, I'll say one thing for you," said Principal Birdwhistle. "You're certainly ambitious."

"Thousands of years ago," Leon began, "before we had telescopes and satellites, people thought the earth, and the whole universe, was shaped like this."

He lifted the first of the four metal domes to reveal a pancake.

"The little stinker cooked it all himself," Frau Haffenreffer announced proudly.

Leon blushed. "The pancake theory lasted a really long time—all the way up until the Greeks. But then, around A.D. 150, Claudius Ptolemaeus—alias Ptolemy—hypothesized that the universe had a different shape. He believed it looked like this."

Leon lifted the second of the four metal domes.

"An onion?" said Principal Birdwhistle.

"Yup," said Leon. "Ptolemy thought the earth was at the center of a giant onion-shaped universe, and that all the planets, as well as the sun, circled around the earth in orbits that resembled the layers of this onion."

"What about the stars?" Mr. Sparks asked.

"The stars were stuck onto the outer layer," Leon said, tapping on the onion skin.

He stepped in front of the third metal dome. "Now, fast-forward to 1609. That's when Galileo used a telescope to find a bunch of moons no one had ever seen before. Galileo also confirmed that the earth was *not*

the center of the universe. Fast-forward again. Relying on Galileo's work, twentieth-century astronomers decided that the universe might not be shaped like an onion, after all. They figured it was shaped like this."

Leon lifted the third of the four domes.

"A glazed doughnut?" sneered Lumpkin, Sr.

"Well, they didn't say the universe was *glazed*," said Leon. "But they did argue that it was shaped like a big fat ring—which they called a 'torus' to sound more scientific."

Mr. Sparks nodded knowingly, but did not say a word.

Leon took another step and planted himself in front of the fourth and final dome.

"That brings me to the theory of the universe I think is the coolest—the one first proposed by Einstein. He hypothesized that the universe has a negatively curved surface." Leon reached for the fourth of the four domes but was stopped by a sudden challenge.

"A negatively curved surface?" Lumpkin, Sr., bellowed. "Give me a break!"

"Mr. Lumpkin, please," said Principal Birdwhistle. "Do allow the boy to complete his presentation."

"What's to complete? I mean, come on. Pancakes? Onions? Doughnuts? Is this a science exhibit or a grocery list? You're not really buying this negative curve crud, are you, Teach?"

"Actually," said Mr. Sparks, "Leon's overview of the universe is grounded in complex higher mathematics."

"You don't say," Lumpkin, Sr., said sarcastically.

Mr. Sparks finally had had enough. "I *do* say, Mr. Lumpkin. And what's more, I say someone needs to be taught a lesson—about mathematics *and* manners!"

Lumpkin, Sr., cracked his knuckles. "Go ahead, Teach," he snarled. "Educate me."

"Gentlemen, please," Principal Birdwhistle said nervously.

Her remarks went unnoticed. Mr. Sparks let loose:

"The surface you're so positive doesn't exist, Mr. Lumpkin, is part of a hyperbolic paraboloid and can be represented by the formula $z = x^2 - y^2$ or, better still, $z = a(x^2 - y^2)$, where a is a relatively small constant, say $a = 0.1$. The sum of the angles of a triangle on this surface would be less than one hundred eighty degrees, contrary to what Euclid might have taught us. This means that it has negative curvature. A whole branch of mathematics, called Lobachevskian geometry, is devoted to such shapes, about which you are completely and totally and hopelessly clueless! So keep your ill-informed opinions to yourself, Mr. Lumpkin, and grant Leon and his classmates the courtesy and respect they deserve!"

Mr. Sparks's tongue-lashing left Lumpkin, Sr., speechless.

"Boy oh boy," said Emma Zeisel, "talk about watching sparks fly!"

Leon waited for the snickers to subside before resuming his presentation. "Just in case you didn't catch everything Mr. Sparks was saying, I have an example of a negatively curved surface that might be easier to understand." He reached for the fourth and final dome, but stopped before revealing the object underneath. "Hold on," he said. "It's Mr. Sparks who should do the honors."

Everyone knew what was coming, but when it came it was still a shocker.

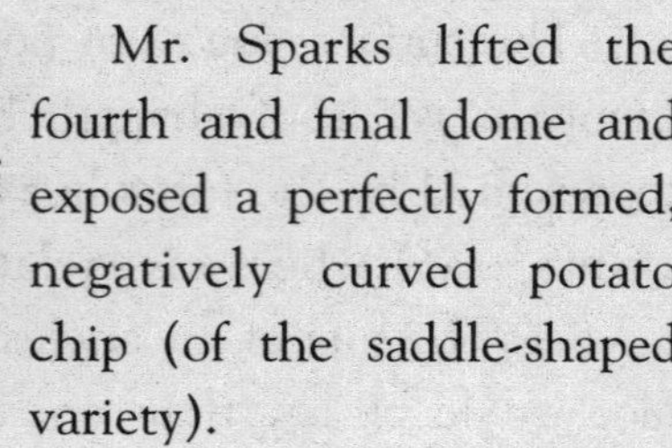

Mr. Sparks lifted the fourth and final dome and exposed a perfectly formed, negatively curved potato chip (of the saddle-shaped variety).

P.W. started a quiet chant: "CHIPS! CHIPS! CHIPS!"

His classmates joined in, and the chant slowly grew louder: "CHIPS! CHIPS! CHIPS! CHIPS!"

And louder still: "CHIPS! CHIPS! CHIPS! CHIPS!"

"Mr. Sparks," said Principal Birdwhistle. "*Please* control your students."

"I'm not sure I can. Besides, Hortensia, it's not just students who need controlling."

Emma Zeisel was the first adult to join the chorus. Then Maria chimed in. Then Napoleon, Frau Haffenreffer, and Regina Jasprow. Then the Dhabanandanas and Warchowskis, and the short, round man with the official-looking briefcase.

Eventually even Mrs. Brede and Dr. Parmigiano joined the one-syllable cheer.

Leon sensed the tide was turning.

This is it, he told himself. Time for the last exhibit.

And so, as the chant began to die down, he gave the short, round man a sign.

FORTY-ONE

The Champion Chip

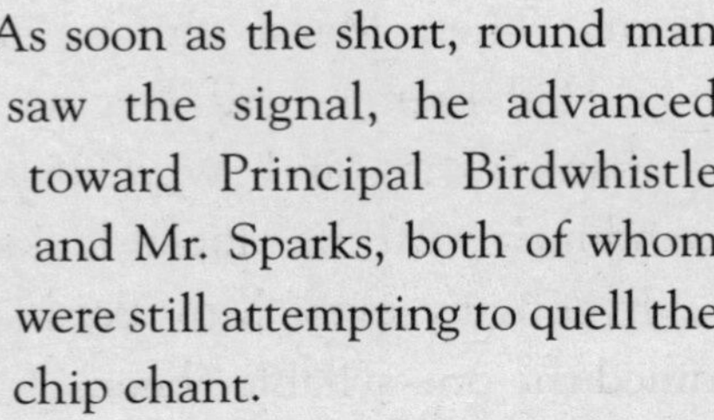

As soon as the short, round man saw the signal, he advanced toward Principal Birdwhistle and Mr. Sparks, both of whom were still attempting to quell the chip chant.

Leon gave a second sign, which alerted Thomas Warchowski, Antoinette Brede, Flossy Parmigiano, Lily-Matisse, and P.W. to shush the room and restore order.

When the gym at last fell silent, Leon introduced the surprise guest. "Excuse me, Mister Sparks? Principal Birdwhistle? I'd like you to meet a special visitor."

Leon may not have pulled an actual rabbit out of his hat, but he came pretty close. "This is Fergus O'Hare," he said.

The short, round man walked up to Mr. Sparks and Principal Birdwhistle.

"How do you do," he said.

"Fergus O'Hare is the executive director of the ASPCA," Leon explained.

"I see," said Principal Birdwhistle.

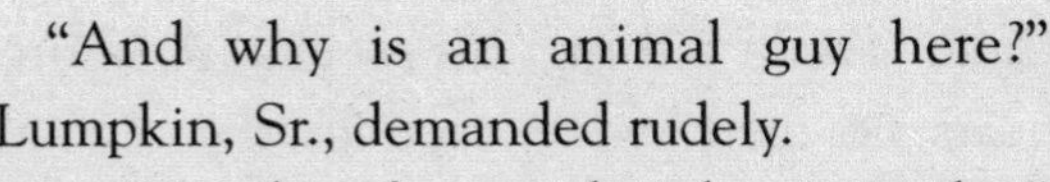

"And why is an animal guy here?" Lumpkin, Sr., demanded rudely.

"People often make that mistake," said Fergus O'Hare. "ASPCA stands for All-State Potato Chip Association."

"Why am I not surprised?" said Principal Birdwhistle.

"Mr. O'Hare is also a topflight research scientist," said Leon. "He used to run the whole entire Potato Division of the Department of Agriculture."

"My word," said Principal Birdwhistle. "That *is* impressive."

"Not nearly so impressive as this glorious chipatorium," said Fergus O'Hare. "Principal Birdwhistle, your students have put together what is arguably the finest display of potato chip science I have encountered since I took over the helm of the ASPCA ten years ago."

"We're honored you think so," said Mr. Sparks.

Fergus O'Hare chuckled. "Honored indeed. In fact, that's precisely why I've come here today." He bent down and clicked open the lock on his briefcase.

The fifth graders, along with their parents and friends, plus Principal Birdwhistle and Mr. Sparks, gathered around Fergus O'Hare and watched him extract a very large, unlabeled bag of potato chips.

"As all of you can see," he said after he stood back up, "this is not your ordinary bag of potato chips—if there is such a thing. It's special. A limited edition. It bears no markings except for the official seal of the ASPCA." Fergus O'Hare pointed to the embossed insignia of his organization. "Mr. Sparks," he said. "Would you kindly do the honors?"

Mr. Sparks accepted the bag. "Hmm. This is far too heavy to contain chips," he said at once. He gave the bag an investigative squeeze.

"What are you waiting for?" P.W. called out impatiently. "Open it!"

"May I?" Mr. Sparks asked politely.

"Absolutely," said Fergus O'Hare.

Mr. Sparks pulled apart the top seam of the foil bag and peered inside. "There appears to be a scroll," he announced.

"What's it say?" shouted Thomas Warchowski.

Mr. Sparks removed the rolled-up parchment. "Principal Birdwhistle, will you hold the bag, please?" He handed the open package to the principal and unfurled the scroll, which he read aloud with pride, pleasure, and embarrassment: "'The All-State Potato Chip Association, in recognition of the fearless protection and promotion of the world's most miraculous munchie, bestows its highest civilian award—The Golden Champion Chip Medal of Honor—upon the fifth graders of the Classical School, who, in a single year, under the guidance of Franklin W. Sparks, used potato chips, without regard to flavor, shape, or size, to explain the principles of classification, taxonomy, chemical and electrical energy, aerodynamics, optics, acidity, wireless communication, recycling, ballistics, and cosmology.'"

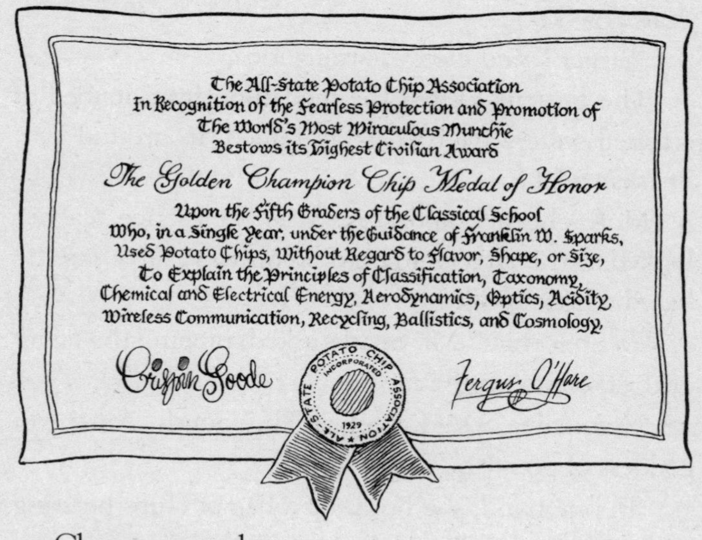
The All-State Potato Chip Association
In Recognition of the Fearless Protection and Promotion of
The World's Most Miraculous Munchie
Bestows its Highest Civilian Award
The Golden Champion Chip Medal of Honor
Upon the Fifth Graders of the Classical School
Who, in a Single Year, under the Guidance of Franklin W. Sparks,
Used Potato Chips, Without Regard to Flavor, Shape, or Size,
To Explain the Principles of Classification, Taxonomy,
Chemical and Electrical Energy, Aerodynamics, Optics, Acidity,
Wireless Communication, Recycling, Ballistics, and Cosmology.

Crispin Goode

All-State Potato Chip Association
Incorporated
1929

Fergus O'Hare

Cheers erupted.

"Hold on," said Principal Birdwhistle, shaking the bag. "There's something else inside here."

"Why don't you do the honors, Principal Birdwhistle?" Leon suggested slyly.

Flattered, the principal removed the second item. It was a yellow leather case. She unhooked the clasp gingerly and lifted the lid. Again, a dense knot of fifth graders, parents, and friends closed in.

"Holy cannoli," cried P.W.

"It's wonderful!" exclaimed Emma Zeisel.

"*Ja! Wunderschön!*" Frau Haffenreffer dittoed.

"Sheesh!" exclaimed Lily-Matisse. "Check out the size of that thing!"

"It's as big as a hockey puck!" said Thomas Warchowski.

"Bigger!" said Flossy Parmigiano.

The principal lifted the medallion from its bed of crushed yellow velvet and draped it around Mr. Sparks's neck.

More cheers erupted. And as the science teacher looked at the large gold coin, Leon was pretty sure he heard a little sniffle.

"Who is that?" Mr. Sparks asked, tapping the figure of the woman on the medal.

"Axomama," said Leon. "The South American goddess of potatoes."

"In one hand, she holds up a bag of chips bursting with light beams," said Fergus O'Hare. "And in the other hand, she clutches a potato plant in full bloom."

"And the Latin that curves around the lower part of the medal?" asked Mr. Sparks.

"*Commissamini sine metu* means 'Feast Without Fear,'" Fergus O'Hare explained. "It's the motto of the ASPCA."

"And speaking of feasting without fear," said Emma Zeisel, "Mr. O'Hare isn't the only one who brought a surprise."

"*Ja!*" said Frau Haffenreffer, holding up the pastry box.

Fergus O'Hare sniffed the air. "Are those what I think they are?"

Frau Haffenreffer nodded. "*Kartoffelchipkeks*."

"Potato chip cookies!" Emma Zeisel clarified.

"Everybody help yourselves!" said Frau Haffenreffer.

The two Lumpkins were the first to attack the snack, but other parents and students eventually displaced them.

"Man oh man, these are awesome!" said P.W., moments after taking a bite.

"They sure beat instant garlic-flavored potato-chip ice cream," said Flossy Parmigiano, eating three of the cookies in quick succession.

The *kartoffelchipkeks* vaporized faster than liquid nitrogen. When the box was empty, Fergus O'Hare turned to Franklin Sparks and said, "It is customary for award winners to make a few remarks."

P.W. started up a new chant: "Speech! Speech! Speech!"

Mr. Sparks raised his hand to quiet everyone down. For a long moment, he gazed at the medallion draped around his neck. "You know," he said at last, "Feast Without Fear' is the perfect motto for the scientist. I'm sure Einstein would have approved."

"Hear, hear!" said Fergus O'Hare.

"And what's more," Mr. Sparks continued, "I suspect—no, I am certain—Einstein also would have endorsed the work exhibited around this gym."

"I am quite convinced you are right," said Principal Birdwhistle.

"I propose a toast!" said Fergus O'Hare. "To potato chips. Our most beloved and misunderstood munchie."

"And to Mr. Sparks!" added Principal Birdwhistle. "Every bit as beloved—and, at least until now, every bit as misunderstood."

"Thank you, Hortensia," Mr. Sparks said, clearly touched. "But I'm not the one who should be honored. Nor should I be the one wearing this beautiful medal. It belongs to all my co-researchers, and to one in particular."

Mr. Sparks removed the ribbon and placed it around the neck of his most devoted student.

But Leon barely had time to enjoy his celebrity.

"Psst!" P.W. whispered in Leon's ear. "We've got a problem."

"What are you talking about?"

"Take a look," said P.W. "Lumpkin didn't stop with the potato chip cookies. He's starting to devour your universe."

Leon broke free from the well-wishers and approached his exhibit. "Shoot!" he cried. "That doofus just ate my pancake!"

He grabbed his backpack and ducked behind a stack of floor mats. Once he was sure he was out of view, he withdrew Lumpy and prepared for some covert finger work.

"You're too far away," P.W. warned. "Try near the pommel horse. You'll be hidden *and* in range."

Leon took the advice and rushed over to the horse. But halfway there, he tripped on his shoelace and took a tumble that sent Lumpy flying. Quick as a whip, he picked himself up and reached for the figure. He grabbed Lumpy and shoved him under his shirt. But he wasn't fast enough.

Lumpkin heard the fall and spotted his spitting image.

"Wlkajdf alkd jfkda!" he shouted, his mouth full of glazed doughnut.

Leon took off like a jackrabbit, weaving in and out of the exhibits in a desperate attempt to flee Lumpkin. He zipped past the Extermitater, past Mr. Molar the Wisdom Tooth, past the cantenna, the volcano, and the Baggied beans.

Leon didn't have to turn around to know that Lumpkin was gaining on him. He could feel it. Yet just when capture seemed certain, Leon caught a break.

"Henry Lumpkin!" he heard the janitor shouting. "Get your hiney back here and pick up the kidney beans you just knocked over."

Leon used those last few moments of freedom to stash Lumpy. Once he had, he rejoined his classmates, fully expecting Lumpkin to pounce.

But Lumpkin did not pounce.

"Do you see him?" Leon asked Lily-Matisse and P.W.

"Maybe Cranky Hankey sent him packing," said Lily-Matisse.

"I doubt it," said Leon. "I'm sure he's lurking somewhere close."

"A lurking Lumpkin?" said P.W. "That can't be good."

Lily-Matisse bounded up the bleachers to get a bird's-eye view. "Spotted him," she called down. "He's poking around P.W.'s exhibit."

"Oh, no!" Leon cried.

"Relax," said P.W. "It's not like my Extermitater is loaded."

"You're wrong!" Leon blurted out.

"What are you talking about?" said P.W.

"Well, I needed someplace to hide Lumpy and—"

Lily-Matisse's eyes widened. "Leon!" she cried. "You didn't!"

"Yup," said Leon. "I did."

FORTY-TWO

An Explosive Situation

"You shoved Lumpy inside my Extermitater?" sputtered P.W.

"Hey, I had to think fast," Leon said defensively. "Lumpkin was chasing me and I needed somewhere safe."

"P.W.'s whatchamacallit isn't exactly *safe*, Leon," said Lily-Matisse.

"Thanks for the tip," Leon said miserably.

The three watched from behind the floor mats as Lumpkin pulled the Extermitater off the wooden display board.

"We better tell someone," said Lily-Matisse.

Leon shook his head. "Hold on," he said. "Let's see what he does first. He might lose interest."

"Dream on," said P.W.

Lumpkin shouldered the Extermitater and fired off pretend rounds at the pommel horse, the water fountain, and the backboard.

"There's no way he's

putting that thing down on his own," said Lily-Matisse. "I'm getting Birdwhistle."

Moments after Lily-Matisse left, Lumpkin pocketed the hair spray.

"He's on the move," P.W. warned.

"I'm going in," said Leon.

P.W. tried to stop his friend but couldn't. Leon marched straight over. "Hey, Henry. Wanna trade?"

"Trade what?" snarled Lumpkin.

"The Extermitater."

Lumpkin raised the business end of the launcher. "For *what?*" he said threateningly.

Leon tried not to stare at the orange hair poking out of the muzzle. "For this," he said, removing the gold medallion from around his neck.

Lumpkin was tempted—that much was clear from the glimmer in his beady black eyes. But before the exchange could take place, Principal Birdwhistle stepped between the boys.

"What is the meaning of this?" she said. "Henry Lumpkin, put down that science exhibit *right now!*"

Lumpkin backed away and shook his head defiantly. "Sorry. No can do."

P.W. leaned over to Leon. "A Lumpkin with a loaded Lumpy launcher?" he whispered. "That *really* can't be good."

"Quiet!" said Principal Birdwhistle.

Lumpkin broke away from the crowd. When half a

basketball court separated him from everyone else, he brought the launcher between his knees and removed the end cap.

"Don't do it!" cried Lily-Matisse.

Lumpkin withdrew the can of hair spray, gave it a vigorous shake, and shot a long, steady stream of aerosol into the ignition chamber.

"I'll say this one more time," said Principal Birdwhistle. "Return P.W.'s apparatus to the exhibit table."

Lumpkin screwed the end cap back in place and dropped the hair spray on the ground. "Sorry, Teach," he said, sounding just like his father. He headed for the exit.

"Stop!" yelled Emma Zeisel.

"*Arrêtes!*" cried Napoleon.

"*Halt!*" screamed Frau Haffenreffer.

"*¡Pare!*" shrieked Maria.

"หยุด!" hollered Ms. Dhabanandana.

Lumpkin turned and shook his head. "Sorry," he said, as if events were beyond his control. "Can't stop now. Besides," he added with a laugh, "it's not like it's loaded."

A shrill whistle blast caught everyone off guard. "Lumpkin!" shouted Coach Kasperitis. "Don't *make* me come over there!"

Mr. Sparks weighed in more quietly. "Henry," he said. "If you don't want to listen to us, at least consider

Newton's Third Law. 'For every action, there is an equal and opposite *re*action.'"

"And while you're thinking about that," Principal Birdwhistle added, "you may wish to consider Birdwhistle's *First* Law—*my* reaction to any further misbehavior will be swift and permanent."

"Listen to the principal!" Leon begged. "If you push that button—*believe me*—you *will get expelled*!"

"Big deal!" said Lumpkin. And with that, he bolted out of the gym.

Leon, Lily-Matisse, and P.W. raced after him, but before they reached the double doors, they were stopped by a gargantuan . . .

FORTY-THREE

A Very Short Chapter

FORTY-FOUR

The Observation of Sparks in Motion

The day after the science fair, Henry Lumpkin failed to attend classes. He was absent the following day as well. And the day after that, too. In fact, Henry Lumpkin was a no-show for the remaining weeks of school.

Most of the fifth graders figured he had been given the boot—end of story. But there was another possibility—another end to the story.

What if, by launching his own spitting image, Lumpkin had launched himself?

Leon's final warning proved correct. Lumpkin *did* get expelled. But the nature of the expulsion remained unexplained.

Lily-Matisse tried to wheedle some information out of her mom, but Regina Jasprow refused to discuss the matter.

"What exactly did she say?" Leon asked Lily-Matisse.

"She told me it was confidential. And when I pushed her, she went ballistic."

"Actually," said P.W., "it was Lumpkin who went ballistic."

Leon rolled his eyes. "You're worse than my mom. She's been going around the hotel saying she always knew Lumpkin was a loose cannon."

"He was," said Lily-Matisse. "And if he actually did send himself into orbit like a potato, I hope he never lands!"

"Me, too," said Leon. "Still, I'm kind of sad we'll never see Lumpy again. I liked the little fella."

"If no Lumpy means no Lumpkin," said P.W., "that seems like a pretty good swap."

"I guess," said Leon. "But I really do want to know what happened."

Just when it seemed as if the fate of Henry Lumpkin would never get revealed, Mr. Sparks came through yet again—this time with news of the discharged bully.

The update took place during the last lab of the year. Mr. Sparks rolled a heavy piece of equipment into class. "Get your mitts off my exhibit and take your seats," he commanded. "We've got a lot of material to cover."

"And *un*cover!" said P.W., eyeing the drop cloth that hid the wheeled contraption.

"How right you are!" said Mr. Sparks. And to prove the point (though not the way P.W. expected) he unbuttoned his shirt and exposed an Einstein T-shirt the fifth graders hadn't seen. This one said $E = MC^2$, and at the bottom, in teeny-tiny type, the famous formula was clarified:

EDUCATION = MUNCHING CHIPS, TOO!

"Cool!" said Thomas Warchowski.

"Sweet!" said Leon.

"Wicked," said P.W.

"It *is* rather darling," Antoinette Brede admitted.

"Glad you guys approve," said Mr. Sparks, "because I had a bunch made—one for each of my champion chippers." From under the tarp, he removed a shopping bag filled with T-shirts and handed one to each of the fifth graders.

P.W. was the last to get his. "Hey, there's one left over," he said, pulling the spare from the bottom of the bag. "And man oh man, it's a *monster*!" He held up the T-shirt for the whole class to see.

"I could use that thing for a sleeping bag," said Flossy Parmigiano.

"We all know who it's for," said Thomas Warchowski.

"*Was* for," Antoinette Brede corrected.

"No," said Mr. Sparks. "Thomas is right. I plan to mail Henry his extra-extra-large."

"Where are you sending it?" Leon asked at once.

"To the—" Mr. Sparks stopped himself. "I was advised not to discuss the matter."

"Come on," P.W. pleaded. "Tell us!"

"*Please*, Mr. Sparks?" begged Lily-Matisse. "You can't tease us like that. It isn't fair. What happened to Henry Lumpkin?"

Mr. Sparks looked around. It was obvious his students were dying to know the destiny of their expelled classmate—and that three of his very favorite students were dying more than the rest.

"Well, I can tell you this much," said Mr. Sparks. "That army jacket Henry loved so much? I'm pretty sure it will come in *very* handy."

"Military school?" P.W. exclaimed.

"I will neither confirm nor deny that hypothesis," said Mr. Sparks, saluting P.W. and adding a little wink.

As *oohs* spread through the room, Mr. Sparks glanced over at the potatoes. "Oh, my, look at the time. I better *speed* things up."

Leon knew a hint when he heard one. "Does that gizmo under the tarp have something to do with cars?"

"It does indeed," said Mr. Sparks. "Henry Lumpkin isn't the only one who can end the year with a bang. Now, without further ado . . ."

He whipped off the drop cloth. "Behold the Chipmobile!" he proclaimed.

"What in the—" P.W. was so dazzled he couldn't finish his thought.

"It looks like . . . like a go-cart with, with a fire extinguisher stuck on the back!" Thomas Warchowski stammered.

"You're not far off the mark," said Mr. Sparks. "However, that 'extinguisher' is actually a power pack of pressurized potato distillate." He saw at once that his description confused the class.

"Think of it as a chemical mixture that's halfway between rocket fuel and rubbing alcohol," Mr. Sparks explained. "I had hoped to use the stuff during Parents' Night—to explore the principles of combustion. But I never got the chance. After I saw all the wonderful potato chip exhibits at the science fair, I modified the application for use with the Chipmobile. Since I started the year with sparks, it seemed only logical to end the year the same way. Antoinette, would you kindly clear the flight path?"

"Excuse me?"

"Open the door," said Mr. Sparks as he strapped a bicycle helmet onto his head and twisted two spongy earplugs into his ears. "Remember," he shouted, "never try this kind of experiment without proper supervision!" He slipped a pair of safety goggles over his eyes and belted himself into the vehicle's curved yellow seat.

The class closed in on the Chipmobile.

"Okay, you guys," Mr. Sparks called out. "Back behind the benches. I'm not blasting off until the flight deck is safe!"

Once the class retreated, Mr. Sparks pulled a metal safety ring from the pressurized tank and gripped a handle duct-taped to the front of the Chipmobile. He gave the thumbs-up, which every student returned.

"And now for *my* science project," he declared joyfully. " 'The Observation of Sparks in Motion'!"

He squeezed the handle.

All of a sudden, there was a giant *whoosh*!

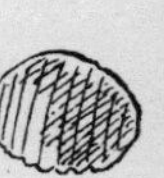

The spud engine zipped past the potato clocks, past the foil bag kites, past the wrinkled gazes of Professor Spud (who now had more "eyes" than body). It zipped past the chip classification chart. Past the specimen case protecting the Golden Champion Chip Medal of Honor. Finally it whizzed through the doors of the science lab, leaving Leon, P.W., Lily-Matisse, and the rest of the cheering fifth graders in a haze that smelled of potato.

When Leon got home that afternoon, he knew something was up. Napoleon accompanied him into the lobby. Maria, Frau Haffenreffer, and Emma Zeisel were all lying in wait.

"You're looking pretty darn chipper in that Einstein T-shirt, sweetie," said Leon's mom.

"Not as chipper as I was when I saw Mr. Sparks cruise out of class in his Chipmobile!" Leon described the extraordinary exit of his extraordinary teacher.

"That does sound pretty terrific," Emma Zeisel admitted. "But I think we have something that will make you even chipperer."

"I doubt it," said Leon.

The three women and Napoleon started to laugh.

"Okay," said Leon. "I'll bite."

"You certainly will," said Emma Zeisel. "Once you open your package."

"Package?" said Leon.

"Package," his mother confirmed. "Follow me." She marched her son past the lobby signboard, which now read:

Emma Zeisel ducked into the back office and returned with a giant carton.

Leon looked it over. "It's from the ASPCA!" he exclaimed. "See? It's got the official seal and motto stamped all across it." He tore open the box and attacked the gift-wrapped package inside.

"Hold it," his mother scolded mildly, pointing to an envelope taped to the wrapping paper. "Always read the note first, sweetie."

"But—"

"Your mother is right, Leonito!" said Maria.

Napoleon nodded gravely.

"*Ja,*" said Frau Haffenreffer. "You heard your mother, you little stinker."

Leon put the gift aside and read the card out loud:

ALL-STATE POTATO CHIP ASSOCIATION
INCORPORATED
1929

Dear Zeisel Comma Leon,
I thought you could
use this.
Happy Snacking!
Fergus O'Hare

"*Now* can I see what's inside?"

"Go for it," said Emma Zeisel.

Leon ripped through the gift wrap. "Rhode Island Monk Chips!" he exclaimed. "You know what this means? It means I've completed New England!"

"See," said Emma Zeisel. "Now don't you feel chipperer?"

"Nope," said Leon. "I feel a lot better than that. I feel—" Leon stopped himself. "Hold on." He whispered to Napoleon, who nodded and dashed through the lobby.

A moment later the cabby was back, with the item Leon had requested.

"Like I was saying," said Leon. "I feel a whole lot better than chipper." He held up his handmade moodometer and nudged the arrow on the dial from PINS AND NEEDLES to PRETTY GOOD to CHIPPER. He kept on nudging, pushing beyond CHIPPER to GREAT!, beyond GREAT! to PUMPED!, and beyond PUMPED! to the very highest reading on the cardboard dial: JAZZED!

MONK
CHIPS

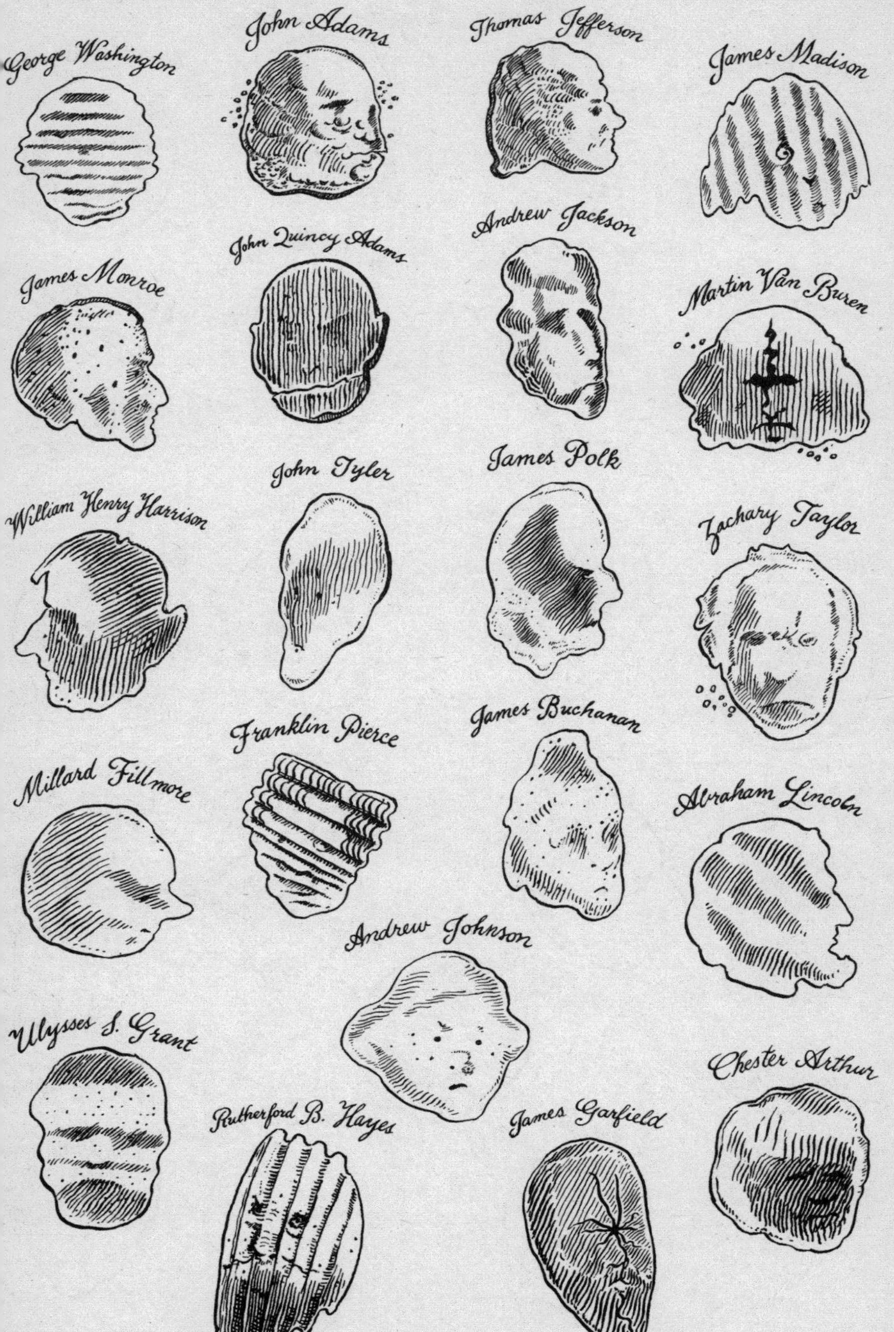
George Washington
John Adams
Thomas Jefferson
James Madison
John Quincy Adams
Andrew Jackson
James Monroe
Martin Van Buren
John Tyler
James Polk
William Henry Harrison
Zachary Taylor
Franklin Pierce
James Buchanan
Millard Fillmore
Abraham Lincoln
Andrew Johnson
Ulysses S. Grant
Chester Arthur
Rutherford B. Hayes
James Garfield

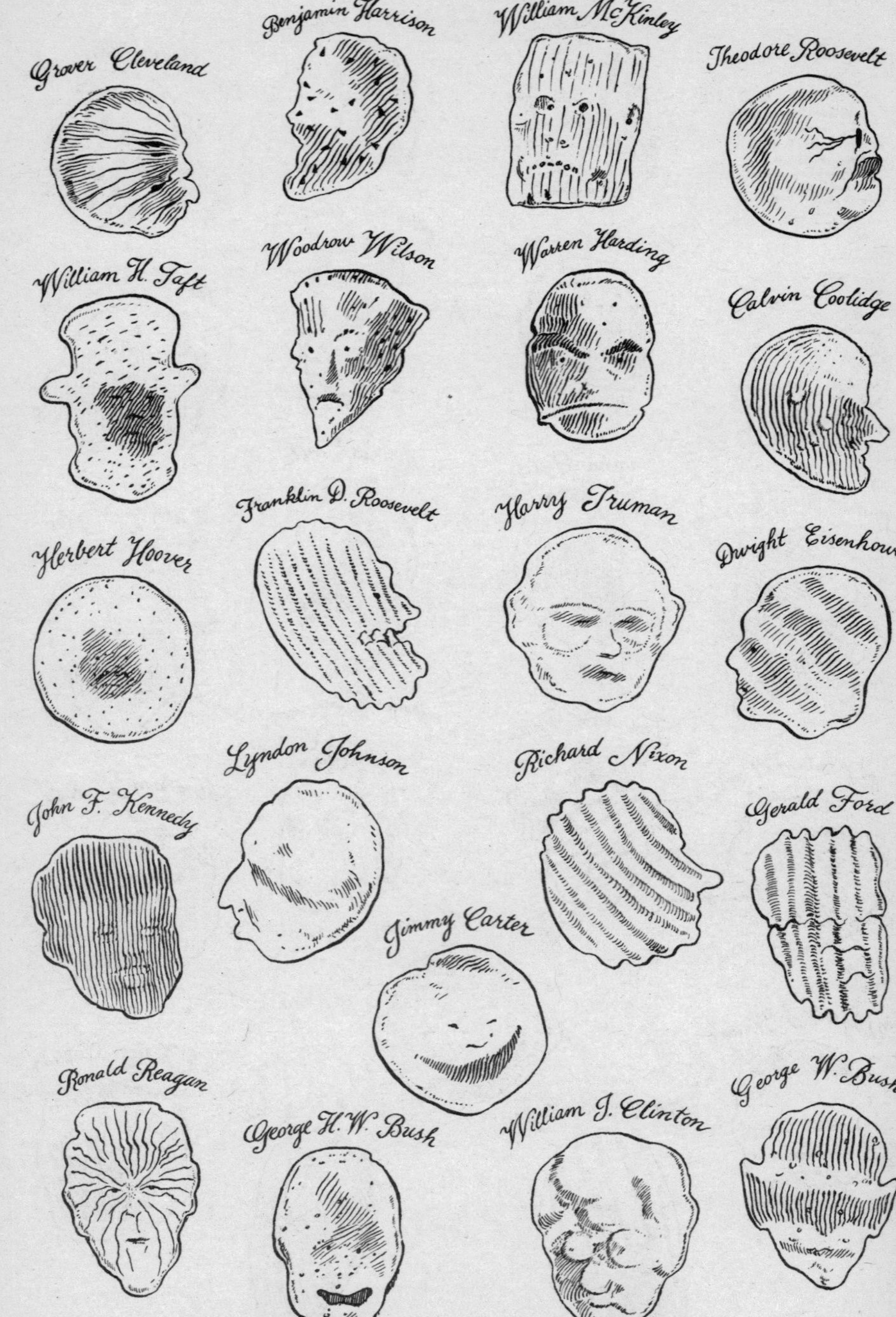

Grover Cleveland
Benjamin Harrison
William McKinley
Theodore Roosevelt
William H. Taft
Woodrow Wilson
Warren Harding
Calvin Coolidge
Herbert Hoover
Franklin D. Roosevelt
Harry Truman
Dwight Eisenhowe
John F. Kennedy
Lyndon Johnson
Richard Nixon
Gerald Ford
Jimmy Carter
Ronald Reagan
George H. W. Bush
William J. Clinton
George W. Bush